the Celebutantes
ON THE AVENUE

ALSO BY ANTONIO PAGLIARULO

A Different Kind of Heat

Antonio Pagliarulo

the *Celebutantes*

ON THE AVENUE

Delacorte Press

Published by Delacorte Press
an imprint of Random House Children's Books
a division of Random House, Inc.
New York

www.randomhouse.com/teens

Educators and librarians, for a variety of teaching tools, visit us at
www.randomhouse.com/teachers

Library of Congress Cataloging-in-Publication Data
Pagliarulo, Antonio.
The celebutantes: on the avenue / Antonio Pagliarulo. — 1st ed.
p. cm.
Summary: When fabulously wealthy sixteen-year-old triplets Lexington, Park, and
Madison Hamilton appear to be involved in the murder of a powerful magazine editor,
they decide to do some investigating of their own before the police and paparazzi
completely ruin their lives.
ISBN-13: 978-0-385-73404-2 (trade pbk.)
ISBN-13: 978-0-385-90415-5 (glb)
[1. Murder—Fiction. 2. Wealth—Fiction. 3. Fashion—Fiction. 4. Triplets—Fiction.
5. Sisters—Fiction. 6. New York (N.Y.)—Fiction. 7. Mystery and detective stories.] I. Title.
PZ7.P148Ce 2007
[Fic]—dc 22
2006017035

The text of this book is set in 13-point Filosofia.

Book design by Angela Carlino

Printed in the United States of America

10 9 8 7 6 5 4 3 2 1

First Edition

For my sister, Maria,
With love and thanks

For Immediate Release
To: The Editors, *Town Magazine*
From: Lexington Hamilton (and on behalf of my sisters, Madison and Park)
RE: Your view of us

I was perturbed by your article "Sexy Celebutantes," which appeared in the April issue of *Town Magazine*. Initially, I read it because I wanted to see how close to the truth a journalist could actually get, but as the paragraphs dragged on, I realized that I was skimming my eyes over trash, trash, trash.

Quote 1: Born into a world of privilege and power, today's celebutantes spend their days in spas and salons, or shopping until their stiletto heels snap under the weight of dozens of designer gift bags lugged to and from parties. They are not merely millionaires; they are moguls-in-the-making, bred to double and triple their familial fortunes.

So not true. We go to school like teenagers everywhere. We sit in our classes, we smile at our teachers, and sometimes we even take notes. Later, if there isn't a premiere or a party, we *might* do a little shopping. And stilettos don't always make the cut. Jimmy Choos also come in graceful and fashionable flats, which are needed to outrun paparazzi. Kindly amend your files.

Quote 2: The uppity St. Cecilia's Prep on Fifth Avenue is the high school of choice for today's celebutantes. At $40,000 a year, the posh academy only accepts students whose fortunes top the fifty-million-dollar mark. For that much dough, the kiddies come and go as they please, and they take classes like Philanthropy 101 instead of more traditional subjects like biology and history.

Get your facts straight. Tuition at St. Cecilia's Prep is actually $88,000 a year, and we don't waltz in and out whenever we want. We do, however, have schedules designed to accommodate the demands of our lives. Occasionally we have obligations before first period. Sometimes photographers can only shoot in the earlier part of the day, and other mornings there are brunches that must be attended. As for "Philanthropy 101" ... well ... my sister Madison took that class, and two months later she organized a fund-raising event at the Mercer Hotel that raised one million dollars for Harlem Hospital. And, for the record, most of St. Cecilia's Prep's student body have fortunes that exceed the hundred-million-dollar mark. Kindly amend your files.

Quote 3: It's no secret that today's hottie celebutantes grow up fast. They take limos, drink the best champagne, and board their private jets to Monaco, Borneo, or L.A. And forget cheap motel rooms for cheap thrills. Romantic rendezvous happen in style—in penthouse suites overlooking Central Park, on yachts docked in the Hudson Marina, or (perhaps more appropriately) in the stately dressing room of the Ermenegildo Zegna boutique on Fifth.

I have never fired up my private jet to go to Borneo. I don't know anyone who has.

Quote 4: The most famous—or infamous—of the celebutante lot are the Hamilton sisters: Madison, Park, and Lexington. These photo-hogging playgirls are the rulers of the roost, sparking scandal wherever they go. They have enough money to buy their own fashion houses, but insist on promoting up-and-coming designers for the sake of "art." Better poster girls for the shameless celebutante lifestyle you simply won't find.

My sisters and I are not ashamed of our wealth, nor do we shrink from the spotlight. Some people are born with bad skin and have to use foundation for the rest of their lives. We were born famous, and the cameras will follow us till we're old and in our thirties. And as for the "shameless lifestyle" thing . . . well . . . you can all kiss my art. Till then . . .

See you,
On the Avenue

You Can Find It on Lex

Night fell cool and crazy over Manhattan, the streets buzzing with the first hint of spring. It was a Friday in May. Lights pulsed along the skyline and traffic clogged the streets. The air was thick with the anticipation of all that can happen in the city on a warm spring night.

Lexington Hamilton stood rigidly at her bedroom window, staring down at the busy stretch of Fifth Avenue. People were definitely in a partying mood. Crowds were thickening by the minute, and there wasn't a free cab in sight. East and west, north and south, clubs and bars were opening their doors and cranking up their sound systems. It was almost eight o'clock. Lex couldn't believe she was still dressed in her red and white school uniform with the tacky St. Cecilia's Prep logo emblazoned on the lapel. She hated the damn thing, but after cutting out of last period she had rushed over to Saks for makeup and Bendel's for a new pair of shoes. The hours had simply slipped through her fingers. Now she was itching to doll herself up.

She turned away from the window and locked her eyes on the garment bag lying across her bed. It held her newest creation—a dress fashioned especially for the sexy and the savvy. Lex had designed it herself two weeks ago and had recently decided to add it to her growing clothing label. There were expensive names in her closet, but she favored her own creations above all others. She used versatile, striking patterns and only the best fabrics. Risky, funky, and tastefully sexy, her collection would be big news one day soon. She had dozens of sketches on her desk—skirts, jeans, jackets, suits, bras, underwear, well-cut lingerie— and she knew it was only a matter of time before her aptly titled Triple Threat label went global. But the first order of business was getting noticed without anyone realizing that you *wanted* to get noticed.

She walked over to the bed, eyeing the garment bag. No one had seen her bring it home. She held it up, drew the zipper down, and smiled. The dress was amazing. White silk and cut well above the knee, it practically *screamed* her name. And the shoes were a perfect match. Christian Louboutins, their cream color accentuated the dress's fringed hem, and the trademark crimson soles were the perfect contrast. She hadn't been invited to this evening's gala at the Metropolitan Museum of Art, but she'd make one hell of an entrance when she arrived.

The very thought of it made Lex giggle. Her triplet sisters, Madison and Park, thought she was under the covers nursing a stomach flu. They had spent the afternoon preening for the gala, too wrapped up in their own worlds to acknowledge Lex's mounting anger. Why should *she* stay home while *they* attended the star-studded event? It didn't make sense. Well . . . it did, but the truth wasn't a good enough reason. The truth was that Madison—with her coiffed hair, classic gowns, and altogether refined manner—was better suited to represent Hamilton Holdings, Inc., at a snooty, conservative gala. Madison always got invited to the boring highbrow functions. Lex, on the other hand, found herself on the wilder, trendier A-lists, where loud music, hot guys, and good booze were in abundance. Park was happy to tag along in either case. Wide-eyed, calm to a fault, and nauseatingly cheerful, Park was the self-appointed peacemaker of the family.

Lex pressed her ear to the closed bedroom door and listened. The long hallway was silent. Lupe, their housekeeper, was busy banging pots in the kitchen. Madison and Park had already left.

All was in readiness.

Smiling broadly, Lex headed for her bathroom and flicked on the light. She tore off the uniform, chucked the skirt and blouse to the floor, and revved up the Jacuzzi. She added a splash of her favorite Mario Badescu body wash to the water and lit one of the Toumbac candles she'd bought in bulk from A.P.C. As the bubbles rose and undulated, she climbed inside, savoring the heat that enveloped her muscles and the scent of Parisian flowers that now filled the bathroom. She was too tense. The anger and frustration of the day had wound her up. She still couldn't believe that their father, Trevor Hamilton, had allowed Madison and Park to go along without her tonight. When Lex had broached the subject last week, he'd simply given her the same spiel about good manners and proper behavior.

You haven't earned the right to attend these types of functions, Lex. Every time I open a newspaper and read through the gossip columns, there you are—dancing on a table at some nightclub, causing a stir at a premiere. I can trust Madison to behave herself. And with me away for a whole week, the company will have to be represented accordingly.

The company, Lex thought bitterly. It was always about the company. A media empire that encompassed three television stations, a radio network, and several real estate branches, Hamilton Holdings, Inc., was their father's first baby. Trevor Hamilton had built it from nothing, deal by vicious deal. Over the years, he had been touted in the press as a ruthless businessman and a tireless philanthropist. In truth, he was an odd mix of both. He was also as much of a celebrity as any Oscar-winning actor. From New York to Beverly Hills, Paris to London, Dubai to Sydney, the Hamilton name was respected, revered, and occasionally despised. It all came with living life in the constant glare of the media.

Lex understood the importance of keeping a good profile, but she hadn't done anything *that* bad in recent months. Yeah, she liked having fun. Yeah, she was a party girl. Where was the crime in that? After all, it wasn't *her* fault the media enjoyed following her around and snapping her picture everywhere she went. It just *happened.* Like last year, at the annual Memorial Day bash in the Hamptons. She had gone to Tavern and hooked up with William Bondurant, a senior at St. Cecilia's and one of the most stunning creations on God's green earth. They'd slipped around to the back of the club, over by the wooded parking lot, and had a little rendezvous. William took his shirt off, Lex took her bikini top off, they were laughing and kissing and groping when *boom*—a flash illuminated the darkness. They'd both looked up, stunned and mussed in the heat of the moment. Next morning, the grainy black-and-white photo appeared in a dozen papers: Lex cuddled in William's arms, her bare breasts two inches from his smiling face. Trevor Hamilton had been less than pleased, but Lex had shrugged the episode off without a twinge of embarrassment. And besides, some good had come out of it. She and William had dated for nearly three months.

Since then, Lex had courted trouble only a handful of times. This past winter she'd been mentioned in the tabloids sporadically, and for minor incidents. Skipping a day of school to attend the unveiling of Chanel's spring collection. Being quoted on Page Six of the *New York Post* saying she hated wearing underwear. Slipping a bartender at Bungalow 8 fifty bucks for a peach martini. Silly things like that. She had been branded the official bad girl of the very public Hamilton family, and wherever she went, scandal followed.

But tonight would be different. Her best behavior would take center stage. She wasn't interested in the gala itself—a fund-raiser for the museum's Impressionist art wing—so much as she was in the people who'd be in attendance. One person, actually: Zahara Bell, arguably the most powerful fashion editor in

New York City and quite possibly the world. A sweet write-up from Zahara in *Catwalk* magazine was an instant fashion initiation, and with her blessing, Lex would be accepted—she had no intention of being the new J.Lo of the fashion world. Zahara Bell was a sugarcoated bitch, but in the last three years she had launched the careers of five major designers. If Lex got her attention, the Triple Threat label would bring the Hamilton name to new heights—and it would convince Trevor that his daughter was more than just a hungry party girl. Maybe then he'd start treating her a little differently. Younger than Madison by six minutes and Park by two, Lex was the baby of the family, the last stop in a sisterhood that went from west to east.

Thankfully, Trevor would be out of the country for several days, traipsing through the rain forests of Costa Rica in search of adventure. His yearly getaway couldn't have come at a better time. Surrounded by dripping trees and furry frogs, he was totally unreachable and wouldn't be able to scold Lex for taking matters into her own hands.

She stepped carefully out of the Jacuzzi and toweled herself off. She stood before the studio-lighted mirror and gave herself a careful once-over. She was thin and toned. Her blue eyes were almond shaped, her nose straight. Her full lips accentuated the smoothness of her complexion. She removed the pins from her hair and shook out the bright blond mass of waves, letting the tendrils fall to the middle of her back. A satisfied smile tugged at the corners of her mouth. She was totally pleased with her appearance.

She padded out to the bedroom. With expert ease, she slipped the dress off its brass hanger and pulled it over her head. Then she took a deep breath, stretched her hands behind her head, and worked the ivory buttons into place one by one. The dress felt like soft butter against her skin. She shivered at the cool kiss of it and thanked God for her good taste. The pair of Louboutins was on the floor; she stepped into them, then went to the door and turned the knob.

The hallway was still mercifully quiet. She looked both ways, noting that the doors to Madison's and Park's rooms were closed. A feeling of excitement washed over her. The plan had worked. "Here we go," she whispered, and went toward the kitchen. On the threshold, she put a hand on her hip, struck a fashionable pose, and cleared her throat.

Lupe, short and thin and wearing her customary stained apron, spun around. Her eyes widened in surprise, and the espresso pot she was holding slipped from her fingers. *"Dios mío,"* she said, her Colombian accent thick.

"That's a good thing, right?" Lex walked across the large kitchen, circling the marble island as she modeled her newest design. "Well, how do I look?"

"Beautiful," Lupe said with a genuine smile. "But not enough clothes."

Lex rolled her eyes. "Come on. I designed it two weeks ago and had this sample made in Milan. Isn't it gorgeous?"

"Mucho bazoomas," Lupe said, staring at the plunging neckline that made a peepshow of Lex's breasts. "A girl so young, there's no need to dress like that."

"But you like it, don't you?"

"Yes, I like it." Lupe's eyes suddenly narrowed. "Where you going, anyway?"

"Out with an old friend," Lex replied casually. "We're having dinner downtown."

"You're not sick anymore, I guess?"

Lex put a hand to her forehead and made a pretense of coughing. "I'm feeling a little better. And I don't plan on eating much, anyway. Where're Madison and Park?"

Lupe shook her head as she turned back to the commercial-sized dishwasher. She had been the housekeeper for the Hamilton family for nearly a dozen years and knew every one of Lex's tricks. Instead of answering, she said, "Your father told me that you're not supposed to go to the gala tonight. You know that."

"I'm not going to a gala. I'm going out for a quiet dinner." Lex tried her best to keep her tone casual, innocent, *and* believable. She didn't know if it was working. She looked down at the marble countertop and started leafing through last month's issue of *Paper* magazine. A minute passed in silence, and she finally glanced up.

Lupe was giving her one of those don't-tell-me-that-cute-guy-in-your-bedroom-is-just-a-gay-friend stares. She slammed the dishwasher closed and began drying her hands on a dish towel. "What I'm supposed to say when you father calls, eh? You gonna go out now and turn off the cell phone. Then I'll be in trouble. Forget it. I'm not lying for you tonight."

Lex's jaw dropped. The excitement she'd been feeling a minute ago turned into sheer panic as she followed Lupe out of the kitchen, past the dining room, through the living room, and into the library. "Lupe, *please*. You *have* to. You don't understand. If I don't go to the gala tonight, I'll never want to wake up again. I'll spend the next year crying my eyes out."

Lupe was dusting off Trevor Hamilton's prized mahogany Civil War–era desk. It was situated in the middle of the library and flanked by four walls filled with books. "No," she said again. "Your father said no, and I can't lie."

"Come on, be a sport," Lex pleaded. "I'll never ask you for another favor again."

"No."

"I'll clean my own room and do my own laundry."

"No."

"I'll vacuum the living room."

"No."

"I'll make my own dinner."

"No."

"I'll load the dishwasher."

"No."

"I'll go to confession with you at St. Patty's tomorrow."

"No."

Lex sighed. She pouted and crossed her arms over her chest. What a waste. After today's exhausting shopping trek, she deserved to show herself off. Two stores. Crowds of people. All that time creating the perfect dress and now—

Dress.

The word echoed through Lex's mind and a little lightbulb clicked on over her head. Of course. That was the answer. Why hadn't she realized it earlier?

She whirled around. "Okay then, Lupe. We'll cut a deal. You lie for me tonight and I'll buy you the Oscar de la Renta cashmere sweater you've been wanting for the past three months."

Lupe stopped dusting off the desktop. Her back straightened. Her fingers clenched into tight little fists. And for the first time since they had begun arguing, she didn't say anything.

Lex walked over to her. "You have a picture of it in

your bedroom. Just think how great it'll look on you," she whispered seductively. "Think how your friends will be staring in envy when you go to your nephew's wedding next month."

Lupe had been listening intently. She closed her eyes, bit down on her lower lip, and then quickly shook her head. "Enough. No. I can't do it."

"Of course you can. It'll be my treat. Our secret. By the time you finish saving up the money to buy the sweater, it'll go onto the clearance rack and into the hands of someone who totally doesn't deserve it."

Silence.

"And I'll buy you great shoes to match," Lex said, fully aware that she'd hooked Lupe in. "Going once . . ."

Lupe sighed loudly. She ran a hand over her fore-head, where a trail of sweat had broken out.

"Going twice . . ."

"Oh, why you do this to me? It's not nice."

"Going three times," Lex trilled. "In five seconds the deal's off—"

"Okay," Lupe cut in. "I'll do it. I'll tell your father you're asleep when he calls."

Lex smiled broadly. She threw her arms around the small woman and hugged her tightly. "Monday after school I'll pick up the sweater. Then we can go to Barney's for shoes! Just you and me!"

Lupe nodded guiltily, then made the sign of the cross.

Scurrying from the library, Lex flew through the living room, past the dining room, and back into the kitchen. She went into the small pantry and clapped her hands vigorously. "Where are you, honey?" she called out. "It's time to go."

Champagne, her tiny teacup Chihuahua, came prancing out of his favorite corner. He was an adorable dog, with closely cropped well-groomed golden hair. A dark brown collar wrapped his little neck, and from it hung a gold charm in the shape of a champagne flute. He stared up at Lex and barked.

She bent down and scooped him into the crook of her right arm. Then she headed for the foyer, where her purse sat on an oval table. Stealing a final glance in the mirror by the front door, she bolted out of the apartment and into the waiting elevator. The floors dinged one by one as she and Champagne descended. The Hamilton apartment was, of course, the penthouse at 974 Fifth Avenue. The prewar building was beautiful, but as far as Lex was concerned, it retained too much of its antiquated charm. The carpet in the elevator was a faded red. Many of the numbered buttons had smudged into shapeless black lines. And it took nearly a minute to reach the ground floor.

She hurried out into the lobby. She could already feel the electric pulse of the streets and hear the controlled chaos of the traffic. Her heart fluttering, she spotted the doorman, Steven Hillby, standing at his usual post by the reception desk. Tall and big-boned, he was the official mayor of 974 Fifth Avenue. He knew everything about everybody.

"Oh no you don't," he said when he saw Lex striding toward him. "A little birdy named Trevor Hamilton told me you were supposed to spend the night *inside.*" He stared down at her with a smug expression.

Without so much as arguing, Lex popped open her purse, took out her favorite pair of Oliver Peoples sunglasses, and slipped them on. Then she dunked into the purse a second time and withdrew a crisp hundred-dollar bill from the bulging side pocket. She held it out to Steven. "Cut the bullshit," she said with a playful smile. "Now go on out there and rev up the engines."

Steven snatched the bill from her fingers and held open the doors for her. "This way, ma'am." His tone was suddenly—and exaggeratedly—sweet.

"You didn't see me leave," she said as she stepped outside.

"And you didn't see me take a bribe."

"I never do."

At the curb, Steven motioned for the gray Mercedes limo parked at the northwest corner of Fifth Avenue. When it pulled up beside him, he waved Lex forward, into the open back passenger door. "Have a good evenin', ma'am."

"Thank you, kind sir." She dropped into the plush leather seats and settled Champagne on her lap. The door closed. "The Met," she said.

The partition that divided the front seats from the luxurious passenger compartment slid all the way down. Striking blue eyes stared back at her from the rearview mirror. Clarence Becker had been the Hamilton family's chauffeur for three years. He was a scrawny forty-two-year-old guy with a good heart and a penchant for booze, loud music, and expensive cigars. Lex often referred to him as a sweet thug.

Now he was staring at her intently. "Lex . . . ," he said, his voice trembling with worry.

"I've already heard the speech, Clarence, and I'm in no mood to hear it again."

He turned around in his seat. "If your father finds out I drove you to the gala, I'll never hear the end of it. He told me you're not supposed to . . ."

As his voice trailed away, Lex reached for the magic purse. She withdrew a long Cuban cigar from the *other* side pouch—the one reserved for rare emergencies that money couldn't solve—and held it out.

Clarence's eyes widened. He reverently took the cigar into his fingers and stared at it. Then he passed it beneath his nostrils, inhaling the expensive scent. "Ohhh," he groaned. "This a hot little number. Yum."

"Straight from Daddy's fine-tobacco collection," Lex said. "He could care less about cigars. Park and I smoke most of them. And there'll be five more for you tomorrow—*if* I get my ride."

Clarence gave her a conspiratorial wink as he dropped the cigar into his lapel pocket and turned around. A moment later the car pulled out onto Fifth Avenue.

Mission accomplished. Lex leaned back and smiled happily. Who said freedom couldn't be bought?

2

West of Madison

The Great Hall of the Metropolitan Museum of Art
was glittering. Candles burned on the tables, and
endless strands of white lights had been draped
across the vaulted ceiling in honor of Van Gogh's
Starry Night. It was like a scene from a fairy tale,
Madison Hamilton thought as she scanned the
crowded floor. She recognized most of the faces
smiling back at her. Some were her father's business acquaintances. Others were old fixtures on the
New York social scene. Dinner had been served, and

now the quiet crowd was mingling as the orchestra played Bach.

She stood up from her place at the coveted President's Table—reserved for patrons who had dropped ten thousand dollars a plate—and looked down, making certain she hadn't spilled any food on her gown. It was vintage Chanel. A simple black lace strapless that fell to her ankles and hugged her waist snugly. At her neck, a Harry Winston ten-carat choker sparkled like the Manhattan skyline. Her dark hair was pulled up in a chignon. She knew all eyes had been on her since the gala had started an hour ago, and she didn't mind the attention one bit. Here, among her intellectual peers, she was being admired for more than just her beauty. Madison had spent the past two months interning in the Met's fund-raising and development office, coordinating many of tonight's decorative festivities on her own. It was no secret that she had the brains to match the influential last name.

Madison yawned just as a photographer approached, his camera ready. She quickly clamped down on her teeth, smiled, and lifted her chin slightly, all too aware that this very picture would appear in the Style section of the *New York Times* on Sunday. As the lens flashed brightly, she prayed for a flattering shot—even though an unflattering shot was rare.

Of the Hamilton triplets, Madison looked most like their mother. Venturina Baci, famed actress of stage and screen, had been a top model in her teens and early twenties. A lean, leggy Italian with wild dark hair and the face of an angel, Venturina made her theatrical debut in London's West End; a year later, while shooting her first movie in New York, she spent a single night partying at a trendy nightclub and fell in love. Venturina was twenty-six. Trevor Hamilton was thirty-two. Their romance had been chronicled in all the major tabloids of the day: the rising star and the ambitious, handsome entrepreneur. They married a few months later and Venturina became pregnant with triplets. But the marriage didn't last. When Madison, Park, and Lex were all of three, Venturina moved back to Italy to jump-start her European film career. And Trevor, already a billionaire, wouldn't hear of his famous girls leaving New York, the city that adored them.

There was never a time when Madison resented being compared to her mother. Venturina Baci was beautiful and accomplished, a European treasure. Her movies were not of the blockbuster variety, but works of cinematic art. All the high-profile directors loved her: Almodóvar, Jeunet, Zhang. Over the years, Madison, Park, and Lex had traveled to the Cannes and Venice film festivals to cheer Venturina on. They shared a special relationship with their mother, a bond that transcended the four thousand miles separating them. Venturina wasn't around to share in all the small, meaningful moments of their lives—shopping on Fifth, vacationing in the Hamptons—but she was always there when her girls needed her.

Madison dropped her pose as the photographer nodded gratefully. Then she turned around and caught sight of her best friend, Coco McKaid, sifting through the crowd.

Coco was small and impish, with pixie-cut black hair and big brown eyes. She always looked as though she was in the middle of an emergency. Like Madison and her sisters, Coco was a sophomore at St. Cecilia's Prep. Her parents owned the Bristol Winery in Napa Valley, California—which was exactly why Coco hated wine and drank only vodka. She came to Madison's side and said, "Can you believe it?"

"Believe what?"

"You mean you haven't seen him yet?"

Madison frowned. "Jeremy Bleu? We all saw him twenty minutes ago. He made the opening remarks. He's gorgeous." As she spoke the words, a dreamy picture of Jeremy flashed in front of her eyes. Hollywood's current golden boy, Jeremy was one of the biggest celebrities in attendance tonight. His upcoming movie, *Knight,* had something to do with swords, shields, and the weapons of those violent medieval days. The flick would probably suck and go on to make a few hundred million at the box on. But it didn't matter what Jeremy Bleu said or did. His looks were downright phenomenal. You could sit there, mute the sound in your home theater, and just stare at him for hours. The black hair. The bright green eyes. The muscles rippling through his shirt. The very thought of him made Madison swoon.

"Not *him*," Coco said, exasperated. She tugged Madison's arm and led her across the room toward the edge of the dance floor. "Look, and then puke."

It took only a moment for Madison's eyes to register the awful sight. Theo West, the forbidden object of her affection, was snuggling close to Annabelle Christensen, who had long ago been elected mayor of Slut City, New York. They were box-stepping to the music and nuzzling at each other's lips. Madison felt her stomach clench.

"How the hell did they get in here?" Coco asked.

"Both Annabelle's and Theo's parents are benefactors of the museum," Madison replied calmly, never taking her eyes off the unseemly pair. "But I never thought Theo would have the nerve to come."

"Well, he did. And so did that bitch."

"Keep your voice down," Madison instructed her friend. "I don't want to let them know we're watching."

But it was hard to ignore either one of them. Theo was tall and well built, and his blond hair fell across his forehead in curly strands. He had blue t teeth, and a butt like Michelangelo's vid. Annabelle's strawberry blond locks d wavy. Her face was fairly hideous, but nnast's tight body and, according to ru- ed that gymnast's body to assume various enticing positions behind closed doors.

"Who made her gown?" Coco whispered. "The house of *Dior,* or the house of *whore*?"

Staring at Theo made Madison want to cry. They had known each other their entire lives. The attraction between them had always been intense, but the mere possibility of a real relationship was a total no-no. The West and Hamilton families were social rivals. It was a decades-old war, rooted in money, greed, and cutthroat business deals. Trevor Hamilton had publicly bashed the Wests on several occasions, and the Wests made no secret of their distaste for the Hamilton clan's "uncouth behavior." The battle had been written up in gossip columns at least a thousand times.

Madison had always thought of the rivalry as a trivial matter. Why couldn't bygones just be bygones? Last year, she had adopted that mode of thinking and approached Theo one day after school. The desire she felt for him had simply boiled to the surface. She'd cornered him in the auditorium and said, "Look. I know we're not supposed to even talk to each other, but I like you. And I think you like me. *We* didn't create the tension between our families, right?" Theo had responded with a broad, sexy smile. And then he'd gently stroked a finger across her cheek, lifted her chin, and kissed her hot on the lips. It was the first time Madison had ever let her guard down. For days afterward, she couldn't think of Theo without feeling those sharp sensations way down in the danger zone. They had talked and kissed in secret for a couple of weeks, but then, one day, he'd simply started ignoring her all over again. When Madison approached him, he told her it was impossible, it could never work, he hated betraying his family, and just leave it at that, okay? Since then, Theo had been shamelessly playing the field and not bothering to even pretend otherwise. It was as though the tender relationship between them had never even existed.

Even now, Madison hated admitting the truth to herself—and the truth was that she had begun falling in love with Theo West. Beneath the playboy image was a smart guy who loved Shakespeare, Mozart, *and* Clarins. She was probably the only girl on the planet who knew he recited sonnets and exfoliated before shaving.

"Stop staring," Coco whispered harshly.

Madison blinked and brought herself back to the present. "It just hurts," she said quietly. "I can't believe he would choose a girl like Annabelle over me."

"He didn't choose Annabelle because he likes her

more. He chose her because she carries condoms in her purse."

Madison looked away as Theo clamped a CPR-sized kiss on Annabelle's mouth.

"Don't let it get you down," Coco said. "I only wanted you to see the proof that he's totally rank. You deserve someone way better than that asshole. Try to stop thinking about him."

"I wish it were that easy." It wasn't. Theo was the first guy who'd made her feel *hot*. Not just physically, but emotionally too. In the path of his lustful stares, she had experienced a new confidence, something akin to sexiness. Would things have been different now if she *hadn't* gone all the way with him? Sometimes she cursed herself for letting it happen, for giving Theo her virginity. That night, there'd been something primal about the passion between them. She could still feel the strength of his body, taste the sweetness of his breath. . . .

"Oh, shit," Coco said, interrupting her thoughts. "Here they come."

Madison looked back at the dance floor and saw, with slowly growing horror, that Theo and Annabelle were striding toward her, hand in hand. It was too late to walk away. Her heart started pounding. Was she supposed to just ignore him? Would it be cooler to greet him?

"Chill," Coco whispered.

Madison held her breath as Theo neared. Her eyes locked on his. She cracked a ghost of a smile and tossed her head back.

He stopped not two feet from her. "Hey," he said.

"Hi, how's it going?" Madison kept her voice cheery. Beside her, Coco grunted a reply.

"Great," Theo replied. "You did one hell of a job here, Mads. This is sure to be a huge success."

Mads. What he used to call her when they were secretly an item. Madison nodded. She noticed the unnatural brightness of his eyes and knew he'd probably smoked before coming here. She didn't know what to do but answer lamely, "It was a lot of fun. We all worked hard."

"You know Annabelle, right?"

"Of course." Madison smiled.

Annabelle stepped between them. The sharp look in her eyes was obvious. "Oh, Madison," she said, a twinge of sarcasm in her tone. "You look so *cute.*"

Cute? Madison kept the smile in place. She didn't reply.

Annabelle turned her gaze to Coco. "Are you kids having fun?"

Kids? Cute? What a bitch.

Coco chuckled. "And who are you wearing tonight, Annabelle?"

"Zac Posen," Annabelle said, doing a little whimsical pose.

"It's an interesting dress," Coco drawled. "And it looks *loose* in all the right places."

Madison bit her tongue.

Theo looked away.

Annabelle's lips pursed into a tight line, and she shot Coco a hateful stare. "Come on, Theo," she snapped, tugging at his arm. "Let's leave the kids to their playpen." And with that, she stomped off, Theo trailing close behind.

Madison finally let out her laughter. But it was a hollow victory. Deep down, she still felt cheated, insecure, inadequate. She felt like the kid Annabelle had labeled her.

"Sluts just have nerve," Coco said. "I was two seconds from telling her it looked like she'd bought that dress off the rack at Macy's."

Madison gasped. *That* was an insult very few people deserved.

Coco's eyes suddenly widened as she stared over Madison's shoulder. "Hey, I thought you said Lex wasn't coming tonight."

"Lex?" Madison asked, confused. She followed Coco's gaze to the hall's arched entryway and nearly lost consciousness.

Yes, it was Lex. In the flesh.

She entered the room as though the event were being held in her honor. She took slow, practiced steps, nodding and smiling at the dozens of guests who had stopped dancing—or stopped breathing—to gawk at her. She brought her hand up in a flat, windshield-wiper wave. Cameras flashed. Someone from one of the tables whistled admiringly. And Champagne, cuddled in the crook of her arm, started barking.

"Oh, my God," Madison said. "I think I'm going to be sick."

"Don't vomit on your shoes," Coco warned.

Too shocked to move, Madison played her usual card and forced a smile to her lips. People were staring. Some were whispering. The air of disapproval wasn't a surprise, given Lex's completely inappropriate attire. Madison watched her sister sashay across the floor, all legs and boobs and flashy grin, and for the first time in her life wished she could just disappear.

"Hi!" Lex said giddily. "I'm not too late, am I?"

Keeping the smile in place, Madison leaned toward Lex's ear and said, "What the fuck are you doing here?"

"What language!" Lex shot back. "Where did you learn to speak like that?"

"Quit being coy and tell me how you got here. Did you bribe Lupe and Clarence again? Oh, Daddy's gonna have a field day with this."

"I didn't bribe anyone," Lex lied. "For your information, I snuck out of the apartment. Lupe and

Clarence have nothing to do with it. I wanted to come, and here I am."

Madison sighed, exasperated.

"Hey, Lex. Welcome to the party." Coco sounded pleased, and she couldn't help herself. A party wasn't really a party until Lex walked through the doors.

Lex nodded. "It's beautiful. I feel right at home."

"How could you come here dressed like that?" Madison snapped. "You look like you're on your way to a nightclub in Queens."

"Queens!" Lex looked horrified. "You're just jealous because everyone's staring at me. Now point me in the right direction and I'll leave you alone."

"What direction?" Madison asked sharply. "Do you expect anyone to take you seriously dressed in one of your cheap designs?"

"My designs are hot, and you know it, Madison. I just need to get noticed by the right person."

"Well, you'll definitely get noticed tonight, but for all the wrong reasons, as usual. Now can you just go sit down and try to stay out of trouble?"

Lex's mouth fell open in melodramatic shock. "I don't understand why you're being so rude to me. You *know* how much I admire Zahara Bell and how hard I've tried to get her to notice me. Instead of helping your own sister out, you're treating me like some intruder from New Jersey."

"Zahara Bell hasn't even gotten here yet. Your

fashion idol never showed up, despite having paid for a seat at the President's Table. Anyway, every other woman in this room is hoping to get noticed by her."

"Oh." Lex pouted. "Well then, I want to meet Jeremy Bleu."

"You'll meet Jeremy next month anyway," Madison snapped. "We're going to the premiere of his new movie."

Lex stared at her sister. "For fuck's sake, what's with you tonight?"

Madison looked away. She knew her eyes had gone watery.

"Theo West was here, dancing with Annabelle Christensen," Coco said quietly. "And Annabelle even came by to insult us."

Lex's jaw hardened into a scowl. "That little bastard had the nerve to show up here? With Annabelle? Where are they?"

"Forget it. I'm fine." Madison held in her tears. She hated showing her vulnerable side, even though both Lex and Park knew about the secret relationship she and Theo had shared. Madison hadn't bothered to hide it from them because, despite their sibling rivalry, they were each other's closest friends and always kept each other's secrets. But now Madison felt downright childish. She hadn't wanted the evening to be this way.

The orchestra launched into another classical

tune, and the dance floor grew more crowded. Candles were being relit. Waiters were clearing the main course from tables and preparing the settings for sumptuous desserts. The latter action did not escape Champagne's attention; he barked and squirmed in Lex's arms as decadent aromas wafted on the air.

"Did you *have* to bring the dog?" Madison said.

Lex nuzzled his little face. "He goes so well with my dress, doesn't he?"

"Totally," Coco agreed.

Without a word, Madison turned and walked to the bar. She ordered a glass of Cristal. Coco requested a vodka and cranberry, Lex a Malibu Bay Breeze. The bartender, in his twenties and marginally cute, delivered the drinks without hesitation.

"Hey," Coco said. "Where's Park, anyway?"

Madison did a quick sweep of the floor, scouring the crowd gathered by the other bar across the room. No sign of Park.

Suddenly Lex said, "Heads up! Flash alert!"

All three girls simultaneously placed their drinks on the bar, then turned to face the photographer. In quick, practiced gestures, they linked their arms around each other and smiled. With the booze out of sight, the published picture would have no reason to stir trouble. The photographer thanked them and continued on his way.

Reaching again for her drink, Madison let her

eyes drift to the dance floor. There they were again—
Theo and Annabelle, making a spectacle of themselves. This time the sight hit her hard. She couldn't
stop the tears from welling up. She heaved a sigh and
looked helplessly at Lex.

"No, no," Lex said worriedly. "Your makeup. It'll
start running all over your face."

"Come on." Coco grabbed Madison by the arm.

The three of them rushed past the tables and
out into the huge hall. Lex reached the ladies' room
door first. She jiggled the knob, which appeared to
be jammed.

"Hurry," Madison urged, sobbing. "I don't want
anyone to see me."

"Just stay calm," Lex said. "Damn thing is locked
from the inside."

"Let me try it." Coco wrapped her hands around
the knob, but it didn't budge.

Madison heaved as mascara-tinted tears ran
down her cheeks.

A moment later, Lex managed to bust open the door.

A collective gasp echoed through the hall. Lex,
Madison, and Coco froze, eyes wide, mouths open.

Jeremy Bleu, superstar and hottie-in-the-flesh,
was sitting on the sink. His white shirt was pulled
out of his pants. His mouth was smeared with lipstick. He stared at the onlookers and cracked an im-
petuous smile.

The girl half-straddling him didn't bother to move. Her arms were locked around his neck, her face flushed and caked with her own lipstick.

"Park!" Madison screamed. "What the *hell* are you doing?"

The shock hung on the air for another tense moment. No one noticed the photographer coming out of the men's room directly opposite, but they all blinked when he lifted his camera over their heads and captured the scandalous scene with a flash.

3

The Lights on Park

She extricated herself from the compromising position very casually. Her long brown hair, flipped to one side of her head, fell around her shoulders as she pulled her legs back and set her feet firmly on the floor. Then she ran a finger beneath her wet, glistening lips and said, "Hi."

It was typical of Park. She never panicked. She assessed a situation, weighed her options, and then cheerfully tried to banter her way out of it. Positive thinking was her trademark. But as she stared back at the stunned faces taking in her every move, she couldn't quite think of anything pithy or profound to say.

"Hi?" Madison echoed incredulously. "Is that what you just said? What the hell is wrong with you?"

Park opened her mouth to speak. No words came out. She turned around and shot a glance at Jeremy Bleu, who was hastily shoving the tails of his shirt back into his pants.

When he realized the silence was focused on him, he cleared his throat. "Uh . . . I guess we got a little carried away," he said quietly. "Sorry."

Park finally let out a long sigh. "Well, what's the big deal, anyway?" she snapped, looking from Madison to Lex to Coco. "You're all acting as if you've never seen two people having fun. Jeremy and I were sharing a beautiful and heartfelt moment. We were just—"

A second flash cut through the bathroom. It was more startling this time around, like a direct hit to the face, and Park found herself blinking rapidly in the confusion of the moment.

Everyone was silent around her.

Until Madison turned and looked directly at the paparazzo.

He was a short, bald man with ruddy cheeks and fat fingers. Dressed in a tuxedo, he wore a press badge around his neck.

"You!" Madison screeched. "Give me that!"

The little man jumped back, cradling the camera against his chest.

"You're in the ladies' room, taking pictures!" Madison ranted, mascara streaking her angry face. "How dare you!"

"Pig!" Coco cried.

"Hand it over!" Lex demanded. "Daddy will freak!"

"Oh, shit! If those pics make it into the paper, my publicist will kill me." Jeremy Bleu raked a hand through his wavy hair. He drew the end of his sleeve across his mouth, nervously wiping away all traces of smeared lipstick. "Dude," he said stiffly, taking a step toward the paparazzo. "That's just not cool. You can't come in here and start snapping pics. That's not right. Hand the camera over."

"Absolutely not!" the little bald man replied. He tried backing out of the doorway hurriedly, but then Jeremy caught him by the elbows and started roughing him up.

Park watched the scene with mounting concern. "Be careful!" she said. "Don't hurt him. Don't pull the strap from around his neck—you could damage his voice box."

"Pig!" Coco shouted again.

"No respect for privacy!" Madison was saying.

". . . not gonna ask you again, dude," Jeremy warned.

The paparazzo, backed against the wall, held the camera out and began to aimlessly snap more pictures. One flash. Two, three, four, five. "Leave me alone!" he yelled back. "Get out of my way!" Then, with a pitiable roar, he charged past Jeremy and made for the hall.

"Stop him!" Madison cried.

Lex tightened her fingers around her purse. She raised it in her left hand and then brought it down with a *whoosh*—smacking the paparazzo broadside in the head.

He stumbled, moaned, and caught himself on the edge of the doorframe.

"Oh, no!" Park cried. "Lex! You hit him with the magic purse? It weighs a ton!"

"Grab that camera!" Jeremy Bleu yelled.

Madison and Coco rushed forward. In unison, they wrapped their hands around the camera and began prying it from the strap at the paparazzo's neck. He resisted, lashing out at them with his hands.

Lex lowered a barking Champagne to the floor. She watched as the dog sprinted toward the door, all three pounds of him, and bit down on the paparazzo's pants.

"I've got it!" Coco cried triumphantly. She held the camera up like a prize, then started tinkering with the buttons.

"No!" the paparazzo screamed. "Don't do that!"

"It's a digital!" Madison said. "There's no film in it. Take it and get out of here!"

As Coco dashed for the door, the paparazzo jumped in front of her. She froze, eyes wide, and nervously scanned the bathroom. "Incoming!" she yelled, and chucked the camera into the air.

Park looked up as it swooped in her direction. Her hands shot out and the camera landed in her palms.

"Stop!" the paparazzo ranted. He lunged forward, grabbing Park's shoulders.

"Don't you touch her!" Jeremy Bleu appeared at Park's side like the proverbial knight in shining armor. He locked his hands on the paparazzo's, trying to free Park from the older man's grip.

Quick as a cat, Park launched the camera into the air a second time, aiming it straight across the room at Lex.

Lex caught it.

The paparazzo instantly dashed after it. But he stumbled and pitched forward as Champagne locked jaws with his ankles again.

Madison was standing not two feet away. Following the path of the paparazzo's plunge, she yanked open the door of the first stall and then jumped back.

There was a loud *smack* as the paparazzo slammed into the toilet. His howl of pain was drowned out by the roar of the flush valve.

Madison kicked the door shut, temporarily trapping the man inside. "Everybody out!"

They filed into the hallway quickly, Champagne trailing behind them. Music played from the ballroom. Mercifully, there was no one around who could have heard the noisy scene.

"What now?" Coco asked breathlessly.

"We have to keep running," Lex said, bending down and scooping Champagne into her arms. "These paparazzi are nuts! He'll follow us straight into the gala!"

"Just delete the picture and leave the camera here," Jeremy suggested. "That way he'll leave us alone."

Park grabbed the camera from Lex's right hand. It was a sophisticated piece of machinery, pulsing with a bunch of tiny lights and buttons. She began stabbing them with her fingers just as the bathroom door flew open.

The man appeared on the threshold, looking dazed and disheveled but totally enraged. "Don't you kids move!" he screamed.

Park hugged the camera to her chest. It was her natural instinct to dispel all traces of panic, so instead of shouting or running, she held her hand out and said, "Stop right there, sir." She locked eyes with the little man and calmly passed the camera to Madison. Then she put both hands on her hips and tossed her head back. "Now, it's obvious that we have an ugly situation on our hands, but we all need something. We need you to let us delete the pictures you snapped, and you need us to return your camera. So if you'll kindly remain exactly where you are, we'll do what's necessary and all will be well. All those in agreement raise their hands."

Looking stunned but hopeful, Madison, Lex, Coco, and Jeremy all raised their hands slowly.

"Great," Park said with a smile. "Now, sir, I know you don't agree, but majority rules. Madison, please begin the deletion process. . . ."

But as her voice trailed off, the photographer took a small step toward them. Nostrils flaring, temples pulsating, he shook his head and said, "If you don't hand over that camera, I'll kill every one of you with my bare hands."

No one moved.

"Fine," he whispered angrily. His right arm shot out and latched on to the hem of Lex's dress.

Lex instinctively jumped back. The force of the jolt tore a jagged line down the middle of the frock.

Madison gasped.

Park bit down on her lip.

Coco stepped back, bringing Jeremy with her. It was a gesture of pure concern, because the girls all understood the severity of what had just occurred.

For a moment Lex looked as though she'd been slapped in the face. When the shock finally subsided, she stared down at herself—at her one-of-a-kind Triple Threat dress—and took a deep breath. "You little piece of shit," she seethed, her eyes blazing at the man. "You tore my dress!"

The guttural tone of her voice was so frightening, the paparazzo started.

"You tore my dress!" Lex screeched. "Now it's war!" Cradling Champagne tightly against her stomach, she locked her fingers on the long strap of the magic purse and raised it above her head.

"Reach for your stilettos," Park yelled, crouching down as she glanced from Madison to Coco to Jeremy.

Her teeth bared, Lex swung the heavy purse like a propeller at full throttle and then took perfect aim at the paparazzo's belly.

The blow found its target. The little man hunched over as the purse nailed him with the force of a brick. His "Oh" came out on a strangled breath.

"Try it again," Lex shouted, "and I'll get you below the belt!"

Park stood up straight again. She shook her head, looking pained. "For God's sake, Lex, you're gonna kill somebody with that thing! Sir, are you okay? Should we call the paramedics?"

"Fuck that!" Coco said.

"Totally," Jeremy agreed. "Dude got what he deserved."

"Did I?" The man balanced himself against the

wall, his voice low, angry. He was sweating and out of breath. But a determined gleam lit his eyes as he stared at Madison—and the camera in her hands. He assumed a sprinting position and let out a dramatic roar.

"Okay," Park said matter-of-factly, clapping her hands. "Everybody run."

Madison moved first. She turned left, away from the direction of the gala, and began powering down the wide empty hall.

Lex and Coco followed.

Jeremy grabbed Park's hand and pulled her into a jog.

And the paparazzo gave chase. "Stop!" he shouted. "You kids! Stop! Give me my camera!"

"Keep going!" Coco yelled.

Lex threw a glance over her shoulder. "He's gaining on us! Hurry!"

Madison was ahead of the pack. Holding the camera in one hand and lifting the ends of her gown with the other, she ran as fast as she could. Up ahead, the wide hallway was cordoned off by red velvet ropes, blocking entrance to another wing of the museum.

"Where are you going?" Coco called out.

"I don't know!" Madison yelled back.

Just then, two uniformed security guards came out from behind the ropes. "What's going on here?" one of them shouted.

Madison ground to a halt. She looked back and

saw Lex and Coco dashing toward her. Park and Jeremy were clumsily trying to outrun the crazed man, who looked like a little bull as he got dangerously close to them.

The security guards began making their way over to Madison. Tightening her grip on the camera, she dodged them and made a sharp right turn down an adjacent corridor.

"Freeze!" the guards said in unison.

Park ran past them with a flurry of her hand. "I apologize for the commotion," she said. "We're just having a little trouble. Thank you for your concern." She nearly tripped when Jeremy yanked her away from the guards and forced her to pick up her pace.

"In here!" Madison finally shouted.

Park kept her eyes on Lex and Coco, watching as they followed Madison through an open door and into what looked like a pitch-black room. Before plunging inside, she caught sight of the bull-man and the guards barreling toward them. "Where are we going?" she asked Jeremy.

"Does it matter?" He pulled her over the threshold and out of sight.

It was like slipping into a dark, silent cave. The voices shouting at them from the corridor dissipated, and Park heard Madison and Lex panting nearby.

"Where the hell are we?" Coco asked, her voice echoing through the blackness.

Leaning into Jeremy, Park sniffed the air. A musty odor pervaded her nostrils.

"Somebody find a damn light!" Lex said. "I can't see a thing!"

"Stay calm," Park ordered. She reached out her hands and took several small steps forward. She bumped into Madison, then pushed past her and felt along the wall for a switch. Finding one, she flicked it up.

Light blasted the space. It was a big rectangular coatroom, jammed with blazers, jackets, and several poufy furs. Sweaters and boots were strewn across the floor. The sudden hum of overhead air-conditioning vents cut through the silence as a cold draft swept over them.

"Oh, great!" Lex cried. "We're trapped in here. They'll find us in a second!"

"What did you expect me to do?" Madison shot back. "I couldn't just keep *running*."

They would have continued bickering, but Coco's high-pitched wail pierced the air like a knife.

She was standing a few feet away from them, in a small clearing beside an empty coatrack. Her mouth was open. Her hands were trembling. And her eyes were locked on the horrible sight that lay before her.

It was a woman's body. She was on her back, legs bent and arms outstretched. Her lips were frozen in an ugly grimace. Her skin was blue-tinged. Around her neck was a thick black scarf, wound so tightly that her head looked as though it might pop off any second.

Park went to Coco's side. Her hands flew to her mouth in shock. "Oh. My. *God!*"

Madison, standing speechless not three feet away, nearly fainted. She stumbled back and into Jeremy's waiting arms.

"She's totally dead!" Coco said. "Murdered!"

Lex shrieked. She held Champagne against her chest, then forced herself to stare. Her eyes widened in disbelief as they traced over the woman's short black hair, straight nose, and lean body. "It's Zahara Bell!" she screeched. "Oh, my God! Someone's killed Zahara Bell!"

"Jesus, it *is* Zahara!" Jeremy said. He held Madison firmly in his arms and at the same time leaned forward to inspect the corpse.

"Oh, this is so *gross,*" Coco whispered.

"Call the police," Park ordered. "Open the door and get security in here!"

But before anyone moved, the door burst open and the two security guards rushed inside. They didn't speak. They didn't even breathe. The shock showed on their faces instantly. They both reached for the radios on their belts and began shouting out codes. "All of you kids, get out of here!" one of them bellowed.

"Wait!" Lex said. "Oh, my God! I don't believe it! *Look!*"

"What is it?" Madison asked, her voice quavering.

Lex pointed down at the body of Zahara Bell, indicating her clothing. The dead woman was wearing a black strapless cocktail dress that appeared to have been hastily yanked over her boobs. The lace pattern running down the center was intricate and unique: At close glance, the hand-stitched seams formed a slender champagne flute that looked as though it had been superimposed onto the delicate fabric. Pinned to the dress's left sleeve was a bright orange silk orchid. "That's one of my dresses!" Lex screamed. "It's a Triple Threat original! *And it should be hanging in my closet right now!*"

"What?" Park asked, her tone incredulous. "That's impossible."

"She's right," Madison confirmed weakly. "My God, she's *totally* right. Lex wore that dress to the opening of Lotus in Vegas two months ago."

"That's right! I did!"

"Enough!" the security guard bellowed. "Get out of here now! *Now!*"

"What about the scarf?" Coco asked, ignoring the order. "You didn't design that too, did you? Looks like it's what did her in."

Lex held a hand to her stomach. "Are you *kidding*? Like I'd make a scarf that ugly."

"The poor woman," Park whispered, recoiling and pushing her sisters and Coco toward the door. "Who would want Zahara Bell dead?"

"You know the deceased woman?" the security guard asked.

Lex whirled around. "*Know* her? She's the most brilliant and powerful fashion editor in the world!"

"For God's sake!" Coco sneered, narrowing her eyes at the guard. "Can't you at least *pretend* to know who important people are?"

"Fine. Next time I will." The guard pointed to the door. "Get out. But don't you girls even *think* about leaving until the cops have spoken to all of you."

They walked out of the coatroom and into the corridor. A crowd had already gathered at the opposite side of the wing, the din of voices drifting through the air. As the girls hurried across the floor and out of earshot, Madison said, "Hey, wait a minute. Where's Jeremy? And what happened to the psycho photographer?"

Park blinked, confused. She looked around, poking her head out at the crowd and scanning dozens of curious faces. Jeremy had, in fact, vanished. And so had the paparazzo.

"The little dick bounced on us," Lex snapped. "See what I mean? You can never trust actors."

"He was holding me up one minute and gone the next," Madison said. "Where did he go? I didn't see him leave."

"Maybe . . ." Park found herself struggling to find the right words. "Maybe he's in the men's room, or maybe he's just hiding out, avoiding the crowd. He knows he can't leave without talking to the police."

"Well, neither can we." Madison looked down at her hands. She was still clutching the camera. She gestured for Lex to open up the magic purse and dropped it inside.

"This is ridiculous," Coco said. "I don't want to stay here. There's a dead body here. There's a *killer* here. Why do we have to stay?"

"Because we found the body," Lex told her quietly. "And that spells a whole lot of trouble. My God—you heard that security guard. We have to talk to the cops. They probably think we're *guilty* of something."

Madison nodded. Anxiety showed in her eyes. "You're right. They probably do. And it makes perfect sense. Zahara Bell was wearing one of Lex's dresses: Does that tie us to the crime? We're probably *suspects,* for God's sake!"

"Don't say that! I can't even hear it!" Coco covered her ears with her hands.

"What are we gonna do?" Lex said, panic rising in her voice. "How are we going to explain this to people? The press will have a field day. We'll all be tried as murderers. It'll be worse than when . . ."

Park didn't flinch as all eyes locked upon her. She stared back at her sisters and Coco and then ran a hand through her hair. "There's only one thing we *can* do," she said calmly. "We'll just have to find the killer first."

4

In *Bleu*

Jeremy was breathless. He had been speed walking
for ten solid minutes, and now a film of sweat was beginning to dampen the exquisite fabric of his Dolce &
Gabbana tuxedo. He finally slowed his pace as he
neared the corner of Fifth Avenue and Sixty-third
Street. Traffic was heavy, crowds thick. The city was
just starting to boom with nightlife. Under normal
circumstances the vibe would have excited him, but
he wasn't in a partying mood anymore. His heart was
thudding. His palms were slick. And for the first time

in three fame-filled years, he found himself wishing for complete anonymity.

Running a hand through his wavy hair, Jeremy eyed the dozens of occupied cabs streaming past. There was no chance of flagging one down. What would be the damn point, anyway? He was only a few short blocks from the Pierre and the safety of his penthouse suite. It made more sense to continue walking, but the possibility of being spotted and fawned over by ten or twenty fans was all too real—and all too dangerous. Cameras would flash. Word would spread. By morning there would be pictures of him in all the major newspapers looking scared and disheveled and totally spooked. And every reporter in the city would put the pieces together and know that he had fled the crime scene. It wasn't exactly the kind of publicity he wanted. One little connection to a dead body and your movie career was downgraded to daytime television status.

He reached the corner of Sixty-first Street. He scanned the endless stream of cars again. Everything was just too damn bright. Here, on the west side of Fifth Avenue, he stood ensconced in shadows, the trees of Central Park camouflaging him beneath a leafy canopy. One more block and the avenue widened to a concrete jungle. There was no safety in the harsh glare of headlights and glowing sky-scrapers. Still, he knew it was only a matter of time before *someone* with a brain recognized him. He had no choice but to keep moving. Holding his breath, he stared at the flashing crosswalk signal and cut quickly to the opposite side of the avenue. He walked with his head down. Several pedestrians zipped by him, but no one threw a glance his way.

Good. Ignore me. Let me be invisible.

Even as the words echoed through his brain, Jeremy knew that becoming invisible was as impossible as going a week without sex. His face was currently gracing the covers of five national magazines, a billboard in SoHo, and countless promo posters for his upcoming film, *Knight.* Yesterday, while in Los Angeles, he had granted Mary Hart an interview for *Entertainment Tonight.* There was also his appearance on the *Today* show to think about. And just two hours ago, he'd been the main attraction of the Met's fund-raising gala. The whirlwind of publicity was constant. It hadn't stopped in three years, ever since he'd starred in *All Cut Up,* his first blockbuster movie. Jeremy had gone from fifteen-year-old Iowa farm boy to international celebrity overnight, and the world's eyes were locked on him. He liked to think it had everything to do with his acting abilities, but deep down, he knew his good looks were the reason for his fame. He was tall and lean and solidly built, with washboard abs and killer pecs. He couldn't take a bad picture. Women went crazy when he stepped out of a limousine and strutted down the red carpet. They went even *crazier* when they spotted him doing everyday things—driving to the gym, shopping at the grocery store, playing with his dog on the beach in front of his Malibu mansion. Getting used to the continuous adoration had been easy, but being photographed a dozen times a day was another story. That was the downside of fame: you couldn't scratch your ass without it making the tabloids.

Now he glanced up and saw the Pierre's well-lit entrance a few steps away. Relief flooded him. He feigned a smile as the doorman, a middle-aged man in a blue suit and top hat, perked up with visible admiration.

"Mr. Bleu," the man said quietly, reaching for the door and holding it open. "Welcome back to the Pierre. Is there anything I can help you with this evening?"

"No, thanks," Jeremy replied tersely. "I'm fine." He stepped into the stately lobby but didn't make eye contact with the front-desk staff. He walked straight to the elevators and jumped into the first empty one. As he rode up to the penthouse suite, he felt his anxiety level kick up a few notches. This was a nightmare. A total fucking nightmare. Once the news broke that he had been at the gala, people would start asking questions. How was he going to handle that?

What impact would the impending scandal have on his career?

The elevator doors yawned open and Jeremy stepped into the privacy of the penthouse parlor. He fished the key from his blazer pocket. He jammed it into the lock, turned it, and slammed the door behind him. He stood for a moment in the darkness, staring out the large windows that overlooked Central Park and the blazing lights of the West Side. The view was spectacular. It had always managed to calm him in the past, but now he felt edgy and totally freaked. He couldn't look down at the grandeur of Fifth Avenue without imagining cop cars, sirens, and crowds of reporters closing in for the kill.

Peeling off his blazer, he went for the bar in the far corner of the room and reached for the bottle of Grey Goose. He grabbed a martini glass. He poured the vodka almost to the rim and then spiked it with a shot of Midori. Then he downed most of it in a single gulp, wincing as the beverage seared his throat. It had been a long time since he'd had a good, stiff drink. Maybe that was what he needed—a few hours of high-flying euphoria to ease his nerves. But even as the first mouthful of alcohol settled on his empty stomach, he knew getting blitzed wasn't going to accomplish anything. In the morning his hangover would be just another obstacle, and he'd still have to face the fact that Zahara Bell was dead.

Not just dead, he thought. *Murdered.*

He closed his eyes against the vision that rose before him, the vision of Zahara's twisted—but very well-clothed—body lying on that coatroom floor, the thick scarf cinched around her neck. It made him want to hurl. He had never in his life been *that close* to an actual crime scene.

Especially not one with personal ties.

He had met Zahara Bell the year before in Milan at the Prada men's show. Jeremy had been escorted to the front row, and ten minutes later Zahara had settled herself in right beside him. She was pretty hot for a woman her age. She'd been dressed immaculately in a tight black miniskirt and leather blazer, and Jeremy had noticed her legs right away: smooth, tanned, and perfectly toned. Her sexy stilettos had sent his equipment into a frenzy. She was in her forties and old enough to be his mother, but that hadn't mattered a bit. For most of the show, Jeremy had watched her from the corner of his eye, making small talk and drinking in the sweet scent of her perfume. A week later, in one of her customarily controversial *Catwalk* magazine interviews, Zahara had referred to Jeremy as "devilishly delicious." The description pleased him. Since then, he had seen her on several occasions, and they had always flirted with each other from a comfortable distance.

Now the woman was plant fertilizer. Jeremy shook

his head to blot out the image of her slender neck straining against the pressure of the scarf. It was such an ugly memory. On movie sets there were all kinds of gadgets and makeup and camera tricks that mimicked murder with stunning accuracy, but nothing compared to seeing the real thing up close. He still couldn't believe it had actually happened. He had heard hundreds of unflattering stories about Zahara Bell over the past three years, and there was no shortage of people who had reason to want her dead. She had been the quintessential bitch, making and breaking the careers of fashion designers all over the world. As editor in chief of *Catwalk* magazine, she'd published scathing articles and humiliated dozens of high-profile celebrities who had simply rubbed her the wrong way. She had ripped through countless frightened assistants as well. In one particularly shocking tale, Zahara had apparently called a board meeting at *Catwalk* magazine for the sole purpose of embarrassing a number of young female employees who hadn't lived up to her fashionable standards; she had identified them one by one using less than flattering names: *Lard Legs, Pimple Princess, Dandruff Drag Queen,* and *Jiggle-Butt.* Zahara herself had also been branded in the press by her enemies. Depending on who was talking about her, she was often referred to as a "bloodsucking python" or a "venomous scorpion." A well-liked woman she was not.

Jeremy set the empty martini glass on the window-sill and peeled off his shirt. It was soaked through with sweat. Cursing, he threw it onto the couch and stomped into the bathroom, where he studied his reflection in the mirror. All that damn nervous energy had caused him to break out in hives. There were two bright red dots on his forehead and another just beside his nose. Thankfully, the rest of his upper body looked good. Park Hamilton had been pressed up against his chest a short while ago. He could still feel the heat of her lips and smell the sweetness of her perfume. She was *so* hot. He wished more than anything that they could've finished what they had started. The only evidence of their little rendezvous was the pinkish purple hickey forming on the left side of his neck. He touched it gently and bit down on his lower lip, trying to control the hormones raging through his blood.

He hadn't meant to ditch her. It had been an act of sheer, stupid panic. As the commotion in the coat-room heightened, Jeremy had stormed down the hallway and out of the museum's front doors. He had even seen that short fat photographer making a run for it. He couldn't imagine how upset Park must have been when she realized he had left her flat and cold to deal with the whole mess. She and her sisters were probably calling him a dickless asshole right now, but dammit, that was totally untrue. Running away from danger wasn't Jeremy's style; it never had been. If he had managed to keep his wits in order, he would've gathered Park into his arms and held her until the cops showed up. He would've showed her that he was more than just a famous face. But fear had gotten the best of him. In those terror-filled moments, he had heard his publicist's voice echoing in his head like thunder.

The biggest rule of fame, Jeremy, is to control your publicity. Don't create a scandal unless it will benefit your career.

And as far as he could tell, there was nothing good about being connected to Zahara Bell's murder.

There was, however, something to be said for snagging one of the Hamilton triplets.

Despite the fact that he and Park had only just met, Jeremy knew the connection between them was fierce. Hell, it might even be love at first sight. It was unlike anything he had ever experienced before. Just thinking about her made his heart pound. He had hooked up with more girls than he could count, but Park was different from any of them. She had style and class and grace. She had brains. They had locked eyes across the crowded ballroom, and next thing he knew they had struck up a flirtatious conversation. But even as the air between them had heated up, she hadn't thrown herself at him carelessly. She had sized him up, stared him down, and reeled him in. *She* had made *him* feel thankful for the gift of her kiss, and it usually didn't work that way. Usually, girls fawned and swooned and clawed their way into Jeremy's jeans. Getting laid had never been a challenge for him. But tonight, under Park's spell, he had felt completely dominated. And he'd enjoyed every second of it.

He exhaled a heavy breath, determined to quell the fire burning in his boxers. What he needed was a cold shower. He settled for a splash of water across his face, then reached for the travel case sitting on the far end of the sink. From it he drew a long silver and blue tube of ZIRH moisturizer. He squeezed a small amount into the palm of his left hand and slathered the cream over his cheeks, forehead, and chin. The red hives started to disappear almost immediately. A good complexion was paramount when going before the cameras, and Jeremy had few doubts that in the morning he would have to make some sort of statement to the press. Thank God for men's cosmetics.

Stepping out of the bathroom, he felt the full force of the martini hitting his blood. He was ever so slightly—and ever so sweetly—light-headed. He settled himself on the plush couch in the center of the suite and stared down at his hands. They were still trembling. A moment later his eyes drifted to the large mahogany and glass coffee table not two feet away. The remote control stared back at him.

No, he thought, *don't turn on the TV. Bad idea. Zahara Bell's murder couldn't have made it onto the news so quickly.*

He hesitated, but curiosity got the better of him. Slowly, nervously, he stretched out an arm and jabbed a finger at the Power button. The plasma television mounted above the fireplace came to life with a flash. The channel was tuned to MTV: Jessica gyrating to her latest hit. Deciding he didn't need to be aroused further, Jeremy grabbed the remote and began cruising through the channels. One, two, three, four . . . no mention of the story on any of the local stations. Good. The more time he had to figure things out, the better. He would spend the night plotting his way out of this one if he had to. He would even—

The remote landed on ABC, and Jeremy gasped. He was staring at a live aerial shot of the Metropolitan Museum of Art. Crowds were gathered at the bottom of the steep steps, and dozens of police cruisers sat motionless along the west side of Fifth Avenue.

"Oh, God," he whispered. "Not already."

He raised the volume on the flat-screen, and Diane Sawyer's unmistakable voice filled the room.

". . . following a developing story," she said as the aerial shot zoomed in closer. "Several sources have told ABC News that internationally renowned fashion editor Zahara Bell was found dead inside the Met just over an hour ago. Bell was apparently a guest at a charitable gala at the Met tonight . . ."

Jeremy shot to his feet, panic seizing him. "Diane, sweetie, don't do this to me!" he shouted.

". . . and we are now being told," Diane continued, "that police are treating this as a *homicide*. You are seeing on your screens now a live shot of the Met, teeming with activity. Tonight's star-studded gala was apparently being sponsored by Hamilton Holdings, Incorporated, and we are being told that the Hamilton triplets—Madison, Park, and Lexington—were in attendance. A number of other celebrities were also in attendance: Gwen Stefani, Lindsay Lohan, and Jeremy Bleu among them. Sources are telling ABC News that all the guests are still inside the museum as police secure the crime scene and begin their investigation into the murder of Zahara Bell. . . ."

"No!" Jeremy screamed. "No! No! *Fucking no!*" He slammed his hand against the remote. The flat-screen blinked out, plunging the suite into semi-darkness again. Breathing nervously, he raked both hands through his hair and stomped over to the nearest window. He stared down at the busy stretch of Fifth Avenue. Traffic. Lights. Ordinary cars. No police cruisers. He was about to make his way to the bar for a second martini when the suite's telephone rang. Cautiously, he picked it up.

"Mr. Bleu?" a female voice said from the other end of the line. "This is the front desk calling. I wanted to let you know . . ." The woman's voice trailed off as background noise filtered through the receiver.

"Yes?" Jeremy said impatiently. "What is it?"

"Well, we thought you should know," the woman continued. Her voice dropped into a whisper. "There are several reporters in the lobby demanding to speak to you."

"Don't you *dare* let them anywhere near those elevators!" Jeremy screamed. "Do you hear me?"

"Yes, sir," she replied nervously. "Yes. I—"

"If even *one* reporter makes it up here and starts banging on my door, I'll have my publicist tear this place apart. I'll let the whole world know that you can't provide adequate security for your guests. Do you understand me? *Do you?*"

"Yes, yes. Of course. I—"

Jeremy slammed the phone down. He started pacing. The word was obviously out that he had run away from the Met only moments after discovering Zahara Bell's body. And if the press knew it, so did the police. He imagined them storming through the suite like wolves on the prowl, eager to tie his bad-boy image to a really bad situation.

Why did you flee the crime scene, Mr. Bleu?

Because I was scared, Jeremy thought now, rehearsing for what would undoubtedly prove to be the most challenging role of his life. *I didn't know what else to do. It was fear. I'm still afraid, Officer. There's a killer on the loose.*

And what did you do after you left?

I came back to my hotel room. The front desk saw me. People saw me.

Did you know the victim?

He would give them a slow, mournful nod. *Yes.*

And then what? Would it really be that easy? What if the cops started poking into his past and found the shit he didn't want them to find?

He went to the bedroom and grabbed his pack of Nat Shermans off the nightstand. He lit up. *You didn't make any mistakes,* he assured himself. *No one will ever find out. Just stay calm.* He paced the room, puffing hard on the cigarette. When the image of Zahara Bell's twisted body flashed before his eyes again, he started. He shook his head. Then he raked his left hand across his neck and shoulder, wanting to squeeze the tension from his muscles. It was the precise moment his heart nearly exploded in his chest.

Oh, shit. Please, don't let it be true.

But it *was* true. Realizing his error, he stared frantically around the room, wondering what to do next.

How could I have been so stupid? Why didn't I think before acting?

He kept telling himself that maybe no one would notice. He hoped to God no one noticed. That was his only chance at escaping this ugly mess. Otherwise, in the morning, he would be *totally* behind bars.

5

Killer Couture

It was all about staying cool. The girls had learned that lesson a long time ago. When scandal erupted and nasty rumors took flight, you had to toss your head back, drop your shoulders, and draw attention to the jewelry sparkling around your neck. Precious gems brightened even the most unflattering light.

Madison knew this. She stood a few feet away from her sisters and Coco, her body turned purposefully toward the crowd that had gathered at the opposite end of the corridor. The Harry Winston choker glittered on her neck like a disco ball. An intricate web of bright green emeralds and heart-shaped five-carat sapphire stones, it was a rare work of art that never failed to attract dozens of admiring glances. Madison lifted her eyes nonchalantly to the ceiling and casually struck a pose. People were staring more than they were whispering, and that was a good thing.

"I didn't notice how gorgeous that piece is until now," Park said quietly.

Coco nodded. "It casts a spell. Look at how quiet the crowd got."

"She's *always* worn jewelry beautifully," Lex commented of her sister. "I can't wear chokers—they don't call enough attention to my boobs."

They stood a few feet away, watching calmly as Madison seized and mastered the moment. She tossed her head back again. She pivoted as if she were standing at the edge of a runway. Then she smiled as three cameras flashed in rapid succession. The cool act worked like a charm. She was representing Hamilton Holdings, Inc., at the gala, so it made perfect sense for her to wow the crowd—especially now, with so many people wondering what the hell was happening.

It was an ugly scene. There were at least fifteen uniformed police officers standing along the corridor, looking grim. Yellow crime-scene tape sealed off the entrance to the coatroom. And a tall middle-aged man with thinning blond hair and a badge around his neck was standing on the threshold scribbling notes onto a pad. He muttered something to one of the cops and then looked up.

Park immediately met his stare and locked her eyes with his. As he came toward her in quick strides, she extended her hand.

The older man seemed taken aback by the gesture. He paused, cracked a nervous smile, and folded his hand in hers. "Detective Charlie Mullen, Homicide," he said.

"Park Hamilton," she replied, making certain to keep her tone calm. "Charmed, I'm sure."

"I know who you are, Ms. Hamilton," Mullen said.

"Please, call me Park." She glanced over her shoulder, introducing Lex and Coco. Before the detective could begin asking questions, she said, "This has been a terrible and unfortunate tragedy. We were simply in the wrong place at the wrong time."

"That's putting it mildly." Mullen cleared his throat. "Would you mind calling your sister over here? I need to speak with all of you."

"Madison," Park said lightly. "Could you join us, please?"

Turning on her heels, Madison made her way over to them with graceful steps, as though waltzing across the floor. She extended her hand to the older man.

Mullen took it, and his eyes fell inevitably to the

shimmering choker. "Those are some rocks you got around your neck," he said, impressed.

"Thank you." Madison smiled.

"Are those real emeralds?"

The question—so innocent and yet so painfully offensive—rattled Madison to the core. She couldn't believe someone would actually think she was wearing *costume jewelry*. Fake emeralds? Fake sapphires? The very thought of hastily cut green glass and those ugly blue plastic nuggets made her dizzy. She blinked, speechless, and looked from Park to Lex to Coco. When the silence got tense, she turned back to Detective Mullen and said, with as much strength as she could muster, "Yes. They're real."

"Amazing," Mullen whispered. "I don't think I've ever seen emeralds that big this close up."

Park knew a cue when she heard one. She also knew an impressed fan when she met one. Detective Mullen might have been in his forties, but he was obviously in awe of the company surrounding him. She wondered if he had a daughter her age, or if his wife was one of those tabloid magazine junkies who enjoyed reading about the infamous Hamilton sisters. Whatever the case, it wouldn't hurt to make small talk. "Do you know the legend behind real emeralds, Detective?" she asked him sweetly.

"I don't," he admitted.

"Well," Park began, "emeralds are among the

earliest gemstones known to man. In ancient times, they were dedicated to the goddess Venus for love, and also because they were believed to improve intelligence. But they were mainly used for love. They say that if you give someone an emerald, she'll be a faithful lover for the rest of her life. They also say that once you own an emerald, you can never lose it. Emeralds always find their way home."

Mullen smirked. "That's interesting. Never heard that before. You some kind of expert?"

"You could say that." Inwardly, Park smiled. She was more than an expert when it came to precious gems and stones. Jewels had been one of her ruling passions ever since she was a little girl, and over the years she had devoted countless hours to studying everything from diamonds and pearls to the rarest sapphires. Her knowledge of the subject was huge. Her personal jewelry collection was even bigger. "Your wife would probably love an emerald for your anniversary this year," she said.

Mullen made a sour face. "I'm divorced."

"A good-looking guy like you?" It was Lex's voice this time. She was standing directly behind Park, and now she feigned a ditzy smile as Detective Mullen blushed. "I find that *so* hard to believe."

"So do *I*," Coco said with mock seriousness, a hand to her chest.

"Well, you know, this is all very flattering, ladies,

but I do have a few questions to ask you," Detective Mullen told them sternly. He flipped open his notepad and began riffling through the pages. "Now, I was told by the security guards that right before the body was discovered, you all ran into the coatroom and then closed the door. Why was that?"

"We were trying to outrun a psychotic paparazzo," Madison said. "We were very lucky. I thought he was going to kill us."

"Uh-huh. And had you ever seen this . . . paparazzo before tonight? I mean, since you girls are used to being photographed all the time."

"Never," Lex said. "He was short and fat and bald. *And* he tore my dress."

"Right," Mullen mumbled as he wrote. "So it was you four girls being chased by this man. And you didn't see where he disappeared to?"

"No, we didn't." Park bit down on her lip. "It wasn't actually us four. I had a . . . guest . . . with me."

Mullen glanced up at her. "Yes, I know. Jeremy Bleu. I guess you have no idea where he is right now, huh?"

"I don't know," Park admitted. "Everything got so crazy after we . . . saw the body . . . and, well, when we came out here, he was gone."

"He ditched us," Lex chimed in.

"He did *not*," Park cut in sharply. She stared at Detective Mullen. "I'm sure Jeremy has a positively good reason for not being here. Like I said, this was all just a misunderstanding."

"Jeremy Bleu not being here is the same thing as Jeremy Bleu fleeing a crime scene, Ms. Hamilton," Detective Mullen snapped. "How well do you know Mr. Bleu? Is this characteristic of him?"

A silence fell as Park considered her response. Was she supposed to tell Detective Mullen the truth? *We met each other tonight, Detective. The attraction between us was intense and I just wanted to jump his bones.* Totally not! The truth sounded way too slutty. She sighed and said, "I haven't known him for very long. But I do know that he's smart and polite and very thoughtful." *And completely gorgeous. Don't forget completely gorgeous.*

"At what point this evening did you first see the victim?"

The girls glanced at each other. Lex, still cradling Champagne to her chest, shook her head. "We first saw Zahara Bell in the coatroom. She was absolutely dead by the time we got there."

Mullen kept writing in his notepad. "Think back now. When you first started running down this corridor, did you see anyone else standing here, or even close by?"

"I was the first one to run down the corridor," Madison answered. "I didn't see anybody."

"What made you run down this particular

corridor? Big museum here. You could've gone down any corridor."

The edge of suspicion in Detective Mullen's voice was very slight, but it angered Madison. "We were being *chased,* for God's sake," she told him sharply. "When a crazy person is chasing you, the most common reaction is to run away. Don't they teach you that when you become a cop?"

Detective Mullen dealt her a cold stare. "We're not talking about me here, Ms. Hamilton. We're talking about you—*all* of you. Where's this paparazzo you're talking about? Where's Jeremy Bleu? A murder has been committed, and I'm not getting very convincing answers from any of you."

"We're telling you all we know," Park said firmly.

"And how well did you know the victim, Zahara Bell?"

"We knew *of* her, and of her stature as the world's greatest fashion editor," Lex replied. "But none of us had ever met her personally."

Detective Mullen flipped through to the front of his notepad. "From what I was told a few minutes ago, your father's company sponsored this gala here tonight. You mean to tell me you invited guests you've never met?"

Madison sighed. What was the point of trying to explain philanthropy to a cop? It was blue blood versus blue-collar, and the two simply didn't mix.

"That's exactly right," she said. "In our world, Detective Mullen, people can know each other without ever meeting each other."

He raised his eyebrows. "That doesn't make sense."

"Sure it does," Madison told him. "You knew my sisters and me before meeting us a few minutes ago, didn't you? That's because we live in the public eye. Same thing with Zahara Bell. I had hoped to meet her tonight, but . . ."

"But what?" Detective Mullen asked.

"But she didn't make it, obviously." Madison had to shut her eyes against the memory of Zahara Bell's body. She felt even worse when she remembered that the body was still behind that closed coatroom door, with that heinous scarf as its last accessory.

"So then, I guess you haven't found him yet," Coco said, breaking the momentary silence.

"Found who?"

Coco rolled her eyes. "The killer. *Helllooo?*"

Detective Mullen glared down at her. "What makes you so sure the killer is a *he*?"

"Oh, come on. Get real." Coco chuckled.

"It's totally obvious," Lex said under her breath.

Park and Madison nodded firmly.

"Is that what you girls think?" Detective Mullen said. "You think only men are killers and criminals because of the statistics you've read in some magazine? Well, lemme give you girls a quick lesson—"

"It has nothing to do with statistics." Madison cut him off. "It has to do with obvious common sense. And glaring evidence. Zahara Bell's killer was a man. There's no doubt about it."

"Of course there isn't," Park said. "I can't even believe we're discussing this."

Detective Mullen crossed his arms over his chest. "What evidence? What the hell are you girls talking about?"

"Didn't you see the body, Detective?" Lex asked him, her tone incredulous. "There's an ugly black scarf around Zahara Bell's neck. It doesn't even *remotely* go with the dress she's wearing. It's not even the right season. It's a mismatch. Only a man could have killed her that way and not noticed how *bad* it looks. A woman wouldn't have anything like that still out of fall storage."

"A hetero man," Coco chimed in. "I mean, that's important, since we're building a profile of the killer."

"Oh, totally," Madison agreed. "A heterosexual man with no sense of style. The kind of man who wears black loafers with navy blue pants. Or boot-cut jeans with white sneakers. Hideous."

Detective Mullen, standing there in black loafers and navy blue pants, didn't say a word.

"Let me tell you," Lex said excitedly, "if the killer had been a woman, all the signs—the evidence— would have been a lot sleeker. A scarf like the one around Zahara Bell's neck would not have even entered the picture."

"Not one that looks like alpaca," Coco offered. "Something like raw silk, maybe, or maybe even cashmere."

"I would never ruin a cashmere scarf," Park said. "Especially not if it meant *leaving* it around someone's neck. Though I guess if it was completely, noticeably last season . . ."

"True, but you get my point." Lex looked at Detective Mullen. "So you see, it's obvious that we're looking for a male killer. The scarf around Zahara Bell's neck was absolutely *not* a part of her outfit."

Detective Mullen sighed. "And how do you know that for sure, Ms. Hamilton?"

"Because that dress is my—" Lex bit down hard on her tongue, and the nick of pain made her fingers clench. Champagne barked and squirmed against her chest.

"That dress is your *what?*" Detective Mullen asked, taking a step toward her. "Finish your statement, Ms. Hamilton. Do you know something about the dress the victim is wearing? Or about the way in which she was killed?"

Lex didn't speak. She glanced nervously at Madison, then at Park. Both of them looked pensive. As the silence hung on the air, Lex felt her heartbeat kick up several notches. *Shit. Shit. Shit.* It was still so damn confusing—her own one-of-a-kind dress on a dead woman's body. She didn't understand it, so how the hell was she supposed to explain it?

"Ms. Hamilton?" Detective Mullen prodded. "You wanna speak up?"

"It's . . . well . . ." Her voice trailed off. She gulped. "It's just that the victim, Zahara Bell, is wearing my dress." Even as the words rolled off her tongue, Lex couldn't help noticing how ridiculous they sounded. Ridiculous. Stupid. And impossible. But nonetheless true.

"What? What did you just say?" Detective Mullen looked as if he'd been slammed in his baseballs with a really big bat. "You'd *better* start explaining that one!"

Lex gave him the abbreviated version: the Triple Threat fashion line; her own gorgeous designs; original pieces that were all hanging in her private closet back home. No one could have gotten their hands on them. Very few people even knew she was about to launch her own line, and so she had no idea how Zahara Bell had snagged that particular dress. Fair enough?

Flushing a vibrant and highly unattractive shade of red, Detective Mullen began scribbling a series of notes onto his pad. He wrote and wrote. His fingers moved across the pages furiously. After what felt like five minutes, he trained his eyes on Lex. "Tell me something, Ms. Hamilton . . . when did you report this theft to the police?"

"Theft? I never reported any theft because I

didn't know the dress was missing until I saw it on the body," Lex told him.

"So you never look in your closet at home?"

"I go into my closet all the time, Detective. But I can't *see* everything that's in it at one time." Lex stared at him, exasperated. "My closet at home is about ten times the size of that horrible little coatroom. I wore the dress we're talking about a long time ago and it never occurred to me to look for it in my closet. But that's definitely it."

"So then, who do you think broke into your apartment and stole it from your closet?" Mullen asked, an edge of sarcasm in his tone. "Do you think the victim, Ms. Bell, was a thief?"

Madison sighed loudly. "Why are you asking us police-related questions? It's *your* job to investigate."

"And that's exactly what I'm doing. As it stands now, the victim is clothed in a dress that was hanging in your home. You all happened to find her body. You girls are also hosting this event. And . . ." Mullen flipped to the last page of his pad without taking his eyes off them. "And one of you has a penchant for jewelry. An interesting mix, if you ask me."

Park cleared her throat. "What does my penchant for jewelry have to do with anything?"

"Oh. Didn't you know?" Mullen asked a little too coyly. "Zahara Bell was wearing the Avenue diamond tonight, and now it's missing. Torn right from her neck, apparently."

"The Avenue diamond!" Park shouted, her eyes bulging. "*The* Avenue diamond?"

"Holy shit," Coco whispered.

"Yes," Mullen replied. "*The* Avenue diamond. You wouldn't happen to know anything about *that,* would you, Ms. Hamilton?"

Park bit down on her lip. Instead of launching into a roll call of facts about the miraculous and stupendous Avenue diamond—or its personal connection to the Hamilton family—she said, "We had nothing to do with this murder, Detective. We were all just in the wrong place at the wrong time."

"You expect me to believe that?" Mullen's voice rose. "You girls expect me to believe *any* of this? It's obvious that this isn't a simple coincidence, and I think it's despicable that you would try to use your celebrity to weasel your way out of this. It's also apparent that there's a lot about this crime you're not telling me."

Madison gasped. As Detective Mullen's words echoed through the corridor, her jaw dropped, her eyes flashed, and her shoulders stiffened squarely. "How dare *you* speak to *us* that way!" she snapped. "My sisters and I are not going to stand here and allow you to try to drag us through the mud because you don't want to do your job and find the man who killed Zahara Bell. That's what's *apparent.*"

"Our publicists will tear the whole police department apart when they get wind of this," Lex added.

Mullen laughed at that. "Your *publicists*? Go home and tell your daddy to call some *lawyers,* not publicists. *That's* what you girls will need. Good lawyers."

"Fine," Park replied calmly. "Does that mean we're free to go?"

"For now, yes." Mullen flipped his notepad shut. "But I'll be speaking to all of you tomorrow."

As Mullen turned to go, Madison, Park, Lex, and Coco watched two uniformed officers emerge from the coatroom, rolling the stretcher that held Zahara Bell's body neatly zipped in a body bag. Gasps echoed through the corridor. The chatter of voices filled the air.

"Gross," Coco said, cupping a hand over her mouth.

They all turned their eyes toward the crowd. Suddenly, a figure began moving through it, pushing his way to the front. It was Theo West. And despite the chaos of the moment—his wavy hair was scraggly, his face was sweaty—he looked hot.

Madison froze as he came striding in her direction.

"I just heard what happened," he said quietly, standing very close to her. "I just can't believe it."

Madison nodded dumbly. She caught a whiff of his cologne and felt as though her knees would buckle. But instead of melting at his feet, she threw her head back and bravely met his eyes. "Neither can we," she answered. "It's tragic."

"Are you okay? You weren't hurt or anything, were

you?" His right hand came up and landed softly on her shoulder.

The motion, Madison realized, was involuntary. She felt his fingers hot against the side of her neck, and his thumb swished along her skin in a gesture that was unconsciously tender. She lost herself in the moment. She lost herself in his eyes. Everything around her disappeared and suddenly there was only the two of them. There was the memory of their last, secret kiss and the electric tingle of his touch.

"Mads?" he whispered. "You okay?"

"I'm fine." She tore her eyes away from him and shrugged.

"We're *all* fine," Lex chimed in, butting her head in between them. "Thanks for asking."

"Jesus, Lex, you don't have to be so cold." Theo stared at her. "I was just about to ask if you were all okay."

"I'm *totally* sure you were." Lex rolled her eyes.

"Hey," Park said, stepping in between them. "Theo, you knew Zahara Bell personally, didn't you? I mean, wasn't she at a magazine owned by the publishing division of your father's company a few years ago?"

The silence that fell between them was palpable.

Theo's cheeks grew red. "I never met her," he said with a sneer. "Now if you'll excuse me, I have to get going." And with that, he turned and disappeared into the crowd, leaving the girls in a tense group.

"Listen," Coco said nervously, "I'm gonna bounce. I have to get home and call my folks."

"Go," Lex told her. "We'll call you later."

Madison and Park were already facing the crowd. Lex joined them, all too aware that they would have to walk through it with their heads held high. Side by side they went forward, into the storm, and a dozen cameras started flashing. Against the glare of the white lights, people eyed them curiously and began to whisper.

The Hamilton triplets. A murder. Front-page news.

It was official: the biggest scandal of their lives had broken wide open.

6

Bust It Like Becker

Exhaling the last smooth, smoky stream of his Cuban cigar, Clarence Becker leaned up against the driver's-side door of the Mercedes limousine and stared across Fifth Avenue. The Met was always lit up at night, but right now it looked like a runway strip at the airport. Police cruisers lined the west side of the street. News vans waited in the shadows of Central Park. The scene was chaotic, and little packs of reporters kept popping out of cabs and news vans to cover the big story unfolding inside the museum.

Clarence had heard something about it on the radio an hour ago—a fashion lady found dead. Big fucking deal. She was probably one of those bitchy types with a stick of dynamite up her ass. Media was making it into headline news just because she had a couple of bucks. Hell, where he came from, crimes were *really* violent. Clarence had been born and raised in Bensonhurst, Brooklyn, the only non-Italian kid in a neighborhood of mobsters. He was seven the first time he heard gunshots booming in the night. Nine the first time he saw a body. He remembered it like it was yesterday: old man Randazzo sprawled on the pavement in front of DeCicco's Restaurant, riddled with bullets and practically floating in blood. Lots of wiseguys had ended up on the meat rack back in the neighborhood, and more than half of them never even made the papers, let alone the television.

Clarence shook his head. It was all about dollar signs in this world. You could buy anything if you flashed the greens. Being a chauffeur for the Hamilton family these past few years had proven that much. Clarence had seen Trevor Hamilton slide his way out of a hundred sticky situations by simply reaching into his wallet. Same for the girls, although Lex was more prone to use money to get her way than Madison or Park. Thinking of them now, Clarence smirked. They were a handful, but they could also be a sweet and cute little trio. They had never uttered a nasty word to him or acted like bitches. They had never made him feel like the poor schlep he was. In fact, they seemed to actually *respect* him in a fatherly sort of way. It was shockingly pleasant. As far as he was concerned, Madison, Park, and Lex were more than just his bosses. They were more than just celebutantes too. In that hidden and totally unmacho corner of his heart, Clarence felt a certain fondness for them. Playing the role of bodyguard wasn't in his job description, but he couldn't help being overly protective of the girls. He looked out for them. He kept their secrets. And he knew every one of their crazy antics.

He scanned the front steps of the museum again. He was parked across the street, directly in front of the Stanhope, and had a bird's-eye view of the activity. What the hell was going on in there? He didn't like the idea of the girls being in the middle of all this chaos. Lots of crazy people walking around. If the girls didn't come out soon, he was going to have to push his way inside and kick some serious ass. He knew they weren't in any imminent danger, but a few more minutes and one of these nosy reporters would figure out who he was and start badgering him. It always happened that way. Got a question about someone famous? Ask the chauffeur! Clarence scowled at the very thought of a microphone being shoved in his face. Any of those pencil pushers so much as approached him, they'd have his fist for dinner.

He was about to get back into the limo when something caught his eye. There was activity up near the entrance of the museum. One set of wide doors yawned open, and out came several uniformed cops. They strolled down the front steps into waiting cruisers without so much as glancing up at the reporters screaming after them. Other people came streaming out the doors too, well-dressed people who were being ushered down the south side stairs to waiting cabs. Damn reporters were calling out questions and flashing pictures.

And then Madison appeared way up at the top of the stairs, followed by Lex and Park.

The reporters began shouting in a frenzy.

From where he was standing across the street, Clarence could just make out Madison's gown. He squinted and watched as they began descending the stairs. They looked confused, exchanging glances as they navigated their way out of the museum. Whistling, Clarence went and stood directly in front of the limo. He waved his hands in the air. But it was no good. The commotion had reached a fever pitch, and his signals disappeared behind a wave of flashes. One more minute and the girls would be swarmed by the media vultures.

Whirling around, Clarence jumped into the limo, gunned the engine, and skidded across the avenue in a diagonal line. He jumped out onto the street and motioned for the girls.

It was Lex who saw him. Her face lit up and she grabbed Park, who in turn latched on to Madison. They flew down the steps in a sloppy, stumbling chain. But just before they hit the sidewalk, four reporters cut a path in front of them and started belting out questions.

"Shit," Clarence muttered, instantly angered.

"Lexington!" one of the reporters screamed. "Did you see the body?"

"Did you see Zahara Bell before she was killed?"

"Madison, what do you have to say about the gala?"

"Lex, is it true that Zahara was found dead in a dress *you* designed?"

"Park, did you and Jeremy Bleu come to the gala together? Are you a couple?"

On and on the questions came, circling on the air like a bad smell. Just hearing them made Clarence's blood boil. He stomped onto the sidewalk and, in one swift motion, shoved the first two reporters out of the way. "Watch it!" he growled. "Move your asses!" He grabbed ahold of Lex and pulled her forward, elbowing another reporter in the ribs as he did so. He popped the back door of the limo and ushered the girls inside as cameras flashed in his face. Then he ran around to the driver's side, climbed in, and slammed the door shut.

It was silent inside the limo. Clarence took a deep breath. He wiped the sweat from his forehead. He turned around slowly.

The girls were staring back at him, breathless and stunned.

"What the hell is going on?" he asked.

The reporters had pushed up against the tinted windows, their voices muffled but determined.

Madison sat up, her eyes wide. "Becker!" she cried. "Bust it out of here!"

"Yes, ma'am!" Throwing the limo into gear, Clarence slammed his foot on the gas and shot into traffic. He kept his eyes trained on the busy stretch of Fifth Avenue that lay ahead. Too many cars. Too many red lights. The paparazzi were probably already trailing the limo in one of their vans.

"Don't take us back home!" Lex said. "They'll all be waiting for us there!"

"I know," Clarence shouted back at her, keeping his hands on the wheel. "Girls, fasten those seat belts! Looks like we've got company." He shot a glance in the rearview mirror and spotted two vans cutting crazily through the traffic.

"Here we go," Park said with a sigh.

"Becker, you have to lose them!" Madison yelled. "We can't answer any more questions or appear in any more pictures. This is insane!"

Clarence nodded. Just ahead, a bus was pulling away from its stop, veering quickly into the middle lane. He floored the accelerator.

The limo shook.

The girls screamed.

Champagne barked and yipped in Lex's arms.

Gripping the wheel tightly, Clarence shot past the bus, narrowly missing its bumper. In the rearview mirror he saw one of the vans skid to a stop. "Ha!" he said. "We lost one of 'em. One more to go!"

"I'm gonna be sick," Lex mumbled. "I *hate* high-speed chases."

Clarence watched in the mirror as the second van, still two blocks behind, cut into the left lane and gained speed. He kept his foot heavy on the metal. He weaved through the traffic smoothly, dodging cabs and cars and a horse-drawn carriage. At the corner of Sixty-eighth Street, he swung a right and sped across Central Park. The narrow lane cutting across to the West Side was mercifully clear. Clarence checked the rearview mirror again and smiled when he didn't see the gleam of the van's headlights. Goddamn photographers. Little shits would sell their own grandmothers for a snap of the lens. He continued driving way above the speed limit, not slowing down until he reached the West Side and the busy intersection at Broadway. He turned right and eased into the traffic. Then he cleared his throat and said, "You girls mind telling me what the hell's going on?"

"To give you the abbreviated version, we're suspects in a murder investigation," Park told him calmly.

Clarence gasped and nearly lost control of the limo. "What? Are you shittin' me?"

"Only about fifty percent," Madison said. "But it's

obvious the cops are going to try and pin some of this on us." She gave a quick rundown, telling him about Lex's dress, the scarf around Zahara Bell's neck, and the psycho photographer.

"Wait a minute," Clarence cut in, panic rising in his voice. "You mean someone broke into the penthouse and went into Lex's closet? That's *impossible!*"

"Apparently it isn't," Lex replied. "I *never* leave my pieces anywhere but my bedroom closet. How the hell it got on Zahara Bell's body is anybody's guess."

"Do any of you even *care* that the Avenue diamond is missing?" Park nearly wailed. She threw her arms up in a gesture of desperation, then sighed dramatically.

Glancing in the rearview, Clarence saw that her eyes had gone glassy. God knew, he had heard the story of the Avenue diamond and its almost mythical connection to the Hamilton family a dozen times. He wished there were something reassuring he could say, but words eluded him.

"Of course we care," Madison said softly. "But the diamond isn't really our biggest concern here."

"The hell it isn't!" Park shot back. "Do you know what'll happen to this city if the diamond isn't found? Do you know what might happen to *us*? It's the reason the three of us even *exist,* let me remind you."

Lex rolled her eyes. "We don't need reminding, thanks."

There wasn't a single person on earth who needed

reminding. Everyone knew the story of Venturina Baci and the Avenue diamond. The night she'd worn it in public—one of the few celebrities ever allowed to do so—was the very night she and Trevor Hamilton had conceived their daughters. While pregnant, Venturina spoke publicly about the diamond's unimaginable beauty—and its mystical powers. It was no ordinary rock. The legend, she told reporters, was absolutely true. Just before her twentieth birthday, doctors had told Venturina that she would never be able to have children because of a rare genetic defect, but then she wore the diamond to a premiere and got a little frisky with her husband and *bam:* babies on the way. Coincidence? She thought not. And in honor of the triple blessing the Avenue diamond had bestowed upon her, Venturina promised to name her daughters accordingly.

It was a glittery, dreamy sort of story. Madison and Lex enjoyed hearing it every so often, but they didn't really believe it. Besides, who would even want to *think* about anything having to do with your parents and sex? *Eeewww.* The thought was totally rank. Unlike her sisters, however, Park accepted the story as the gospel truth; this had everything to do with her innate love of jewelry, not fantasy. She recited the tale to anyone who would listen and took pride in the fact that she was inexorably linked to something so powerful and so beautiful.

Now she was sitting tight in her corner of the limo,

arms crossed over her chest. "I mean . . . *really,*" she snapped. "The two of you should be ashamed of yourselves. What do you think Mom will say when she finds out the diamond has been stolen?"

"Personally, I think she'll be more concerned that one of my dresses was found on a murder victim," Lex shot back. "*That's* what's really important right now."

"Like hell it is!"

"Both of you, *stop it.*" Madison exhaled loudly, and her tone went tight and terse as she assumed her no-nonsense businesswoman persona. "Now, let's talk seriously. We're going to have to mobilize our publicists and our attorneys as soon as we get home," she said. "This is the kind of terrible publicity that leads to financial damage. Hamilton Holdings' stock will plummet at the first mention of the word *murder.* And with the fiscal reports due in two months, we just can't have that."

Clarence smiled. He got a kick out of listening to them shift gears. He eyed Park and Lex.

They both knew to follow suit. It was time to forget about their carefree lives as rich famous girls and assume their roles as well-trained miniprofessionals. They were, after all, the future vice presidents of Hamilton Holdings, Inc. Trevor Hamilton had made certain to expose his daughters to every piece of the empire he had built from scratch, and there wasn't a single aspect of his dealings the girls didn't understand.

Their attendance at monthly board meetings was mandatory. Twice a year, they accompanied him on trips to Hong Kong, Sydney, and Dubai to meet with foreign affiliates and potential real estate investors. They even had their own small offices at Rockefeller Center, where the headquarters for Hamilton Holdings, Inc., was located. It was all part of the master plan. Eventually, Madison, Park, and Lex would take the reins from their father and multiply the company's profits by a few billion bucks. That was still several years away, but even now, at sixteen, they knew the full scope of their duties.

Being a celebrity was all about fame. Being a debutante was all about money. But being a celebutante was about making money—and doing it famously.

Park settled herself deeper into the limo's plush leather seats and said, "Right now, I think it's a bad idea to get our lawyers involved. We haven't been charged with anything. We haven't even been accused. I think the company will be okay so long as we ride the scandal out cleanly without legal ramifications."

"Nonetheless," Lex chimed in, "we'll need hourly NASDAQ updates to monitor what's publicly traded. And I hate to say it, but I have to: the West family will be up our asses on this, waiting for the perfect moment to steal our newest investors overseas."

Clarence, listening intently as he cruised up Broadway, smiled even wider. "So what's the newest business venture?" he asked, not wanting to be left out of the conversation. "What the hell can those fat-ass Wests steal?"

Madison hesitated only a moment before replying. "Right now, we're working to secure investors for new cell phone and Internet technology that's coming out of Korea. Amazing stuff that we haven't even seen here yet. It took Daddy almost a year to convince those guys to agree to take a meeting with Hamilton Holdings. It's huge money. A little bit of bad publicity is dangerous, and it gives our competitors ammo to steal the deal right out from under us. That's what the Wests want—to be as powerful as us. They've always wanted it but they haven't managed to get it. That's why they hate us so much." The last few sentences came out sharply, defiantly, and she turned her head to stare out the window.

"Not *all* the Wests hate us," Park said, hinting at Madison's former relationship with Theo.

Madison ignored the comment.

"What we're trying to say," Lex told Clarence, "is that there's a lot at stake. We have to proceed very carefully or we could end up in a lot of trouble."

"I wouldn't worry about it," Clarence said reassuringly. "You girls know what you're doing. You're all smart as whips. And right now, the good news is that the coast is clear. No vans following us. No freakin' paparazzi on the prowl."

"Thank God for that." Madison shifted in her seat. As she did so, she dropped her purse onto the floor of the limo. Sighing, she leaned over and hastily began chucking the fallen items back in where they belonged. It was dark, but she raked her fingers over the carpet, grabbing at a tube of lipstick, a pack of mints, and, way up against the front seat, a compact. "I hate this damn purse," she said. "It's always falling open on me."

"You wouldn't have that problem if you carried one of *my* purses," Lex commented briskly.

Suddenly, Madison leaned forward, half-hanging over the partition and nearly butting her head against Clarence's face. "Becker, how long were you waiting in front of the Met tonight?"

He shrugged. "Since I dropped Lex off. I didn't move from that spot in front of the Stanhope. Just like always. Why?"

"Did you by any chance see a short fat bald guy running out of the museum looking totally fried and sweaty?"

Clarence laughed. "You're kidding, right? You think I sat there and *stared* at the museum for almost two hours? I read the paper, smoked a cigar. Who's the guy, anyway?"

"Forget it," Lex said, pulling Madison back into her seat. "It's useless. No one saw that ugly little man leave the building. He's not important anyway."

"Of course he is!" Madison retorted. "He's the reason we're in this mess. And for all we know, he could be the killer. I think we should go to the police right now and turn the camera in."

"No," Park said. "We have too many things that still need figuring out. Let's get home and then we'll decide what to do."

Clarence slowed the limo down to a crawl as he reached the East Side again, having cut across Central Park at Ninety-seventh Street. The ride had been more stressful than he'd anticipated. His head was buzzing and his shoulders felt tense. Turning around halfway, he eyed the girls and sighed. "Listen to me. Park is right. You take that camera to the cops and it'll only add more fuel to the fire. That's what they want— to use you and exploit you as much as they can because it'll buy them more time to figure out what the hell really happened inside that museum."

"I guess so," Lex said quietly. She reached into the magic purse and pulled out her cell phone. As she turned it on, Madison and Park did the same with theirs.

Almost in unison, all three phones fired up and beeped, announcing messages.

"That's weird," Madison said, studying the screen of her flip phone. "Mine's a text message."

"So is mine," Park and Lex blurted out simultaneously.

An ominous silence fell. Clarence stared at the girls through the rearview mirror.

"My message is from a restricted number," Lex said.

Madison and Park nodded. And then they all read their messages and let out little high-pitched squeals.

Clarence slammed his foot on the brake, threw the car into park, and turned around.

"Look," Madison said, her voice shaking. She held her cell phone out to him.

Clarence stared down at the phone's neon screen. His eyes almost popped out of his head. The message was cold and clear:

THREE MINUS ONE IS MUCH MORE FUN.

"Oh! My! *God!*" Lex shrieked. "Do you know what this means? Someone just threatened our lives. Or *one* of our lives! *One of us is the target of a killer!*"

7

Royally Clucked

The cab sped up First Avenue in typical New York fashion. Diego Marsala—aka Chicky—sat in the backseat with his head pressed against the dirty window. He barely noticed the crowds on the sidewalks, the cluster of cars at the Ninety-sixth Street entrance to the FDR Drive, or the stream of police cruisers heading west. He was too engrossed in worry to think about anything but his own stupid mistakes. And he had made a lot of them tonight.

"Hey, *papi,* step on it, will you?" he snapped at the driver.

The driver, a quiet, skinny man of obviously foreign origin, nodded, but the cab didn't gain speed.

Hopeless, Chicky thought. He turned around in the seat and looked through the window. There were no cars following him. The cops were probably still too busy responding to the crime scene at the Met, and that was perfectly fine. But he knew it was only a matter of time before they'd come looking for him. He had been through the legal system repeatedly in the last twenty years, and one way or another, the law always seemed to sink its teeth into his ass. That was the unfortunate result of a lifetime of petty crimes.

Chicky had turned thirty-six back in January, but he looked at least ten years older. He was short, fat, and bald. He had stubby cream-filled fingers. And his small eyes too often flashed hate and anger. Not at all the kind of guy who looked good in pictures. But, ironically enough, he was quite good at taking them. So good, in fact, that he had managed to make a respectable living snapping celebrity shots for several national tabloid magazines. It was tough, sketchy work that required more guts than skill. A paparazzo wasn't merely a photographer; a paparazzo was a photographer with a *mission*. These days, the security that surrounded celebrities was thicker than the pack of brides at a Vera Wang sample sale. You had to maneuver your way through a series of nearly invisible holes to get close enough to click a good shot. And only the good shots got you cash. To date, he had scaled the sides of private mansions, slept on rooftops in the freezing cold, and hid in more bushes than he could count. All for the perfect pics. It wasn't easy, but it was amazing what the tabloids paid for relatively simple shots of famous people picking their noses, peeing on parkways, or just sunning themselves butt naked in the supposed privacy of their own opulent backyards.

Two years ago, when he'd decided that being a "celebrity photographer" was his true calling, Chicky had surpassed dozens of veteran celebrity-chasers by way of sheer guile. His years in prison had paid off. He knew how to create fake identification badges and press passes. He knew which security guards to bribe. He knew which paparazzi to lock in closets and bathrooms, and how to get close enough to screw up their shots with a simple nudge of his finger. They weren't major crimes, but they were as good as he would ever get.

Chicky had been branded with the feathery nickname while in the slammer, after his fellow inmates found out that he'd been convicted of robbing a poultry factory in upstate New York and holding a frightened farmer—and several fowl—hostage. But in all this time, and despite all his dirty tricks, Chicky had managed to stay somewhat beneath the radar, thanks to his ever-changing disguises. He had dressed up as a priest, a nun, a forklift operator, a waiter, a surgical technician, and a telephone repairman. In the process, he had taken tremendously scandalous pictures and banked a lot of sweet cash. But not enough cash to get him a good lawyer.

And right now, he was sure he needed a good lawyer. He stared out the front windows of the cab. The silent driver wasn't half bad. The guy had gotten him to the outskirts of Harlem in under seven minutes. "Right here," Chicky called out, already opening the back door. He pulled a ten-dollar bill from his pocket and tossed it over the partition. Then he stepped out onto the dark stretch of Third Avenue, his feet breaking into a run. Every extra pound of his stocky frame jiggled as he trotted up to the small, dilapidated apartment building at the next corner. It was one of those gritty almost-a-tenement structures, with barred windows and broken concrete steps. Rats the size of cats skittered up the flanking alleyways. The cockroaches in the stairwell looked big enough to wear sombreros. But it was a cheap and forgotten place, and Chicky needed as much cover as possible.

Inside his second-floor studio apartment, Chicky tore off his tux and chucked it onto the floor. He grabbed a pack of cigarettes from the top of the battered dresser and lit one up. *Stupid,* he thought. *I'm just stupid.* Pacing the narrow room, he cursed himself for hanging around at the gala longer than was necessary. If he'd listened to his instinct, he would have left ten minutes after sneaking in. One of the security guards had eyed his doctored press badge suspiciously, but hadn't said anything. That was when Chicky had known he had to take some good pics and split. But he'd made the mistake of loitering just outside the Great Hall, enjoying the view. All those swanky rich people, with their amazing clothes and pampered faces. Snapshot of a drunk well-known socialite picking the wedgie out of her ass. Excellent close-up of two snotty teens getting filthy with each other on the dance floor. He'd wandered around, snagged a drink from the bar, and then decided to take a little walk. It was a walk that led straight to hell.

Chicky hadn't meant to catch a distant glimpse of the guy hurriedly leaving the coatroom. He hadn't meant to peek inside the coatroom either. But he had. And he'd gotten the shock of his life. Initially, the sight of the woman's body had spooked him. He'd recognized Zahara Bell. In fact, he'd photographed her ten minutes earlier, alive and well. He'd gasped. He'd stifled a cry. And then he'd seen dollar signs floating in front of him, as big and bright as beacons. The camera had flown up to his eyes.

Focus, steady, *click:* the first shot was lengthwise, capturing the fashionable fatality clearly.

Focus, zoom, *click:* the second shot was of the thick, ugly scarf cinched around the woman's neck, wound so tight that he'd wanted to barf.

They were priceless pictures. In the underground

market, he could've gotten *big* money for them. Those were the deals he liked best—all cash, no paper trail, and no questions asked. A pocket-the-dough-and-fly-down-to-Mexico payment. Standing there, looking down at the body, Chicky had felt a surge of excitement. Hot luck! Kill-pics were a paparazzo's dream. Running out and calling the police would've been the right thing to do, but in his world there was no difference between right and wrong. There was only survival. He'd stepped out of the coatroom as if nothing had happened and walked down the corridor. The male figure he'd seen only a minute earlier— the assailant, of course—had been nowhere in sight. Not that it mattered to Chicky: he was happy with his beloved camera and the lurid pics he'd snapped. But then he'd gone into the men's room to take a leak, and when he'd come out . . .

Disaster. The big mistake.

Damn those Hamilton girls! And damn that buff airheaded movie star! If only they hadn't stolen his camera. Chicky had tried like hell to get it back, but skinny rich kids ran very fast.

His camera. The six-figure pics he'd snapped.

All of it gone.

Chicky took a long last drag of the cigarette and stubbed it out. Had the Hamilton girls turned the camera over to the cops? If so, the law would be knocking at his door in just a couple of hours. They'd know that he had seen Zahara Bell's body and not reported it. They'd probably even suspect him of killing her. Chicky couldn't have that. Another conviction and he'd go back to the slammer for life. And oh, how the other inmates would love teasing him.

Itsy-bitsy Chicky, cluck cluck cluck!

Hey, who likes their chicky fried?

The thought made his blood boil.

Running away wasn't an option either. That would be an admission of guilt, and besides, how far could he possibly get?

He knew what he had to do.

He would sit here and wait till morning. If the cops didn't show up, he'd know the Hamilton girls hadn't turned the camera in. After all, they had their own reputations to think about. With the camera in their possession, Chicky had a good shot at getting it back. Not legally, of course, and not very easily. But there was always a way. . . .

He raced over to the tiny closet in the corner of the room. The contents nearly spilled out when he opened the door. Boxes and boxes of junk, hangers, and old clothes that smelled of mothballs and cheap cologne. He cut through it all, tossing items across the floor until he found what he was looking for.

The black and white French maid's uniform was at the bottom of the heap. It had been at least a year since he'd used it to sneak into one of those ritzy uptown buildings in search of a good picture. Now he'd have to use it to bust into the Hamiltons' penthouse. At the back of the closet, Chicky found the curly blond wig and the bag of makeup that would accentuate his feminine look.

I can do this. I can outsmart those silly Hamilton girls before they ruin my life.

Yes, he would do what was necessary. He would get that camera back no matter what.

8

The Plan

Standing in the bright kitchen, Madison yanked open the refrigerator door and plunged her hands inside. From the bottom rack she grabbed a carton of milk, a container of imported Belgian chocolate syrup, and an unopened bottle of Dom Perignon. Her stomach was in knots. Her nerves were an inch from cracking. There was only one remedy that would alleviate the stress, and she needed a whole damn lot of it.

She moved like a robot on speed, lining the items up on the counter while reaching into one of the cabinets for a tall glass. She tore the top of the milk carton. She opened the spout on the container of chocolate syrup. Then she wrapped her fingers around the bottle of champagne and popped the cork with a quick jab of her thumbs. The cork ricocheted across the kitchen, as loud and fast as a bullet. The boom didn't scare her. Madison was too consumed by impulse to notice anything but the tall glass on the counter, now bubbling richly with champagne and milk. When the mixture foamed at the rim, she shot it with the chocolate syrup and gave it a little stir.

She lifted it to her lips and took long, slow gulps, closing her eyes as the strange cocktail soothed her nerves. It was her own personal concoction, an elixir that drowned all traces of anxiety. She only drank it in cases of extreme stress, and when no one was around to tell her how disgusting it looked. In truth, Madison didn't care what Park or Lex thought about her penchant for milk, champagne, and chocolate syrup. When panic took hold, she fell prey to excess and impulse. She lost herself completely in the hazy zone between control and surrender. She was a woman possessed, the ultimate poster girl for gluttony. There had been times when she'd plunged huge tablespoons into a jar of peanut butter and eaten the sticky globs until her mouth felt glued shut. Once, when she was thirteen and worried about failing an art history class, she went all the way to Zabar's and polished off half a babka right there in the dessert aisle, her lips and chin caked with cinnamon.

It always happened this way: tension rose and her willpower tanked.

She pulled the glass away from her mouth. She was dizzy from the swift shock of bubbly booze and sugar, but ugly images kept flashing in her mind's eye. Zahara Bell's body, Lex's dress, the dozens of cameras zooming in on them as they descended the steps of the Met. Madison couldn't begin to understand how it had all happened, how a perfectly lovely evening had gone from magic to murder in the blink of an eye. And she certainly couldn't bring herself to imagine the wall of scandal tilting in their direction.

A spasm hit her stomach. Unable to control herself, she refilled the glass, pouring in the champagne and milk and chocolate syrup in one messy swoop. Then she brought it to her lips and chugged.

"Madison!"

She started as a voice sliced through the blessed silence of the kitchen. Turning around, she saw Lex standing at the opposite end of the long counter, her jaw wide open.

"Look at you!" Lex shouted. "Making a pig of yourself with that disgusting drink. And you didn't even have the decency to change out of your gown!"

For the first time since they had arrived home,

Madison glanced down at herself. She was still clothed in the black Chanel, and now it was stained with tiny white dots from the champagne's bubbly spray and the drops of milk that had dribbled down from her chin. Slowly, she placed the glass on the counter. She brought a hand to her mouth, where a thick brown mustache glowed just beneath her nose. Shame washed over her in waves.

"What is *wrong* with you?" Lex snapped, stomping toward her. "You know *exactly* what happens when you guzzle too much champagne."

"I can't help it. I'm too nervous," Madison told her. "I held on to my cool for as long as I could . . . but once we got home . . . I . . . I . . ." Her voice died down, and she felt a rumble in her stomach. She hunched over slightly. She grabbed the edges of the counter for support. And then it happened—what always happened when she drank too much champagne: she burped like a runaway freight train. The sound boomed all the way into the living room.

A moment later, Lupe came into the kitchen. *"Dios mío,"* she whispered. She crossed herself, then went to Madison's side and rested a hand on her back.

"Ugh." Lex shook her head. "It serves you right!"

Madison looked down, embarrassed. She clamped a hand over her mouth.

Lex stormed to the other side of the counter and grabbed the glass, which was still half full.

"No!" Madison screamed. "Leave it! I'm not finished drinking!"

"Not finished?" Lex's eyes nearly popped from her head. "One more burp and you're gonna blow us out of here!"

"Shut up!"

"Stop it, Lex. Let her drink what she wants to drink." Park's even voice cut through the bickering. She had just walked into the kitchen.

With a nod, Madison slowly reached out her right hand and wrenched the glass from Lex's fingers. She downed another gulp, then stared at Park, who was holding a snifter in one hand and two cigars in the other.

"There's no time for arguing," Park told them. "We have a lot of work to do, so let's get started."

The very thought of discussing Zahara Bell's murder made Madison's anxiety spike a notch. She drained what was left in the glass and slowly refilled it.

"That's your last one, Madison. I mean it." With that, Park set her snifter down on the countertop, giving it a little swirl as she did so; it was filled halfway with cognac. She dipped the back ends of the cigars into the smooth brown liquor and held them under for exactly eight seconds. Then she handed one to Lex and they both lit up.

Lupe waved her hands at the stream of smoke.

She hurried out of the kitchen, giving Park one of those if-your-father-only-knew stares.

"Come on," Madison said quietly, finally relenting. "Let's head into the library."

It was the room of the penthouse reserved for family meetings. The oak-paneled walls, rich red carpeting, and plush leather couches created a warm atmosphere. But the air was charged tonight, the tension palpable. Madison began pacing the floor almost immediately. Park and Lex took their seats beneath the ornately framed Picasso sketches that were only a small part of Trevor Hamilton's extensive art collection. They puffed slowly on their cigars, exhaling thin swirls of smoke and sharing sips of the cognac.

"So what do we have here?" Park spoke up first. "Zahara Bell is found murdered in one of Lex's Triple Threat sample designs, and the Avenue diamond is missing. Either way you look at it, the whole damn mess revolves around *us.*"

"Totally," Lex said. "How much more obvious can it be? First the diamond, and then my dress. And don't forget: I created the Triple Threat line with all three of us in mind, and people know that. My designs reflect our unique and different personalities." She tossed her head back dramatically, but the expression on her face remained serious, as if she were sitting across from a journalist, being interviewed for a cover story in *Vogue.* "Only the best designers can accomplish something like that, you know. It's such a trying job. But my inspiration comes from the fashion greats: Galliano, Armani, Westwood—"

"*Please!*" Madison cut in sharply. "Can you keep your mind focused for just a few minutes? We have to figure out who stole the dress from your closet, and how he got in here. As it stands, we've been totally set up." She paused and chugged another mouthful of her drink. This time, when she burped—like the flat crack of a gunshot—she wasn't embarrassed.

Park and Lex didn't flinch; they had obviously been expecting it.

"Lex," Madison went on, "who could have stolen that dress? Are you even sure it was in your closet? Did you maybe leave it somewhere? Think."

Lex shook her head vigorously. "That dress was in my closet. I *know* it was. I didn't leave it anywhere."

"So then we had an intruder and didn't even know it," Madison whispered. "And he came specifically for that dress, because nothing is missing from my closet."

"Or mine," Park said. "Which means that this little plan was put together a long time ago. The killer stole the dress knowing that he would kill Zahara Bell and shove her body into it." She puffed hard on the cigar. "We have to solve this crime before the scandal gets huge—and before we're hauled in as suspects."

"We're *already* suspects," Madison said. "You heard the way that detective spoke to us."

Park sighed. "I know, but I don't think he *really* believes we killed Zahara Bell. I mean, that whole theory doesn't make sense. What motive would *we* have?"

"And how would we even have the time?" Lex added. "With our schedules? With our lives as busy as they are? *Puh-lease.*"

"So who *did* have a motive to kill Zahara?" Madison set her drink down on the mahogany coffee table and clenched her hands together. "She was a revered woman, but also hated. Anyone at the gala could have wanted her dead. The list is endless."

"No, it isn't. The list is actually very short." Park stood up. She walked across the room to one of the perfectly lined bookshelves. Scanning it quickly, she spotted a hardcover copy of *Rebecca* and pulled it back; behind it was the small ashtray she and Lex used when they smoked their father's cigars. Trevor Hamilton didn't know about this particular hiding place, and he wasn't likely to find out. Park grabbed the ashtray and flicked her ashes into the tarred bottom, then brought it over to Lex.

"Could you explain your theory, please?" Madison snapped. "Every minute counts here."

Park took a long, slow puff on the cigar. "The two biggest items in this case—Lex's dress and the Avenue diamond—are both connected to us," she began. "Whoever killed Zahara Bell planned this so that all the fingers would point to *us*. Or so that the scandal will be mostly about *us*. The killer could have chosen any young, beautiful celebutantes in this city to pin it to, but he chose *us*. That doesn't leave a very big list."

Lex cleared her throat, rolling the cigar in her fingers. "You think the killer is someone we know?"

"Maybe," Park answered. "But not necessarily."

"So then, who are the suspects?" Madison asked, her voice rising. "You're not adding anything new here."

"I said the list was short," Park answered. "I didn't say I knew who was *on* the list."

"Brilliant. Just brilliant." Madison clenched her hands into fists and started pacing the floor again. "Your theory doesn't solve anything. Right now, the only real suspect is Jeremy Bleu. Did you even think of that? How much more obvious does it need to be?"

Park frowned. "Of course I've thought about it. But does he really make sense as a suspect? He's a movie star, he has plenty of money—"

"And he fled the crime scene!" Madison screeched. "How do we know that he didn't have a motive for killing Zahara Bell? You've known him for a total of twenty minutes, Park. He could be a total serial killer in the making."

"Serial killers usually *are* very intelligent and

charming," Lex chimed in. "That's why it takes years and years for them to get caught." She popped the cigar back between her lips.

"Who's to say he didn't have this whole thing all detailed and tagged?" Madison went on. "And that you weren't just another part of his master plan?"

"You both sound ridiculous," Park told them coldly. "I know Jeremy's innocent, and I know I wasn't only a quickie plaything for him. We have a connection. I felt it the second we set eyes on each other, and so did he. I'm not his little pawn. I'm smart enough to see through that kind of bullshit. And besides"—she lowered herself into one of the plush chairs—"how on earth would Jeremy Bleu have gotten ahold of one of Lex's dresses? We've never met him before tonight, remember?"

"*That's* why it's a mystery!" Madison exclaimed. "Because we *don't* know. He could very easily have had a motive to kill Zahara Bell, and the Avenue diamond is worth a pretty penny. Maybe he's one of those people who believes the diamond has some sort of mystical power. Maybe he's not as wealthy as we think. Maybe he made bad investments, blew it all. *Maybe* he's sitting in his hotel room *right now* staring at it."

"While we're here preparing to walk through a major scandal," Lex added. "I checked the news when we got home. We're all over the channels."

"I'm telling you," Park said calmly. "You've both

got it wrong. Jeremy Bleu is not a killer. He has a killer body and a killer smile, but he's not actually a killer."

Madison felt a wave of angry heat flush her face. She looked at Park. She looked at Lex. She looked around the room and then back at Park again. "I won't stand for it!" she shouted. "I won't wait around here and let this horrible scandal take root. Jeremy Bleu owes you—us—an explanation. And he's going to give it to us before midnight! Do you hear me? *Do you?*"

"The streets of SoHo can hear you," Park said quietly. "Just calm down."

"Don't tell me to calm down!" Madison whirled around and stomped out of the library. She flew down the hall and into her bedroom, pulling the Chanel gown over her shoulders and tossing it onto her bed. Without giving it much thought, she started ruffling through her closet for something else to wear.

Park and Lex appeared on the threshold. "What are you doing?" Lex asked her worriedly. "You look like you're gonna explode."

"I'll tell you what I'm doing," Madison replied sharply, disappearing into her closet. "I'm going right over to the Pierre, and I'm going to drag Jeremy Bleu kicking and screaming onto Fifth Avenue."

Park sighed again. "Madison, I won't let you go out there. Not with all those reporters on the prowl.

Not with a killer on the loose. And not after that text message."

"Well, *I* won't let *you* ruin our name and our reputations just because you're under the spell of Jeremy Bleu's banana," Madison snapped. She pulled two pairs of jeans off their hangers and, deeming them inappropriate for what she was about to do, hurled them across the room.

"Wait a minute, Madison." Lex walked into the room and held her hands up in protest. "How the hell are you gonna go outside without causing a stir? Reporters will follow you, and they'll have a field day with it. What if you can't get to Jeremy? How bad will that look for us?"

"Not as bad as the newspapers, and definitely not as bad as pictures of us being hauled in for questioning in a murder we didn't commit." Madison came out of the closet holding a tattered pair of black jeans and a bulky sweater she'd purchased in Aspen the year before.

"*What* are you gonna do with *that* horrendous outfit?" Lex's hands flew to her throat in fear and shock.

But Madison didn't answer. Quickly, almost effortlessly, she slid into the jeans and pulled the sweater over her head. Then she went to the bureau in the far corner of her room and opened the bottom drawer; from it she grabbed a Yankees baseball cap. She flipped her long hair up and yanked the cap down over her head. Running back into the closet, she dug out a pair of brown Timberlands and jumped into them. In under a minute, she had transformed herself into a hapless-looking, boyish figure. The jeans were baggy and loose, and the sweater was bulky and completely missed the outline of her bust.

"Utterly tasteless, and just a little crude," Park observed. "I don't even want to know what you're planning to do."

"I'm planning to solve a murder before it nails us," Madison said. "If I disguise myself enough, maybe I can sneak out of here and slip into the Pierre unnoticed."

Lex's jaw dropped. "And then what? Jeremy Bleu will never agree to see you, and you won't get past security."

"Look," Madison said, whirling around to face her sisters. "We have to figure out what's going on here, and that means we have to work together to solve this crime. No one's going to do it for us. And we have to do it fast—before Dad gets wind of it, and before Mom hops on the next plane to New York."

Park crossed her arms over her chest. A smug expression played on her face. "Even if Jeremy *is* guilty, you honestly think he's going to admit that he committed the crime? I mean, I totally agree with you that we should all be suspicious of his behavior tonight, but you're acting on impulse. And, most important of all, you're *not* thinking the way a good detective would."

Madison tensed. She had caught the unmistakable edge—the certainty—in Park's voice. That meant it was time to shut up and listen. Along with the ability to remain calm in the most trying of circumstances, Park had been blessed with the gift of insight: she could dissect a situation, turn the broken pieces around in her mind, and then link them back together again easily. Madison hated yielding to her younger sister, but given the confusion of the moment, she did just that.

Park was visibly pleased. She began pacing the floor, her strides fluid and assured. "Now," she began, "detectives usually operate by the forty-eight-hour rule. They try to solve homicides in two days, because the trail goes cold after that. The most important person in an investigation isn't the killer—it's the victim. Most people are killed by people they totally know, so if you find out enough info about the victim, you're more than likely to find your way to the killer." She stared at Lex, then Madison. "Get it?"

"But everybody knows the details of Zahara Bell's life," Lex said. "She was a public figure."

Park shook her head. "That doesn't matter. There are always skeletons in the closet, secrets that aren't meant to go public."

"Or secrets that someone might kill for," Madison chimed in. "Right?"

"Exactly." Park smiled. "When you think about it, how much do we really know about Zahara Bell? Someone hated her enough to kill her, and that someone is using us like Wal-Mart dish towels to clean up the mess. Maybe Jeremy Bleu did kill her, but how would we ever prove it without evidence? What if we uncover info that leads us to someone else? If we're leaving here, we're going to Zahara Bell's apartment, not the Pierre."

"She lived on West Fifty-sixth Street," Madison said quietly. "Forty-one West Fifty-sixth Street."

"Yeah, and the building is probably already crawling with cops!" Lex shrieked. "Are you two crazy? That's the apartment Zahara Bell spent most of her time in, and everybody knows that."

"What do you mean?" Park asked, confused. "How many apartments did Zahara Bell have?"

"She moved to the one on Fifty-sixth Street three years ago," Lex said. "Right after her divorce. When she was married, she lived with her husband in a town house off Washington Square, on Waverly. She kept the town house as part of the divorce settlement, and that's where she held all her parties during Fashion Week. I mean, like, *majorly exclusive* parties. *We* weren't even invited."

"That's interesting," Park said. "The apartment

on Fifty-sixth was her main residence, probably because it's pretty close to the executive offices of *Catwalk* magazine. She lived there most of the time because it was convenient, but I'll bet she kept her personal life—the things that mattered most to her—in the town house."

"And if that's the case," Madison said, "the apartment on Fifty-sixth is where the police will go first, because it's where she spent most of her time."

Lex blanched. "Are you two saying that we're gonna go and break into Zahara Bell's town house?"

"Why not?" Park shrugged. "Someone broke into our house and stole a dress from your closet! This is no time to play fair. We have to at least *try*."

Madison nodded. She gave herself a once-over in the floor-to-ceiling mirror that hung to the right of the closet. In the dark, and from a distance, the ugly getup worked: she resembled a fifteen-year-old boy. She turned around and faced her sisters. "You two can't go out looking like yourselves," she said firmly. "Go and try to make yourselves ugly."

Lex ran a hand through her hair and stepped in front of the mirror. She pouted her lips in a mock kiss. "Is that really possible? I mean, *look* at me."

Park rolled her eyes, pulling Lex with her as she strode out of the bedroom and into the corridor. "I'll bring a weapon," she said calmly over her shoulder. "Just in case someone tries to kill us."

As those ominous words swirled around her, Madison felt a nervous tremor rip through her stomach. She tasted the thick, chalky milk-and-champagne mixture at the back of her throat. And when the burp shot past her lips—frighteningly loud, dangerously sharp—she wondered if they would need a weapon after all.

9

West Goes South

Theo was trying hard to keep up with Annabelle. They were fully entangled in Calvin Klein sheets, but his body wasn't responding as swiftly as it usually did. What on earth was the matter with him? Instead of enjoying the moment, he kept glancing around the dimly lit splendor of Annabelle's bedroom, hoping the answer to his problem would pop up on one of the walls.

"Oh, Theo, you're *so* hot," she cooed. "I knew the moment I saw you that we were meant to be together." Annabelle was pretty in an odd sort of way. Her eyes were intense and exuded emotion, but it was her body that attracted attention from nearly every guy in school.

Theo smiled. He closed his eyes. He tried to concentrate on the task at hand. Unfortunately, nothing was happening. The electric tingle of arousal was alive and well in his brain, but the lower half of his body simply couldn't respond. Sex was by far his favorite pastime and he had enough testosterone in his blood to fill a football stadium. Why the hell was his equipment stalling?

"Theo?" Annabelle whispered. She could tell that something was wrong.

He opened his eyes and forced himself to study every inch of the pure hotness before him, but the moment was as good as dead. Finally, with an irritated sigh, he rolled onto his back.

Annabelle sat up. A worried expression played on her face. She smoothed a hand over his chest, tracing a playful little circle. "What's wrong?"

"I don't know," Theo replied through gritted teeth. "I think maybe I'm just tired. Plus I'm kind of stressed."

"It was a crazy night. I don't blame you for feeling out of sorts."

In truth, he felt like a failed fireman: Annabelle's flames were burning, but his hose was out of order.

This was supposed to happen to old guys in their thirties and forties, not to a healthy, virile sixteen-year-old like him. Shit, what if Annabelle mentioned to her girlfriends that he couldn't perform? The word would spread through the halls of St. Cecilia's Prep faster than a fierce winter wind. *West is a softie. West can't please the ladies. West went south.* It was every guy's worst nightmare.

He tore his eyes from the vaulted ceiling and stared around the bedroom aimlessly. The walls were creamy white, the moldings pink. Elaborately framed pictures created a chronological display of Annabelle's life, from the day she was born right up to last month, when she won a gold medal in a gymnastics competition. Cute. Traditional. Warm and toasty for a duplex apartment that faced Columbus Avenue and not Central Park West.

The Christensen family was big money, but not *huge* money. The Christensen furniture line was sold in various retail outlets all over North America, grossing slightly over one hundred million dollars annually. As far as Theo was concerned, it wasn't an empire by any stretch of the imagination. *His* family had built an empire. *His* family warranted international attention. That photographers chased him frequently was no surprise. He wondered what his parents would say if they knew he was courting a Christensen. His mother, Renee, would likely disapprove; she'd smile and nod and run a hand through her perfectly blown-out hair before saying something like: *Annabelle's darling, isn't she? But don't be fooled by girls from economically challenged families, Theo. She probably sees your fortune and not your beautiful mind.*

He turned and looked at her just as she reached onto the nightstand for her pack of Nat Shermans. "Hey, gimme one of those," he said. Pinching the thin brown cigarette in his fingers, he lit it, took a long drag, and exhaled. Then he sat up.

Annabelle wrapped her arm around his shoulders, pressing her naked body against his. "Tell me what's wrong, Theo. I know you're out of it."

He nodded slowly. The cigarette was menthol, and the hint of mint reminded him of the cloves he used to smoke back when he was a freshman. "I'm pretty freaked about what happened tonight," he said. "Just to think that we were standing in the same building where a murder took place . . . it freaks me out."

"Me too. I always wanted to meet Zahara Bell. I totally worshipped her style. Tell me about her, Theo."

He cut Annabelle a short stare. "I never really knew her."

"But . . . you told me you did on our first date," Annabelle said with certainty. "I asked you about her because I knew your father's company published the first magazine she worked for—*Women's Style*. Right? I asked what Zahara Bell was like and you said she was pretty cool. Don't you remember?"

Theo remembered. He remembered and at the same time cursed his big mouth. Why had he told Annabelle that? Well, *duh*. To impress her. To get into her red lace Agent Provocateur panties. It had worked. He took another long puff of the cigarette and said, "Zahara Bell wasn't really that cool. In fact, she was a royal bitch. There're probably a lot of people secretly applauding the guy who killed her."

"Theo!" Annabelle shouted, drawing away from him. "That's pretty sick. The woman was killed, for God's sake."

"Sick or not, it happens to be true."

Annabelle was silent, the cigarette smoldering between her fingers. She stubbed it out in the ashtray hidden behind her lamp. "What did Zahara Bell ever do to *you*?"

As the words circled him, Theo recalled the numerous occasions in which he'd had the distinct misfortune of being in Zahara's presence. Back in February, he had attended the Hugo Boss menswear fashion show with his father, Richard West, president and CEO of West International, LLC. As Theo and Richard went to take their seats in the front row, they'd spotted Zahara coming toward them. Richard had stood there, thinking she was going to kiss his cheek in front of the press and make one of those superficial displays of affection that always ended up in the Sunday Style section of the *New York Times*. But instead of fussing over them, Zahara paused, lowered her sunglasses just enough to peer over the rims, and said to Theo and Richard, "Those seats you're sitting in are taken by *my* guests. I think you should try the second row." Then she turned around and started gabbing on her cell phone. Theo and Richard, utterly humiliated and shocked, had crept into the second row to watch the show. But the worst part was that queen gossip columnist Cindy Adams had witnessed the entire exchange, and wrote it up the next day in the *New York Post*. Theo had despised Zahara Bell ever since.

Now he looked at Annabelle. "She did plenty to disrespect my family," he said. "And she was on her way to disrespecting it more. She's better off dead."

"What does that mean?"

Shit, Theo thought. *My big fucking mouth*. "Eh, what difference does it make now? She's gone. It's just a shame that it all happened tonight, at the gala. Poor Madison Hamilton did a lot of work to make that event a success."

Annabelle gasped. "*Poor* Madison? Since when do you care if shit hits her fan? Are you the only one who doesn't know that your family and *her* family hate each other?"

Theo sighed. He ran a hand over his face and wished he had a bottle of Stoli at his fingertips.

"What I meant is that it's a shame all her work was ruined. She doesn't deserve that. No one does."

"Since when do you care about *her* so much?"

"Since always." The words slipped out. Now he bit down on his tongue.

With a violent jerk of her hand, Annabelle pulled the bedsheet off Theo and wrapped it around her body, leaving him entirely exposed to the elements.

Theo dropped the cigarette into the glass of water on the nightstand beside him, then reached down and scooped his silk Dior Homme boxers from the floor. He slipped them on. He didn't want to face Annabelle because he knew her mouth would be set in an unattractive angry scowl. But after several moments of strained silence, he turned his head toward her.

"You *like* her, don't you?" Annabelle spat.

"Who?"

"Madison Hamilton. I saw the way you kept checking her out tonight, looking at her like she's some sort of goddess. The whole time we were dancing, you kept sneaking peeks in her direction."

Theo didn't respond. He couldn't respond. Annabelle's stinging words rang hopelessly true.

"Answer me!" she demanded. "Do you like her?"

"Come on, Annabelle. Let's not do this. You're totally overreacting."

She hopped off the bed and onto her feet. Her cheeks were red with rage. "*Mads.* That's what you called her tonight. I heard it. Is that some sort of endearing nickname? A little secret between the two of you?"

"No, of course not. There's nothing between us," Theo lied. He half-kneeled on the edge of the bed, one hand splayed over his chest, his head cocked to one side. It was the sexy pose that had always managed to drive Annabelle wild with lust. But this time out, he was losing the battle.

"I guess the rumors are true!" she ranted. "The ones about you and Madison and your little forbidden fling!"

Theo started as though he'd been slapped. His heart was hammering in his chest. "Where did you hear a stupid thing like that?"

"Kelly Peabody told Rebecca Plexer and Stephanie Gilston that she saw you and Madison kissing in the empty gymnasium at school. Then Stephanie told Marcia Killian, who told Aidan Cryer, and Aidan told *me*." She tightened the sheet around her body in a gesture of satisfied defiance.

"Oh, please!" Theo said. "Aidan is gayer than Broadway. He gets off on any gossip about me. He gets off just *thinking* about me."

"Ha!" Annabelle scoffed. "Don't kid yourself. Aidan happens to be dating Marcus Kinney right now, and Marcus is *way* hotter than you."

Theo's jaw clenched. He grabbed his slate-gray Armani tuxedo pants and still pristine white shirt from the floor and pulled them on sloppily. "I'm not gonna stick around if you're just gonna insult me," he said with a sneer.

Annabelle's eyes glassed over with tears. "Is that where you went tonight when you left me alone at the gala for ten whole minutes?" she asked him. "Did you go outside the ballroom and talk to Madison?"

"*What?*" Theo said sharply. And he knew, an instant after the word escaped his lips, that he'd spoken it too quickly, and too nervously. How the hell had Annabelle even noticed he was gone? He had left her carefully and strategically, while she'd been immersed in conversation with Kelly Peabody and Rebecca Plexer at the President's Table. He had slipped out of the ballroom just as Jeremy Bleu took the stage; the guests were staring up at the young superstar, their eyes definitely *not* on Theo as he'd made his exit.

But Annabelle had noticed. She knew he'd been gone for ten minutes.

Shit.

"Annabelle," he said calmly, "I . . . I didn't leave the room. I just went to the bar to get myself a drink."

"Liar!" she screamed. "I *saw* you leave the room, Theo. I might've been talking to Kelly and Rebecca, but I *saw* you leave. Ten whole minutes. Was that enough time to talk with poor Madison?"

"I *didn't* talk to her," he blurted out. "Please—stop saying I left the room. You *can't* say that."

Annabelle stared at him, silent and tense. Her eyes, though brimming with tears, lit up reflectively.

Please don't say it, Theo thought. *Please don't let that steel trap of a mind of yours kick in.*

"You're right," she finally whispered. "You couldn't have been talking to Madison because Madison was standing next to Jeremy Bleu as he made his little speech."

Crap. Theo licked his lips, which were suddenly dry. He didn't know what to say. He could spew out some silly lie, but he knew Annabelle would see right through it. That was the bad thing about dating an incredibly smart and observant girl: you were screwed even when you weren't *getting* screwed.

Annabelle took a deep, slow breath. The sheet had gone loose around her chest, and she hiked it up slowly, never taking her eyes from Theo's face. "What did you mean when you said Zahara Bell was better off dead?"

"Oh, Jesus, Annabelle," Theo snapped. "You're not seriously asking me that. You're not seriously thinking anything stupid, are you?"

"Tell me what you were doing for ten minutes. If it's not a secret, you shouldn't have anything to worry about."

"You wanna know?" Theo said, throwing up his hands. "Okay then. Fine. Great. I'll tell you. Here's the big mystery—I went to the bathroom. That mysterious enough for you?"

Annabelle didn't move. "Who did you see on your way out, or even inside the bathroom? Or better yet, who saw *you*? There had to have been someone, Theo. And don't tell me I wouldn't know the person, because we know all the same people."

"No one, Annabelle. No one saw me. My bad luck." He shook his head. He felt his cheeks burning. "So what are you saying? That you think I left the gala, killed Zahara Bell, and then came back and danced with you? Is that what you're saying?"

"I didn't say it. You did. And you also said that Zahara Bell had disrespected your family, and that she's better off dead. Why don't you explain yourself?"

Theo turned around and shoved his feet into his shoes. "I didn't think I had to explain myself," he said quietly. "I was under the impression that you cared enough about me to trust me. And what the hell difference does it matter if Madison Hamilton and I ever had a fling? Even if it's true—and I'm not saying it is—it's in the past."

"Well, dammit, Theo. I just don't believe you." She wiped a tear from her eye but continued staring at him. "And you still won't answer my question. Where were you for those ten minutes? Why did you hate Zahara Bell so much? Is there something about her and her connection to your family that you're not telling me?"

Theo couldn't contain the rage that fired his eyes.

"Don't *ever* say stupid things like that—especially not in public," he seethed. "And don't go around telling people that you *think* I disappeared for ten minutes while we were at the gala, because no one will believe you. It's *your* family name against mine, and there's no room for competition between us."

Annabelle took a big step back, bunching the sheet up around her entire body as though seeking warmth from a sudden, stinging chill. "You're lucky my parents aren't home, or my father would kick your arrogant ass. Maybe I should just tell the police I know who the killer is. How about that?"

He was silent, his head aching.

"Get out!" Annabelle finally screamed.

"Fine!" Theo whirled around and stormed out of the bedroom and out of the apartment. His heart was whacking against his ribs. He was trembling like a virgin on prom night.

Outside, he walked up Columbus Avenue, feeling cold and exposed. With a sigh of frustration, he realized that he'd left his tux jacket in Annabelle's bedroom. Fine. Let her keep it. He was too disgusted—and too frightened—to care.

A cab skidded to a stop at the next corner. Theo climbed in and cursed his big mouth and his bad luck. As he cradled his head in his hands, it occurred to him that losing Annabelle also meant losing his only alibi.

10

The Hunt

Headlights were the enemy.

Lex stood at the corner of Third Avenue and Seventy-sixth Street, nervously eyeing the traffic. She tensed every time a car slowed down. She feared being spotted as the bright beams cut through the night and momentarily illuminated the sidewalk. Would anyone recognize the famous face hidden beneath the outrageous getup?

It was past midnight. The streets were bustling. People were walking east and west and police sirens sounded in the distance. She felt strange in the purple Betsey Johnson ankle-length skirt and white Donna Karan tank top; she felt even stranger with the black silk scarf draped over her head and across the front of her face. Nothing matched. Nothing accentuated the curves of her body. Silver rings lined her fingers, and several gold chains clinked at her neck whenever she moved. The look was ghetto-gypsy.

She had worked fast to create the new identity, running around her closet, pulling clothes off hangers, checking and rechecking her appearance in the mirror. Then she and Madison and Park had convened in the living room, mapped out their plan, and taken the elevator down to the lobby. They had rushed toward the building's side entrance at breakneck speed and avoided the front doors. Reporters were parked on Fifth Avenue and embedded in Central Park. No easy way out. They had decided on timing their respective escapes at exactly seven minutes apart. The corner of Third Avenue and Seventy-sixth Street was the designated meeting spot.

In the beginning, Lex had managed to keep her cool. Now she was totally scared. Standing out here in the so-not-her-style outfit, she felt vulnerable and exposed to danger. She kept thinking of the text message—*three minus one is much more fun*—and wondering if a killer was hanging out nearby. It wasn't such a silly thought, considering the fact that Zahara

Bell had been murdered in a museum filled with people. She hated seeing that violent image flash before her eyes. And she hated knowing that she was somehow connected to the murder. Once the story hit the papers, the whole world would associate her clothing line with a corpse. *Not* the best way to launch a new brand.

So maybe it *was* a good idea to grab the shoes by the heels and bust into Zahara Bell's town house. Lex hadn't agreed with it an hour ago, but now she was beginning to understand Park's point. They couldn't just sit in the penthouse and let the fire rage around them.

A car slowed at the corner, and its headlights illuminated her for a split second. Lex turned around as inconspicuously as possible. Her heart skipped a beat. Pedestrians walked by, but their glances were harmless. Only in New York could someone get away with standing on a street corner dressed like a gypsy from Bed-Stuy.

Come on, Park, she thought anxiously. *Where are you?*

Lex scanned the busy stretch of Third Avenue again. It had been exactly nine minutes since she'd left the building. Where was Park? Why was she taking so long to walk a few blocks? Had something happened? Then, just as the panic spiked, Lex spotted her.

Park was dressed in gray slacks and one of Trevor

Hamilton's gray double-breasted suit jackets. A white oxford shirt peeked up over the collar. She wore shiny loafers and a black fedora tilted forward on her head, and the shadow it cast obscured her face. She clutched a briefcase in one hand. Moving with a slow, steady stride, she passed easily for a man—a thin, short man, but a man nonetheless. She approached the corner, gave Lex a quick glance, and then walked toward the public pay phone, where she pretended to chat with the receiver pressed to one ear.

Lex breathed a little easier. Not wanting to look bored, she pulled her cell phone from her purse and flipped it open. She stared at the glowing screen, then brought the phone to her ear and mouthed a fake hello. If a suspicious reporter passed by, he'd think her just another ordinary New Yorker burning up free nighttime minutes. She kept the scarf secured over her head and the bottom half of her face.

Exactly seven minutes later, Madison came powering down Third from the opposite direction. She moved with a decidedly rough-and-tumble gait, swinging her arms out and shifting her weight from side to side, like a gang member en route to a hip-hop club. The baseball cap was pulled sideways over her head. She had fashioned a goatee around her mouth with a black eyeliner pencil and fake eyelashes.

They were all in position: Madison and Park on

the southwest corner, Lex on the northeast corner. Now it was time to bounce.

Lex stepped off the curb and into the street. She lifted her arm to hail a cab. It was her cue. She saw that Madison and Park had done the same from their corner.

Good.

A minute later, a cab pulled up and Lex jumped inside. She slammed the door shut. "Washington Square," she said through the Plexiglas partition.

The driver, dark-skinned and wearing a turban, nodded and flicked the meter into place.

Lex turned around in the seat and shot a glance through the back window. She caught a glimpse of Madison climbing into her own cab, but there was no sign of Park. *Please,* Lex prayed, *let this go smoothly.* The Technicolor glare of the city zipped past her as she groped in her purse for her cell phone. Clasping it tightly, she turned it to walkie-talkie mode and waited.

Minutes ticked by. Her heart was pounding.

Then she heard the loud beep announcing an incoming call. She held the phone up.

"Madison on Second, en route to George," came the warbled voice.

Lex smiled, relieved. "Copy that," she replied. "Lex turning east on Third and glad to hear about Madison on Second."

Suddenly, the driver braked at a red light and turned around to face her. "Eh, lady? You wanna me take Lex? I hear you say Madison too. Lotta traffic dat way."

"No," Lex told him. "Take the FDR. It's the fastest way."

"Then why you say Madison?" he asked, confused. "You say Second on Third?"

"I said Madison on Second, not Second on Third." Lex gestured outside with her head, at the green light shining above them. When the cab moved again, she held the phone back to her lips. "Madison on Second, do we have Park on Park, or is Park still on Third? If Park is still at Third we need to make sure Park crosses over toward First and doesn't go down Second all the way."

"Eh?" the driver grunted loudly.

Static crackled from Madison's end of the line. "Madison got a brief visual of Park heading west, maybe toward Madison but then back again on Park. Rest assured that Park is east of Fifth and heading south. You copy that, Lex?"

"*Eh?*" The driver turned around halfway, raking a hand over his face. "Lady! What hell you say?"

"Copy," Lex said. "Over and out." She cut the line and stared at the driver. "Listen, mister. Just get to Washington Square. Is that easy enough? Not Union Square or Tompkins Square or Times Square, and definitely not *Herald Square*. And not even Columbus *Circle*. Washington Square. Okay?"

He shook his head so hard, the turban rocked.

Another beep sounded from the phone. Lex held her breath and waited.

"Park to Lex," came the calm, assured voice. "Park on First heading toward York, had to take a quick detour up Madison before heading back east. Thought Madison was on Madison but I think Madison's on Lex, right?"

"Copy that," Lex replied. "Madison's on Second following departure from Third. After you exit on First, make sure you de-cab on Fifth but only after riding past Madison."

"Gotcha," Park came back. "See you on Fifth but not too far from Fourth, next to Madison who'll be waiting for Lex, who'll be waiting for Park. Then we'll head to the park by way of Fifth, with Lex leading."

"Ten-four." Lex flipped the phone closed. Outside the windows of the cab, FDR Drive was clear, the East River illuminated by a sliver of moon. She caught the driver eyeing her angrily through the rearview mirror but ignored him.

Ten minutes later, the cab was slowing down on Fifth Avenue. The Washington Square arch loomed in the distance, as bright as a beacon. Lex opened the window and scanned the busy stretches of side-walk. Amazingly enough, Madison was standing at the corner of Ninth Street, still looking boyish in her jeans and cap. "Stop here!" Lex shouted.

The cab screeched to a halt.

Lex waited in the silence for close to a minute. Then she spotted another cab slowing to a stop across the street. She watched as Park emerged, the semblance of a sly, sophisticated young man with a briefcase in hand.

Showtime.

Lex paid the driver and hopped out onto the avenue. She began walking toward Washington Square, moving along the west side of Fifth, while Madison and Park followed from the opposite side of the street. Lex kept the scarf wound tightly around her head. Her eyes took in every car, every pedestrain, every stoned college student heading toward the square. She felt a chill snake up her spine as she neared their destination.

Crossing to the east side of the street, she made eye contact with Madison and Park. Finally they were standing together, three oddly dressed people among dozens of other oddly dressed people in an oddly shabby but oddly chic corner of the city. It was a typical Friday night—early Saturday morning, really—in Greenwich Village: college students leaving the nearby dormitories in packs, hot girls and guys on their way to the clubs for a few hours of dancing, couples heading to one of the countless little cafes on

MacDougal or Cornelia. Lex fought the impulse to join the partiers and kept her mind focused on the mission at hand. She led the way through the quaint tree-lined streets that seemed shockingly deserted compared to the bustle of the square.

Waverly was lined with parked cars, but only a few lone tourists were walking around, snapping pictures of the old, elegant brownstones. Lex spotted number 12 easily enough: it was smack in the middle of the row, a four-story brick structure with a splash of ivy trailing along its left side. The large white-frame windows were dark. The house looked as though it had been slumbering in the darkness for a long time.

"Is that it?" Madison asked. "The one right across the street?"

"That's it," Lex confirmed.

"Then why are we just standing here?" Park shifted the briefcase to her left hand. "Let's try to get in and find out who the hell killed Zahara Bell."

"I know, you're right," Lex said. "But it's just that . . . I'm scared. I mean, what if we can't get in? What if an alarm goes off?"

"We won't get caught," Park told her firmly. "If an alarm sounds, we get out of here, jump back into the crowd, and grab a cab home. Now let's go."

Lex reached into her purse and pulled on a pair of black leather gloves. Park did the same, handing an extra pair over to Madison. They approached the town house with their heads bent and their eyes staring straight ahead. It was Lex who mounted the stairs first, walking right up to the front doors. She looked down at the thick brass knobs, then over her shoulder and onto the street. Two cars whizzed by. She and Park had loaded up their purses with various tools—hairpins, a screwdriver, an old credit card—in hopes that they would be able to pry back the locks. They did it at school all the time. St. Cecilia's Prep was a beautiful old building on the Upper East Side, but like many of Manhattan's turn-of-the-century structures, it suffered from a severe lack of modern appliances. On more than one occasion, Lex had picked the lock to the principal's office to get an advance copy of her report card, just in case some of the grades needed a little editing. Park and Madison had done the same.

And maybe, she thought now, this wouldn't be any different.

"Hurry," Madison said through gritted teeth.

Before reaching into her purse, Lex wrapped her gloved fingers around the knob to her right and turned it slowly.

To her sheer astonishment, the door opened.

Park gasped.

Madison held her breath.

Lex, trying to contain her fear and exhilaration, eased the door open and slipped into the dark foyer. Frantically, she waved at her sisters to follow her.

They stood motionless in the shadowy space for several seconds, their breaths steaming the air, their hearts thudding. Just ahead of them was the main door that led directly into the town house.

"How was it open?" Madison whispered. "That's totally weird!"

"Be quiet!" Park shot back.

Lex tried the door directly in front of her. It opened, and a large, ornately furnished living room came into view. Shiny parquet floors, Oriental rugs, a dark wood wet bar in the far left corner beside a spiral staircase. At first glance, everything looked perfect and untouched. The silence was deafening.

They tiptoed inside, standing close together. The light above the staircase was shining, but otherwise, the entire first floor was dark. Huge wood blinds had been pulled down over the windows, blocking out the glare of the street.

Park moved toward the couches on the right, which were situated around a rectangular coffee table littered with books, magazines, and stacks of paper. She pointed silently to them.

Lex nodded, yanking Madison along. They had just begun shuffling through the magazines and papers when a sound boomed from the floor above them.

Footsteps.

Lex froze. She turned and stared at Madison, whose face had gone ashen.

"Shit," Park whispered.

Lex knew the look on her face said it all: *Let's get the freak out of here!* But in a matter of seconds, the footsteps began moving more rapidly above them, swift hard patters that echoed through the living room like cracks of thunder.

Of course there's somebody in here, Lex thought. *Why else would the door be open?*

And now the footsteps were clearly moving toward the staircase.

Holy shit.

It was too late to make a dash for the door.

Holding her breath, Lex yanked Madison and Park by the arms and together they squatted directly behind the couch. They slammed against each other as they vied for room in the small space. Pressed back against the wall beneath the window, they had a clear view of the living room, but if the person coming downstairs decided to sit, they'd be knee-high in horse dung.

Just stay still, Lex mouthed to her sisters. She gave Madison's arm a reassuring squeeze, because at the moment it looked as though Madison was going to barf, burp, or be one with the floor. Park eased the fedora off her head and silently slid it down the length of her chest.

A brief silence descended over the town house. Then a long shadow appeared at the top of the staircase and started moving down it. *Clank, clank, clank.*

Lex dared to peek over the edge of the couch.

Through the darkness, she saw a distinctly female figure walk down to the first floor.

The woman was tall and thin, with a body like an hourglass. She was dressed in simple blue jeans and a starched white shirt. When she stepped into a pale stream of light close to the window nearest the door, her face came into full view.

Lex swallowed her gasp. She recognized the woman instantly.

Julia Colbert Gantz was a former supermodel. Her exquisite face had graced hundreds of magazines. She had modeled for Versace, Armani, Prada, Ralph Lauren, Dior, Chanel, and countless others. Two years ago, she'd joined *Catwalk* magazine as Zahara Bell's executive assistant.

Lex couldn't stop staring. Julia Colbert Gantz was a beautiful woman, but right now she looked like a train wreck. Her hair was wiry and uncombed. Her face was sweaty and pale. And she was visibly nervous, juggling an armful of papers and folders while scanning the living room for something.

Please, Lex thought, *don't come over to the couch.*

Julia Colbert Gantz didn't seem interested in the couch, or anything near it, for that matter. Huffing and puffing, scraping a free hand through her hair, she appeared totally desperate. When she moved into the light again, the dampness beneath her eyes shone. She had been crying.

Suddenly, she spotted what she was looking for:

a small red handbag, half hidden on the love seat under a pile of papers. She ran to it and scooped it up. Then, turning around toward the door, the heel of her boot got snagged on the end of the Oriental carpet. She lurched forward with a squeal, managing to regain her balance on the edge of the love seat. A single sheet of paper spilled from the bunch cradled at her chest and drifted silently to the floor. But in her haste to leave the town house, Julia Colbert Gantz didn't see what she had dropped. She held tight to the handbag, bolted for the front door, and was gone.

Lex shot to her feet. She sighed dramatically.

"Get down!" Madison whispered harshly. "There could still be someone here!"

"There was no one else here." Lex stepped out from behind the couch. She looked down at her trembling hands and saw that her palms were slick with sweat. "Did you see who that was?"

Park, rising up slowly, shook her head. "I was too scared to look."

"Julia Colbert Gantz," Lex told them. "Zahara Bell's assistant."

"What was she doing here?" Madison asked, sounding more frightened than she had a moment ago. "I know she wasn't at the gala tonight—she wasn't on the guest list."

Lex swung the long end of her scarf over her

shoulder. "That's what we have to find out. Let's go upstairs."

"Wait a minute." Park's voice resounded through the dark living room. She was standing closer to the door now, in the exact spot where Julia Colbert Gantz had tripped. In Park's hand was a tattered sheet of paper. She was staring down at it intently. When she understood what she was reading, she pursed her lips together grimly and held the sheet out for Madison and Lex to peruse. "It looks like part of a headline, or a news story," she said quietly.

Lex looked down at the crinkled sheet of paper.

The words across the top half were in boldface print:

ACTOR JEREMY BLEU LOSES MILLIONS.

"Oh, my God," Lex said.

Madison clucked her tongue. "I *knew* it. What did I tell you? *He* killed Zahara Bell and stole the Avenue diamond."

"Now wait a minute," Park shot back. "We don't even know what this is. It's a torn sheet of paper, for God's sake. I've followed Jeremy's career since his first movie and I never read anything about him losing millions of dollars."

Lex grabbed the sheet and studied it closely. "This is a proof," she said. "It's a story or an article that hasn't made it to print yet. See how the letters are a little tilted? And there's no copy to go along with it."

"So what?" Madison shrugged.

"It means this story hasn't been published." Lex held the sheet up to what little light peeked in through the windows. "I guess maybe Zahara Bell was getting ready to publish it in one of the upcoming issues of *Catwalk.*"

"And Jeremy killed her for it," Madison whispered.

"I thought you said he killed her for the diamond." Park eased the fedora back onto her head and rolled her eyes. "Make up your mind, Sherlock."

"You have a better explanation for this?" Madison asked sharply. "It's sickeningly obvious. Julia Colbert Gantz came here because she wanted to salvage this stuff before the cops got to it."

Park crossed her arms over her chest and turned her head away. She was devastated: the pieces of the puzzle were falling into place, and the picture wasn't pretty.

Could this be it? she wondered. *Is Jeremy Bleu guilty? Why don't I believe it?*

Lex folded the sheet of paper and stuffed it into her purse. She glanced up, looking toward the top of the staircase landing. She wanted to see what was on the second floor. Were there more little clues about Zahara to unearth? More clues about who might have killed her? She felt a sudden chill in her bones. She hated being here, in a dead woman's dark house, but they needed answers.

Swallowing her fear, she walked to the staircase. She motioned for Madison and Park to follow her. Single file, they tiptoed upstairs. The long corridor on the second floor was narrow and led to a series of bedrooms. The first door on the right was a home office: a desk, a file cabinet, several issues of *Catwalk* strewn on a chair. Next came a room nearly filled to capacity with clothes, fabric swatches, and hangers. The room at the very end of the corridor had obviously been Zahara's: a framed publicity picture of her hung on the door. They entered, and Park found a small Tiffany table lamp and flicked it on. The light dimly illuminated a huge brass bed and bright white walls.

Lex went to the large bureau in the corner. She quickly but carefully pulled open the drawers and began rifling through them. More clothes in one, more papers and notebooks in another. When she came across a book titled *The Sexy Older Woman's Guide to Pleasure,* she nearly barfed.

"Look at this," Park said from across the room. "Dozens of clippings about the Avenue diamond—including two old stories about Mom and *us.*"

"Was tonight the first time Zahara was granted permission to wear the diamond in public?" Madison asked.

Park nodded. "Totally—and I still don't understand why she was allowed to wear it. I mean, the diamond is generally something you'd wear to the Oscars or the Golden Globes, not a fund-raiser."

There was a sudden commotion outside. The noise cut through the air and made them all stand up a little straighter. Lex ran to the window. Peeking through the blinds, she stared down at the street and gasped when she spotted three police cruisers parked out front.

And the familiar face of Detective Charlie Mullen staring up at the town house.

11

The Escape

There was no time to panic. Even though Madison felt like a fist was squeezing her heart, she followed Park's lead and kept her mouth shut. She didn't think about the fact that they were in a town house without a back exit. She didn't think about the jail term that would follow a charge of breaking and entering. She merely clenched her fists at her sides and watched as Lex flicked off the small lamp.

Darkness plunged over the room. Voices rose up from the street as the police neared the front door.

Madison heard Park shuffling in her briefcase for something, and a moment later a small beam of light cut a path to the corridor. The flashlight worked like a charm.

"Come on," Park whispered. "We have to get out of here."

"How?" Lex's voice sounded strained. "We can't go out through the front door, and the back door leads to an enclosed garden. We're totally trapped."

"No we're not! Don't say that!" Madison snapped. "There has to be a way out of here."

The flashlight trailed over the walls as they bolted out into the corridor. The thin beam bounced and spun and then finally stopped above their heads. Park was tracking it slowly along the ceiling. There was a small alcove to the right that led to a bathroom. Just beyond it, half hidden by a series of hanging plants, was a door.

Madison knew what they were about to do—what they *had* to do—and the very thought of it sent a wave of dizziness washing over her. She stared numbly as Park and Lex ran to the door and pried it open. It wasn't a closet; it was a short narrow stairwell that led up to the rooftop. A draft blew past her. She instinctively stepped back.

Park turned around. "Madison, we have no choice," she said gently, shining the flashlight at her. "It's the only way."

Madison hated heights. It was a miracle that she'd managed to live in the penthouse all these years. She rarely looked out the windows and *never* ate dinner on the terrace during the warm summer months. She didn't understand people who enjoyed those dizzying panoramic views from the Empire State Building. You got that high up and a gust of wind could float you like a piece of paper. Now she shook her head vigorously. "Forget it," she whispered. "I can't do it."

"Of course you can!" Lex shot back, annoyed. "There's no time to discuss this. We have to—"

Downstairs, the front door opened and the din of voices echoed through the town house. It sounded as though five or six cops had entered; almost immediately, they began shuffling through drawers and barking orders at each other. Detective Mullen's voice was the loudest: "See what you can find, boys. Dust for prints just in case, and tag anything that looks to be of interest. I'm heading upstairs to see what else I can find out about the vic."

The fear that surged through Madison was monumental. Her eyes widened, and in that moment she realized how close they were to getting caught. She hurried forward and clasped Lex's outstretched hand. Quietly, carefully, they mounted the stairwell as Park closed the door behind them.

The sky yawned wide open as they reached the upper landing and stepped onto the rooftop. It was a beautiful sight—skyscrapers twinkling in the distance, a bright sliver of moon—but Madison nearly dropped to her knees when she realized that there was nowhere to go but *down*. She clutched a hand to her stomach. The rooftop was flat and built out with a deck, the wooden railings on each side about four feet high; a small professionally landscaped garden occupied one corner, and several rosebushes were just beginning to bloom.

"Come on," Park urged them. "We can't just stand here."

"Where else are we gonna go?" Madison cried.

Park pointed across the expanse of rooftops: the town houses were all the same height, four of them connected like a single block of cement. There were no alleyways in between. Zahara Bell's town house was the third one in the row.

"The last one, down at the corner—it's actually an apartment building," Lex said. "Maybe we can re-enter there and make it down to the street."

Park nodded. She dropped the flashlight into her briefcase, then stuffed the briefcase tightly under her left arm.

"You—you're both crazy!" Madison stammered. "We'll never make it! And can't you feel the wind? It'll blow us right off!"

"Of course it won't," Park assured her. "All we have to do is scale the walls of each roof deck. Come on."

Madison watched as her sisters edged though the deck railings and ran to the far side of the roof. She hated that they were so fearless. She took a single step forward and winced. Her legs wobbled as if she were standing in cheap stilettos. She made it to Lex's side and finally allowed her eyes to focus.

Park wrapped her hands around the top of the wall running along the edge of the building, struggling to maintain her grip. She climbed, swung one leg over the side, and paused to study the next rooftop. Straddling the wall, she looked down at Lex and Madison and said, "Perfect. It's almost identical to Zahara's. Piece of cake."

Lex went next. She wrapped the long scarf around her head and neck and made it to the top of the wall. But she didn't jump over to the next rooftop. Instead, she stared at Madison and held out her hand.

Madison took a deep breath. She studied Lex's outstretched hand as if it were something foreign—an imitation Prada purse or, worse, a slab of costume jewelry.

"Come on," Lex said. "I *so* know you can do this."

"You can," Park echoed from the other side of the wall.

Madison thrust her hand into Lex's and closed her eyes. She felt herself being instantly pulled up. She glimpsed the wall's edge as her left leg swung over. Her stomach bounced into her throat. *Don't look down*, she told herself. *Just don't look down.*

But of course, she did.

Perched on the flat top of the wall, her butt against the cold brick, Madison experienced a spell of vertigo so intense, she nearly fainted. The street five stories below looked like a board game spinning out of focus. The cars were little animals zigzagging in every direction. The people were stick figures taking flight. Her jaw dropped wide open, and the energy vanished from her body. "Incoming," she said weakly, and keeled over the side of the wall.

She fell back against Park's hands. Then she was sitting on her booty again, dazed and blinking as a cool gust of wind swept past her.

"Up!" Lex ordered, pointing a finger at her. "There's no time for this!"

Whimpering, choking back tears, Madison got to her feet and followed her sisters. They dashed across the next rooftop, slipping and sliding on puddles, skirting little tiled gardens and beach chairs left out from last week's warm weather. This time, the wall was easier to mount. Madison did it without squeezing her eyes shut, but the nervous tension roiling in her stomach produced two powerful burps that echoed in the night like a wolf's howl.

When they reached the last building, they saw that Lex had been right: it wasn't a private town house like the others but a brownstone converted into several apartments. This was obvious just from glancing around the rooftop: there were dozens of wires snaking along the edges, and a grid beside one of the television antennae detailing the layout of the building.

Madison saw the rooftop door and ran to it breathlessly. Her hopes sank when she realized that it was locked. She whirled around, a fresh wave of panic surging through her blood. "Great!" she cried. "Now what? We're stuck up here."

"No, we're not." Park set the briefcase down on the tarry ground and flipped it open. Arranged neatly inside were several useful tools: two screwdrivers, pliers, three nail files in different sizes, a bottle of nail polish remover, four hairpins, and a small tube of Clarins moisturizer. She handed Lex the flashlight and instructed her to hold it up in front of the knob. Then she went to work.

Standing off to the side, Madison watched silently as Park kneeled down and picked a small screwdriver from the briefcase. "Hurry," she whispered.

Park slipped the screwdriver into the thin space between the doorknob and the frame, jiggling it until she found the latch. She held the screwdriver in position with her left hand and took the bottle of nail polish remover in her right. Uncapping it with her teeth, she splashed a dollop into the space, then handed the bottle to Madison. Another jiggle. There was the faintest click, but Park knew she hadn't gotten the job done completely. She yanked the screwdriver out, dropped it into the briefcase, and retrieved from it the longest nail file. She plunged it against the latch, aiming it at an angle; it stuck, remaining in place after she took her hands away. With the medium-sized hairpin, Park picked the latch with a series of twisting motions—her wrist went left, right, left, up, down, right, left, and then up swiftly. The hairpin stuck as well.

Park rose to her feet, wiped the grit from her pants, and casually opened the door.

Lex flicked off the flashlight and flung it into the briefcase, apparently not at all surprised at Park's success.

Madison gasped. She clapped her hands together, giddy and relieved.

"There," Park said. "Faster than I thought it would be." When all the tools were securely replaced, she removed her leather gloves and reached for the tube of moisturizer. She squeezed some into her hands. As easily as if she were standing in front of a mirror, she slathered it on her face and neck.

Lex followed, oozing some of the moisturizer onto her own palm before passing it along.

Madison closed her eyes as the coolness of the moisturizer kissed her face. After all these hours of worry and work and exposure to the elements, it was no wonder their skin needed hydrating.

The door led to a descending staircase; it was gray

and dank and poorly lit, but it took them directly inside the building. Almost instantly, the sound of blaring music cut the air. It grew louder as they followed a narrow hallway that smelled of cigarette smoke, pot, and rotting food. Somebody down the hall was singing above the raucous beat. When they rounded the next corner, Madison came to a complete stop. Her mouth fell open.

Spread out before them in the next hallway was a full-fledged frat party. They weren't standing in an ordinary apartment building. They were in a college dormitory, replete with overcrowding, bad lighting, and totally stinky air. Students were all over the hallway: up against the walls, squatting on the floor, clustered by their suites like ants in a sugar bowl.

Madison had never seen so many beer bottles in one place.

"How lucky could we get!" Lex said. "This looks like so much fun!"

"Forget it," Park shouted over the music. She nodded to the very end of the hall, where a red Exit sign glowed brightly. "We have to make it through here and get outside."

"But how?" Madison called back. "We're not students. What if we get stopped by someone? We don't have IDs!"

"Just try to blend in." Park tightened her grip on the briefcase and pulled the fedora down over her head as far as it would go. Then she plunged into the milling crowd.

Lex followed.

Madison wanted to cry out for them to wait, but it was too late. She watched as Park boogied herself down the hallway, stopping every few feet to nod politely at people when they shot her almost curious glances. Lex knotted her scarf over the bottom half of her face and instantly blended with the wild crew of students; when she got to the small mosh pit raging just outside one of the suites, she literally jumped in, rocking back and forth like a headbanger at a heavy metal concert. Then she made her way to the Exit sign with a little two-step dance, looking like another drunk freshman heading outside for a smoke.

Forcing the stiffness from her body, Madison stepped into the crowd. Bodies bumped against her as she yanked the baseball cap tighter around her head. There was no way to get past the craziness without mimicking some of the craziness, so she threw her arms up over her head and reluctantly stumbled into a dance. She felt completely out of place. She couldn't seem to fall in synch with the music. Moving down the hall, she flattened her hands and stuck them out, walking like an Egyptian as a guy dressed in jeans and a sweat-soaked tank top jumped in front of her.

"Hey!" he said, giving her a smile.

Madison smelled the beer on his breath and fought the urge to shove him away. "Hey," she replied, dropping her voice so that it sounded guttural.

The guy was marginally cute but had nice muscular arms. He ground his crotch against her thigh and smirked. "I've never danced with a dude," he screamed over the music. "It feels totally weird, but kinda hot."

"I gotta be careful," Madison told him in the deep manly voice. "My boyfriend's here." She ground against him one final time, then slipped away. She spotted Park and Lex beneath the Exit sign and ran toward them. "Ugh. This is so rank."

Park shrugged.

Lex, who was still thumping her feet to the music, said, "I can't *wait* for college."

Madison and Park grabbed her by the arm and together they rushed down another two staircases. Outside, they discreetly glanced up the street and saw that the police cars were still parked in front of Zahara Bell's town house.

"Meet at the corner of Ninth and Fifth," Lex said quickly.

They dashed in opposite directions to avoid the possibility of being spotted together. Madison made it to the designated spot first, breathless and panting. Two minutes later, she spotted Park coming up Fifth and waved at her.

"What now?" Madison asked, raising her arm to hail a cab. "Do we go to the Pierre and hustle Jeremy Bleu into giving us back the diamond?"

Park shook her head. "We can't risk it. We've had enough close calls as it is."

"Do you think the cops have already gotten to Jeremy?" Madison sounded sympathetic. She knew Park was taking Jeremy Bleu's obvious guilt hard.

"Who knows? At this point, *I* don't even know what to think. I just wish I could speak to Jeremy face to face for a few minutes." Park looked away, visibly upset. "It still doesn't make sense to me—how he could be guilty. But I guess if you've lost millions and you're in trouble, stealing the Avenue diamond makes sense."

It was four a.m. The crowds were still thick, the traffic busy. Nightclubs were just beginning to unload the first round of partiers, and the second round was making its way east and west through Greenwich Village.

Suddenly, Lex came tearing up the avenue at breakneck speed. She looked like a marathon runner nearing the finish line. The scarf was flapping behind her neck, and strands of blond hair tumbled down past her shoulders. Her energy was so unchecked, she nearly crashed into Park. "Look!" she said, reaching into her purse. She pulled out a folded copy of the *Post* and held it out.

"How did you get this?" Madison asked, her eyes wide.

"There was a delivery truck on Sixth, so I lifted a copy and ran like hell." Lex bent over slightly, trying to catch her breath.

"I don't think I want to see it," Park said. "Thank you very much."

Madison unfolded the newspaper, a knot tightening in her stomach. In that moment, she didn't care about the tilting baseball cap on her head or the streetlight shining down on her. No disguise would be able to shield her, Park, or Lex from the imminent media storm.

They were front-page news.

12

The Avenue Diamond

The legend of the Avenue diamond had intrigued Park her entire life. She had first set eyes on it at the tender age of six, while accompanying her father on a Fifth Avenue shopping spree. Hand in hand, they had bought up a storm at Bergdorf's and Bendel's, then crossed the street to study the windows at Tiffany. And there, encased in glass, was the most stunning object she had ever seen. The enormous diamond was as thick as a crystal showpiece, the strands of light surrounding it as bright as the moon in an

Aspen sky. It was a kind of celestial radiance, and Park was sure she had glimpsed a view of heaven. Looking up at her father, she had asked the questions befitting a young celebutante: *Why didn't Mom buy it? How many carats is it? May I please have it?* She had left the sidewalk empty-handed but utterly transformed.

Even now, years later, Park equated the diamond with the divine. Precious gems were the work of angels. Gold was a gift of the saints. But the Avenue diamond was God's way of saying, *Yes, my daughters, I have style.* There wasn't a sane person on earth who would disagree with her. The diamond evoked awe and wonder, mystery and romance. Much more than just a rare rock, it was a one-of-a-kind gemological masterpiece steeped in legend and lore.

And Park was determined to recover it.

Outside the windows of her bedroom, it was dawn. Officially Saturday morning. The sun was just beginning to rise. Buildings gleamed against the pink backdrop of the sky and traffic sounded on the streets. Park was sitting at the L-shaped mahogany desk that occupied a small corner of her big bedroom. She hadn't slept since getting back home. She had lain awake for a couple of hours, her mind buzzing with fear and anger and worry. Now she pushed aside the day's newspapers and flipped open her laptop. She clicked through her private files slowly; most were several pages long, comprising her years of research on gemology. She had separate folders for emeralds, sapphires, rubies, pearls—both white and black—and, of course, diamonds. She also had the names of the private jewelers and overseas dealers she'd purchased rocks from in the past, along with their corresponding dollar amounts. Last year alone, she had dropped $60,000 for three pairs of ruby earrings, $110,000 for a 7-carat emerald ring, and $1.6 million for a 15-carat diamond bracelet. The pieces were exquisite, but she had chosen them for more than just their beauty. A smart collector didn't just buy; she *invested.* Park never spent her allowance without ensuring a profit for herself in the future, and one day, her vast jewelry collection would be worth far more than she had paid for it.

She located her personal file on the Avenue diamond and clicked it open. It was nearly twenty pages long and contained all the information a girl passionate about jewelry could ever hope to find. She began perusing the paragraphs. She knew many of the facts by heart, but it was the legend of the Avenue diamond that intrigued her. Park had a hunch that whoever had stolen it was in for a shocking—and potentially violent—surprise. You didn't just grab an incredible piece of jewelry and bounce. There were severe consequences for disrupting the energy of midtown Manhattan shoppers.

A whopping 110 carats, the Avenue diamond was

valued at $21 million and owned by Tiffany. It was not for sale. It was not on regular display in a store front window. It was released for public viewing only twice a year: in late April, to coincide with the spring spending frenzy that affected every serious shopper, and the day after Thanksgiving, to mark the official start of the holiday season. Long lines thronged Tiffany at both times, with hundreds of tourists pressing up against the windows to experience the sparkle of the magical stone's light. The diamond was a Manhattan fixture, but it had toured the world a decade ago, wowing the citizens of every continent and drawing admiring stares from the kings and queens of Europe and the Middle East. And whether prince or pauper, people always asked the same questions: Was the legend true? Did the diamond really possess otherworldly powers? Could it heal or harm depending on the situation?

Yes, it can, Park thought, the questions reverberating through her own mind. She and Madison and Lex were living proof of that. Had their mother not worn the Avenue diamond that night so many years ago, they probably wouldn't even have been born. Or—worse—they could have been born to a pop star and given trashy names like Broadway, Columbus, and Amsterdam. Park shivered just thinking about it.

No, she couldn't wait for the police to track down the diamond. It meant too much to her family.

She scrolled down to page ten, finding exactly what she was looking for. It was the section of her research she had collected directly from Long Phat, PhD, an internationally renowned gemologist with offices in Hong Kong, Tokyo, and Johannesburg. Park had met Dr. Phat two years ago on one of his rare trips to the United States. He'd been impressed by her jewelry collection and, following a sizeable donation to his scientific institute, had agreed to a brunch date at the St. Regis. Park had interrogated Phat for nearly two hours and in that short expanse of time learned his personal beliefs about the Avenue diamond. The legend and lore—replete with their supernatural overtones—were real. The diamond, he told her, was as old and wise as the earth itself. He had seen its unearthly power create and destroy. It was a stone to be cherished, admired . . . and feared.

The 110-carat diamond had been discovered nearly fifty years ago in the wilds of the Amazon jungle. Bitsy Bellingham Bard, an American socialite on safari with her explorer husband, Gaston Parpedieu, had stumbled down an embankment during a violent rainstorm. When Bitsy landed facedown in a puddle of mud, she felt several bones in her body snap like twigs. She couldn't move. She couldn't see her husband in the lashing leaves and fronds. Pain wracked her body and she struggled for breath. Certain she was dying, Bitsy saw a pinprick of light emanating from a nearby rock bed and felt an instant sense of peace. The light undulated; it shimmered and shook. Then the earth shook too, a jolt that raised the ground and ripped a crack through the sodden floor of the forest. The quake was fast but powerful, and the sudden seismic shift created a small opening in the rock bed. Bitsy dragged herself toward the cave, following the same brilliant stream of light. But it wasn't an angel taking her to the Saks in the sky. It was a stunning stone formation catching its first hint of the sun. Weak and broken, Bitsy touched it and felt a comforting heat surge through her body. She stood up. She wiped the muck from her boots. Her broken bones were healed, her pain gone. For two days, she and Gaston hacked away at the rock wall until the diamond came loose.

Bitsy, a worldly and cultured woman, had friends everywhere—even in the Amazon. As the story went, she took the diamond to a tribal shaman, who held it in his hands and saw a vision in the glimmering rays. It was a vision of Fifth Avenue. It was a vision of shoppers and stores and stunning opulence. He told Bitsy the diamond had been revealed to her by the gods in trust and honor. She was not to squander or sell it. She was not to destroy it. The shaman chanted an incantation over the diamond, did some sort of two-step dance, and handed it back to Bitsy and Gaston. They chartered a private plane back to New

York, and Bitsy soon unveiled the diamond to the world. She christened it the Avenue diamond because she said it would forever protect and preserve the eminent expanse of Fifth—from Central Park right down to Washington Square. Shoppers would always feel at home, and the world's greatest retailers would flourish and expand. The diamond, Bitsy told countless interviewers, had incredible powers; it was to be guarded at all costs from loss or damage, lest its wrath take hold. If the diamond ever *was* stolen, Bitsy promised that it would find its way home within forty-eight hours, leaving the thief "broken and burned."

The world got its first glimpse of the diamond's mysterious pull shortly after Bitsy died. Her greedy nephews, Amos and Arnold, inherited the diamond but quickly sold it to an Arabian prince, pocketing major bucks. That very week, Amos slipped on his toupee, cracked his head open like an egg, and died instantly. Arnold, a notorious drunk, downed a martini in one gulp and choked on the accompanying olive garnish. A few years later, the Arabian prince sold the diamond to Tiffany for an undisclosed amount, citing numerous odd health problems, including impotence and huge diamond-shaped hemorrhoids.

Since then, Tiffany had proven a good home for the Avenue diamond, though Park couldn't understand why the store agreed to loan it out to celebrities, royalty, and other important people these days. Venturina Baci should have been the *only* exception. But Julia Roberts had worn the diamond one year to the Oscars, and it had also graced the necks of Sarah Jessica Parker and Jennifer Lopez. Had Zahara Bell been killed for the diamond? Park wondered. Was it an act of robbery? What unsuspecting, nonsuperstitious person *wouldn't* want to get his or her hands on the Avenue diamond?

In Park's file were several JPEGs of the ravishing rock. Long ago, it had been delicately attached to a thick gold chain—only suitable, Park thought, for long thin necks of the celebutante variety. Now she studied the pictures, which showed the diamond from various angles. The four *C*s that comprised a diamond's worth—color, clarity, carat, and cut—were supremely evident here. The Avenue's color was the best color possible: none. An absence of color was a rarity in diamonds and signified the highest quality. This allowed light to be reflected and dispersed as a rainbow, enchanting even the most astute eyes.

The Avenue's cut was a "round brilliant" one, the most popular cut for a diamond because it ensured optical beauty without damaging the stone's natural atomic framework. When cut to exact and mathematically proven proportions, a diamond's symmetry produced unerring beauty and luster. The Avenue was no exception; light entering it from any direction was reflected through the top, allowing flashes of vibrant color.

In terms of clarity, which measured the surface and internal characteristics of a diamond, the Avenue was perfect. There were no blemishes or inclusions, nor were there any polish lines or marks that clouded its radiance. Many years ago, the Avenue had received the highest clarity grading possible—an F, which stood for *flawless*.

Just reading the notes made Park's heart beat a little faster. She was getting antsy in the chair, her panic levels rising. What if the psycho who had killed Zahara Bell was on his way out of the country by now? He could sell the Avenue diamond on the black market for a whopping amount of cash. That would mean the end of an era for jewelry admirers like her. It would leave a *huge* void on Fifth Avenue, and in the elegant fabric of this magnificent city she called home.

She stood up. She shook the tension from her body. She glanced out the window at the brightening sky and imagined what the day would bring. More reporters and cameras. More questions. Lex's stolen dress. The three of them stumbling on a body. A missing legendary diamond. And the fact that someone—a stranger—had gained access to their home with the sole intention of framing them and tarnishing the Hamilton name. Would anyone believe that she and Madison and Lex were innocent? How would the general—and generally adoring—public react to the scandal? And did Detective Mullen, with his suspicious comments and terrible clothes, believe them?

Turning her eyes back to the laptop, Park felt overcome by a sense of anger she had never before experienced. She was incredulous. She was outraged. Huffing and puffing, she slammed her hands down on the desktop and let out a little unladylike grunt. It was one of her rare and unexpected forays into the world of negative thinking and loss of control. It happened to her maybe twice a year. She hated it.

We have to find the killer. And we have to find the diamond!

"I *know*," she murmured, closing her eyes in a sudden rush of emotion.

It was time to up the ante on their investigation. She knew it. She had denied the inevitable for too many hours now. But as Jeremy Bleu's face flashed before her, she felt a hot tingle shoot through her body.

She hadn't meant for it to happen that way. Not *completely*.

Physical attraction was a weird thing: when it hit you and took over, your knees got wobbly and you did things without thinking clearly. Park hadn't had a boyfriend in many months and she didn't necessarily want one now, but she *did* acknowledge the fact that warmth and body contact were good things. She missed them. At this point, Jeremy wasn't much more than a fling, yet she couldn't dispel him from her mind. There'd been a connection between them, an instant electric current. This, she thought, was what people called *chemistry*.

But why *had* he ditched her last night? Did he know that Zahara Bell had some sort of information on him—a little newsworthy nugget about him losing millions of dollars? What was he so afraid of? She and her sisters hadn't run away in those moments of panic. Neither had Coco. *They* had nothing to hide. Did Jeremy really think he was going to disappear and leave them to clean up this mess? The very thought of it enraged Park.

Running out on her had been the wrong move. She felt hurt and belittled, as discarded as the items on a clearance rack.

Why did you run, Jeremy? What are you trying to hide?

She paced the floor. She forced herself to retrace every minute of last night, from the moment she and Madison arrived at the gala to the moment her and Jeremy's eyes met. She pictured him in that split second, freezing the image in her mind's eye. Gorgeous. Hot. A tall Roman god dressed to the nines in a sleek D&G tux. Crisp white shirt and gleaming gold cuff links. The dark scarf draped around his neck—

She blinked. The image vanished. Her heart slammed in her chest.

The scarf.

Jeremy had been wearing a scarf at the gala, a dark silk and wool scarf that blended softly into the charcoal color of his suit. He hadn't been wearing it when they were making out in the ladies' room. She was sure of it. She remembered pushing the suit jacket off his shoulders and sliding it down his arms as their lips met. She remembered kissing a trail to his neck, her face hot against the starched white fabric of the shirt. He hadn't been wearing the scarf. And with a rush of clarity, Park realized why that little detail was making her stomach churn.

She saw that same scarf again several minutes later—around Zahara Bell's neck.

Oh, my God.

Her cheeks flushed. Blood roared in her ears.

It can't be.

But it was.

Taking a deep breath, and determined to maintain her composure, she walked calmly to the nightstand beside the bed and picked up her cell phone. She flipped it open. She retrieved the text message she, Madison, and Lex had received from the anonymous number.

Three minus one is much more fun.

A scare tactic. Cute.

She slammed the phone shut.

It didn't make sense, but the thought that Jeremy could have actually killed Zahara Bell, stolen the

Avenue diamond, and *then* made out with her was too twisted to believe. She wasn't afraid of him. She was too pissed off to be anything but outraged. What he needed was a good shakedown, a proverbial kick in the ass.

She flipped open the phone again and began scrolling through her address book. The Pierre Hotel. He'd told her he was staying in one of the penthouse suites. Park found the number and waited for the line to connect. A laconic-voiced operator answered at the front desk. "Penthouse A," Park said. "It's an emergency." Nearly a minute went by before a male voice answered.

"Hellooohh?" It was Jeremy—in disguise and suddenly sounding very British.

"Cut the bullshit, Bleu," she barked into the phone. "I know about the scarf. I made the connection. Would you like to explain yourself, or should I just call the cops?"

Silence. And then his breath filling the distance between them. He said, "I can explain, Park. I can explain everything. Please don't doubt me."

She tightened her grip on the cell phone. "There'll be a limo outside your hotel in exactly one hour. My chauffeur's name is Clarence. We can talk, but we're doing it on *my* turf. Got it?"

"Yes. I'll be there. I can explain, Park. Please let me explain."

"Fine. See you soon. Oh, and Jeremy?"

"Yeah?"

She stared across the room at the picture of the Avenue diamond gleaming on her laptop. It inspired her. "Don't fuck with me. It'll cost you *big-time.*"

13

Who's That . . . Girl?

Clad in a black and white French maid's uniform, a blond wig covering his bald head, Chicky Marsala studied his reflection in the smoky mirror that hung on the door of the overcrowded closet. By his own account, he looked *hot*. Several layers of drugstore-purchased Maybelline foundation had transformed his blotchy skin into a smooth and radiant complexion. There was no trace of stubble on his chin, and the short hairs that usually peeked out of his nostrils were all but gone. The only problem was the bra hooked behind his back: the rolls of clean underwear stuffed into the D-sized cups kept shifting, which made one boob droop and the other bounce. Maybe no one would notice. It was early, and from a distance he was the epitome of a big sexy chick with lots of junk in the trunk.

Turning sideways, Chicky gave his profile a once-over. The wig was an expensive model that he had purchased in a high-end retail costume shop on Broadway; the blond tendrils tumbled down to his shoulders but didn't hide the big silver hoops hanging from his ears. The uniform was good quality too. It was polyester and Lycra, and it rose up nearly to his neck. His lips, naturally thick, were painted a bright shade of red. Now he faced the mirror one last time and pouted seductively. He blew himself a kiss and smiled. He was ready to complete his mission.

My camera, he thought. *My pictures and my money.*

He flicked off the lights in the studio apartment and reached for the black purse by the door. He opened it carefully, checking to make sure he had packed all the necessary tools. He had pliers, string, duct tape, three old credit cards taped together to form a thick lock buster, and a pair of leather gloves. At the very bottom of the purse was his most prized possession: a handgun. He had enough rounds to take out a small army, but he hoped it wouldn't come to that. He really didn't want to kill anybody today, especially not those Hamilton girls.

Outside, Chicky hailed a cab and instructed the driver to head south. Scrunched in the backseat, he reviewed the plan in his mind several times. Get into the building, preferably through the front entrance. If that proved fruitless, he'd hit the hidden side doors. Having weaseled his way into countless luxury high-rises in the past, Chicky knew all the secrets. Those side doors usually weren't alarmed because the housekeepers and maintenance crews came and went at all hours. It cost millions of dollars to live in Fifth Avenue digs, but all those ritzy residents didn't know squat about what went on way down on the ground floor. After getting in, he'd ride the elevator up to the penthouse—everybody in New York knew the Hamiltons lived in the penthouse—and then he'd start scratching on the door. He wouldn't knock. He'd *scratch*. Always worked like a charm. People wouldn't open their doors if they thought a human being was on the other side, but they'd pop the locks in case a little kitty or puppy was hungry. When someone answered, he'd shove his way into the penthouse and hold the gun up. Then he'd *force* those girls to hand over his camera.

Sure, they'd probably recognize him. But in between pissing their pretty panties and grabbing each other for support, they'd turn the goods over. Then he'd bind their hands together with the string. A few quick slaps of tape across their lips and they'd have no choice but to shut up. Then it was back down to the lobby and out through the way he came in. Hop into a cab, get home, chuck the clothes, put on jeans and a jacket, and hop the subway to Penn Station. He'd catch a bus upstate and be in the woods by the time the cops sorted through his aliases and positively identified him. He knew exactly whom to call after that. The underground picture market people weren't interested in turning him in. They were only interested in getting their hands on lurid images they could print and sell all over the world.

"Did you say the corner of Madison and Eightieth, ma'am?" the cab driver asked.

Chicky smiled. The guy had called him ma'am. "Uh, yes," he replied in a low, squeaky voice. "Thank you." He stared straight into the rearview mirror and gave a girly giggle.

The cab came to a stop. Chicky paid and stepped out onto Madison Avenue. Traffic was light for a Saturday morning. He looked down at his legs and checked to make sure the seams of his stockings were straight. Satisfied, he set off on foot, walking at a brisk pace. Only a handful of other pedestrians shot him odd glances. Otherwise, he totally passed for a woman.

As he approached the building, he stared up at it. Cars zoomed down Fifth Avenue. He turned up Seventy-third Street and walked west. As he reached Fifth, he spotted a news van parked across the way.

Chicky ambled past the building's front entrance, throwing a hard look inside as he did so. A tall doorman was staring out from behind the doors. That was bad. The guy wasn't at a desk watching TV or reading the paper; instead, he was on alert, eyes wide.

Damn.

Chicky continued walking. He went around the block, across Madison, and then up Seventy-third again. This time he stopped when he recognized the building's side-entrance doors. They were shadowed by a small awning. He reached into his purse and retrieved a few of his tools. Quickly, methodically, and with expert hands, he went to work.

A click.

A snap.

A cut.

A shove.

Bingo.

The door budged.

Laughing to himself, Chicky shook his head. How stupid were these maintenance workers? This big, beautiful, prestigious building was *old,* and the upkeep was awful. It hadn't taken him more than a minute to get the job done. That was the problem with rich people: they thought they were above everything, even getting robbed and roughed up. Their smug superiority pissed him off. Thinking back on the events of the night, Chicky couldn't contain his rage. How he had fought that group of spoiled kids to get his camera back. How they'd tripped him and sent him flying into the toilet. And how that Hamilton bitch had clocked him over the head and in the gut with her ten-ton purse.

He hadn't deserved that. He hadn't deserved the humiliation after all his work.

My camera. My pictures. My money.

Chicky was glad he had decided to undertake this mission. Next time the Hamilton girls and their haughty friends tried to toss their weight around, they would remember tonight. They would remember the gun against their heads, the tape over their mouths, the fear beating in their chests. Most of all, they'd remember *him*—Chicky Marsala, paparazzo extraordinaire.

With a final grunt, he pushed one of the doors open and slipped inside the building. Darkness. A musty smell. He bumped into a cold wall, followed it with his hands for several paces. Then he heard the groan and whine of an elevator overhead and knew he had succeeded in his mission. The rest was gonna be easy. Pinching his fingers around a light switch, he smiled a brilliant smile.

It was his last one.

14

A Killer's Kiss?

The book's title—*Catching Killers: A Journey into the Dark Realm of Homicide Investigations*—was scary. The chapter about questioning potential psychos was even scarier. Park read through it with a little tremor in her tummy, chilled by the possibility that she might soon be facing a strangler. She had removed the gold from around her neck. She had also practiced the few kicks and punches she'd learned when kickboxing had been the cardio of the moment. Sitting on the edge of her bed in a ring of lamplight, she tried to memorize the cop techniques as best she could while envisioning a gun at her hip.

It was a crash course in criminal justice. After slamming her cell phone shut on Jeremy's trembling voice, she had rushed into the library and scoured the volumes; there, on the lowest shelf behind the desk, was Trevor Hamilton's collection of legal literature. Park had grabbed the book hurriedly and flipped through the pages as if her life depended on it. She wasn't an expert, but how hard could it be to get a killer to confess?

According to the book, a good interrogator always kept her cool and never showed irritation—at least not initially. The beginning stages of interrogation were all about forming a bond with a suspect, softening up his edges so that he'd reveal the truth little by little. As a cop, you weren't supposed to exhibit signs of pity or concern for the perp; good old-fashioned camaraderie worked best. And, of course, you were as good as dead the moment you let your guard down. Criminals had wicked minds: they could see through the slightest bit of weakness and use it to their advantage.

Park knew what this meant. She was going to have to hide her fears but hold on to her suspicions—not to the point of being downright abrasive, but just enough so that Jeremy would understand her wariness. There was a trick to this, however, and it had everything to do with body language and vocal tone. The book suggested strong posture and an overall dominant demeanor. No twitching. No slouching or yawning. If the perp remained indignant, then an interrogator had to get a little rough with the questioning; this was the "scare tactic," when every good cop showed her authority and slammed her hands down on the table or jabbed the perp with a sudden accusatory line.

Setting the book aside, Park got up and began pacing the room. She imagined Jeremy sitting down across from her, his leg bobbing nervously, a line of sweat beading his forehead. *So, Jeremy, tell me why you hated Zahara Bell. Jeremy, when did you decide to kill her, and why with that terrible scarf?* She paused before the mirror beside her bureau and practiced her hand gestures. She pointed. She closed her fingers into a fist. She held her palms up and out. Then she added subtle tilts of her head—the left-side serious stare; the chin-pointed-downward look of suspicion. There was a strong chance that the calm and resolved technique wouldn't work on Jeremy, in which case she'd have to pull out the mean method. She practiced it now, whirling around suddenly to face the empty chair at her desk, a cold gleam in her eyes; then she'd stare down at him and scream: *You knew you had to kill her, so you did it last night! Isn't that right, punk? Isn't it? Isn't it?* She curled her upper lip in a sneer for effect. She was totally good at this.

As she stood there practicing in the middle of her

room, Park got the signal from Clarence—two rings on her cell phone. Time was up. She walked to the door of her bedroom and pressed her ear against it. Silence. Quietly, she stepped into the hall and tiptoed past Madison's room, past the kitchen and dining room. She exited the penthouse as silently as a ghost.

This was something she had to do on her own, without Madison or Lex hovering nearby, ready to interject their opinions and suspicions. They were excitable by nature and would likely instruct Park simply to call the police and turn Jeremy Bleu in. Wash your hands of it. Sweep the dirt under the flokati rug. The faster the Hamilton name was cleared of this whole pesky murder thing, the better. Park understood that thread of logic perfectly well, but she also knew that getting to the bottom of a crime with such personal ties had to be done . . . well . . . *personally*. The cops would only complicate matters right now. Not involving them meant not involving the press.

In truth, she didn't want to believe that Jeremy was guilty of anything. She didn't want to believe that her own judgment—sudden though it had been—was flawed and somehow at fault. The first truth: she knew very little about Jeremy. The second truth: it was quite possible that he had a motive for murder. The *strongest* truth: she was on fire with lust for him. This last realization was the most dangerous one of all.

Don't let him charm you, she warned herself. *Don't melt in his presence. And for God's sake, don't imagine him standing naked in a hot shower.*

She stepped into the elevator and rode it down to the lobby. She checked her reflection in the filmy steel doors, pleased with what she saw. Given the darkness of the last twelve hours, she'd felt compelled to clothe herself in colorful attire. She was dressed in blue J Brand jeans, a bright white Calvin Klein shirt, and her favorite pair of Marc Jacobs ballet flats. A vintage Camerino silk scarf was knotted loosely around her neck, its red and blue tones accentuating her smooth complexion. The outfit was funky and slightly boyish, and she liked that it projected strength and coolness.

When the elevator opened on the ground floor, she saw Clarence waiting for her. He was still dressed in his black all-purpose uniform. There were deep circles under his eyes, and his face looked sticky and worn.

Park had given him strict orders to pick Jeremy Bleu up in front of the Pierre. Then Clarence was to personally escort Jeremy into the building and wait for her. Now she was glad to see Clarence. Glad—and a little guilt-ridden. Walking toward him, she smiled and said, "You don't look so good. Are you feeling okay?"

He shrugged. "A chauffeur's work is never done." A yawn rose in his jaw, but he clamped it down and shook his head.

"I'm sorry I had to call you so early," Park said. "But this was kind of an emergency."

"I figured. But is everything okay?"

"I hope so. So long as the press doesn't get ahold of us yet." She put a hand on his shoulder. "You left here really late last night, and here you are, back again. Go home. Madison and Lex and I are perfectly safe upstairs."

He frowned. "Safe? You think so? With your father out of town and the shit hitting the fan, what am I supposed to do? Pretend like I shouldn't be workin' overtime? Someone's gotta look after you girls."

She studied him closely and felt a guilty knot in her stomach. She knew her father worked Clarence to the bone, but she wasn't about to do the same thing. "Go home now," she told him firmly. "There's no reason to stay. If we need you, we'll call."

"I think I should—"

"The conversation is not open for discussion, Clarence. I'm relieving you of your duties right now."

He nodded. "Okay." He cocked his head toward the lobby. "Mr. Pretty Boy is waiting in the conference room, fully out of sight."

"How was he on the drive over?"

"Eh, kinda scared. Looks to me like he's ready to shit a solid gold brick. Why'd you ask him over here so early?"

Park sighed. "I'll tell you later." She started to turn around, but then stopped and slipped her right hand into the pocket of her jeans. She pulled out a Cuban cigar and handed it to Clarence. "For your troubles, kind sir. Take a couple of good puffs for me."

A broad smile creasing his face, Clarence accepted the cigar, sniffed it lovingly, and then dropped it into the lapel of his blazer. "Thanks, honey." Yawning, he shuffled past her and headed for the doors.

Park took a deep breath. She walked toward the lobby, then made a sharp right turn down a narrow adjacent corridor. The conference room was really a small but opulently decorated antechamber that granted residents extra privacy. Away from the well-lit lobby, she and Jeremy would have a chance to speak without the threat of eavesdroppers or the overly curious doorman, Steven Hillby. Her heart pounding in her chest, Park wrapped her hands around the doors' handles and licked her lips.

Don't melt. You have a job to do here. Be smart.

She threw open the doors.

And melted.

Jeremy was standing in the far corner of the windowless room. He was dressed in battered blue jeans and a form-fitting black and gray checkered shirt that she instantly recognized as Michael Kors. His biceps bulged through the delicate fabric. A Yankees baseball cap was pulled forward over his head. He stared at her and smiled broadly. "Hey, you."

Just his smile got her. She felt as if a ticklish, cold

wind had just blown through her body. *You're in danger,* she thought, unable to tear her eyes from him. *I'm gonna throw you down on that floor and ravish you.* But instead of jumping his bones, she tossed her head back and forced herself to assume a rigid posture, as she had read about in the book from her father's library. "Hello, Jeremy," she said coolly. "Thank you for coming. Please have a seat." She walked toward him and stopped beside the love seat nearest the door. She indicated the one directly across the glass coffee table.

He smirked. "What's with the formality?"

Remember the book, remember the techniques. Don't let your guard down. "I just think it's best if we talk, that's all," she told him. "We have serious business to discuss here. Like, totally serious things. I won't stand for anything but the truth."

"I'm prepared to tell you the truth, Park."

"Yes, I understand. Now, tell me, when did you first meet Zahara Bell?"

He sighed. "Listen, all this isn't really important. I know what you're thinking."

"Interesting. The first time you met her, did she ask you a lot of questions? Maybe you told her a little more than you wanted to?"

"Park, I don't get what you're saying." He looked at her with questioning eyes. "I wanna explain to you how my scarf ended up around Zahara Bell's neck."

"Right. Did you strangle her first and then put her

in that cocktail dress? You know, there's really no point in trying to talk yourself out of this, Jeremy. Forensics experts always find evidence at a crime scene." She paused and cleared her throat. She remembered a particular passage from the book and said, "Did you know that eighty-nine percent of homicides in New York City are solved, and the matter of guilt or innocence adjudicated by the courts?"

"What the hell are you talking about?" he snapped. "Park, you sound like some robot. I came here because I want to—"

Her back wasn't to him, so she had to whirl around twice to project the whole scare tactic thing; this gave her an extra second to pull the cold look up into her eyes. "Admit it!" she shouted. "You followed Zahara Bell when she came into the Met and forced her into the coatroom. There was a struggle. You took the scarf off your neck and you—"

Without a word, Jeremy strode toward her in two steps, hooked his hands around her waist, and locked his lips on hers.

Park tried to feign shock and disapproval, giving little squeals of protest, but her attempts proved futile. She was consumed in an instant, swept up in a dizzying haze of desire. She slid her hands along his arms and dug her fingers into his thick shoulders. The kiss exploded on all of her senses, and in the midst of the stars and fireworks, she saw an image of the Avenue diamond sparkling in the morning sky. It was a revelatory experience, for there wasn't another guy in the world whose kiss had the power to induce glorious visions of jewelry.

She broke away from him with a tremor. She turned her head, wanting to avoid his gaze. There were words to speak, movements to make, but the heat between them was like a vortex, sucking every last drop of energy from the air. She waited for Jeremy to say something. Instead, he grazed his lips against her cheek.

Don't melt, you moron.

As the voiced echoed in her head, Park extricated herself from his embrace, pushing him gently away with the palm of her hand. "Stop," she said breathlessly.

Jeremy stared at her. "What's wrong?"

"Everything's wrong." She closed her eyes and forced the dizziness away. She inhaled deeply. When she at last regained her composure, she looked him squarely in the eyes. "I didn't ask you here to make out. I asked you here because you ditched me last night. Because you didn't even have the decency to show up here. Because—"

"Show up here?" he interjected with a chuckle. "You kidding? How? There were reporters everywhere. There still are. You know what that's like, Park. You know I couldn't rush over here and play the knight in shining armor."

"And why's that?" she snapped. "Because you have to protect your pretty face?"

"Because I have to protect my career. I want to avoid a scandal as much as you and Madison and Lex do."

"Too late for that. It's all over the papers already. You should've stayed with us last night and acted like a man. Why did you disappear?"

"I told you why."

"No, you didn't."

"I took off because I got scared."

"Because you're a wimp is more like it! How do you think we all felt standing there with the cops and the cameras on us?"

"Okay, fine. I can say it—I acted like a pussy. There. You happy now?"

"Ugh." She splayed a hand over her chest. "So crude you are. So *crude*. But then, I guess I understand why you *were* wearing the murder weapon, after all." A little cheer went up in her stomach. She'd hit him right in his safe-deposit box—and she could tell he was hurting.

He closed his eyes, looking as though he had just seen something awful. "But I didn't kill Zahara Bell."

"And what about the diamond?" Park said quickly, ignoring him. "Where is it? I know you don't make twenty million a movie yet, and I have a certain feeling that you might be in some sort of financial trouble." She couldn't say *I know Zahara Bell was writing something about your lost millions* because it would mean admitting that she, Madison, and Lex had broken into the town house.

Jeremy stared at her blankly. "I don't know what you're talking about. What diamond?"

"The Avenue diamond. Several cool millions on the black market. Is that why you killed her?"

Laughing, Jeremy lowered himself into the love seat. He stared up at her, fearlessly amused. "I know what you're doing, Park. You're stalling because you don't know what else to say. You know I didn't kill Zahara Bell or steal some diamond. And why the fuck do you care about some million-dollar rock, Miss One Billion Bucks?"

"One point seven billion," she corrected him. "Now tell me how the hell your scarf ended up around her neck."

The smile disappeared from Jeremy's face. He looked down at his hands. "Last night, after I gave my speech at the gala, I went outside to use the bathroom. Sometime between leaving the bathroom and going back into the ballroom, the scarf slipped off—which, I might add, happens to people a lot."

Park's eyebrows raised. "So then you're telling me that someone else—the killer—picked your scarf up off the floor and used it to kill Zahara Bell."

"That's what I'm telling you. I know it sounds like a bullshit excuse, but it's the truth. And when I saw it around Zahara Bell's neck and realized it was mine, I panicked. I full-on freaked. All I could think about was a scandal, a trial, then *jail.*" He pulled off the baseball cap, releasing his mass of scraggly waves. "I didn't know what else to do."

Park didn't know how to react to what he had just said. In all truth, it *was* entirely plausible. She had lost scarves from around her neck more times than she could count. In the moment of silence that rose up between them, what she saw in his face was sincerity, fear, desperation. He wanted her to believe him. He wasn't nervous or fidgety either, the way someone telling a lie would be. Well, *that* sure as hell didn't help her little interrogation session. According to the book, most psychos displayed at least some measure of visible angst.

Damn.

He stood up and took a step toward her. "Ask yourself this: what motive could I have had for killing Zahara Bell?"

"I can't answer that," she replied. "I don't know you well enough to answer that. Maybe you hated her. Maybe you were afraid she was about to write something about you in her magazine, something damaging and scandalous—"

"I'm a fucking movie star, Park. How much of my life do you really think is private and hidden these days? How much of *your* life is private and hidden?

We both know what it's like. If I were a psycho with a violent past, don't you think it would've hit the tabloids already?"

"Maybe you're a psycho with a violent future?"

He laughed at that. He reached out and stroked her cheek. "Look at me and tell me you think I'm lying," he whispered. "Tell me you think I'm a cold-blooded killer."

She couldn't. His touch was honest. His eyes were brimming with warmth. She felt it. This stranger standing in front of her was familiar—not just a hot guy she'd met last night, but someone whose life paralleled her own. The cameras. The public. The fame and the pressure. He understood.

And he was waiting for her reply. Her trust.

She looked up into his eyes. The raw emotion must have showed on her face, because he broke out in a bright smile despite her silence. She smoothed a hand over his chest in a gesture of warmth, of unspoken forgiveness. "Do me a favor," she said. "Wait here. I'll be right back."

He nodded.

Park turned and left the room, closing the door securely behind her. When she got to the elevator bank, she raked her hands through her hair and expelled a heavy breath. What was she doing? She had never felt so sure about a guy in her life, and yet she couldn't dismiss the fact that he had ditched her at the scene of a crime—a murder, for God's sake! Was he telling her the truth, or was he merely acting, putting on a performance? It *was* his job, after all. She had succeeded in getting an answer from him about the scarf, and it wasn't necessarily a bogus answer. The more she thought about it, the more she realized how preposterous Jeremy's guilt seemed.

She paced the floor for several minutes. What she needed was support. She reached into the pocket of her jeans and pulled out her cell phone. She was about to dial Madison when a guttural scream tore through the air.

Park's heart leaped in her chest.

It was Jeremy's voice, thundering out of the antechamber and echoing through the entire lobby.

She turned and ran back toward the closed double doors. As she did so, she caught sight of the doorman, Steven Hillby, dashing in her direction, his eyes wild with worry.

"What's going on?" he shouted.

Park threw open the doors.

Jeremy was standing against the wall, his face contorted by fear. Across the room, a body lay on the floor in front of the open closet door.

"Oh, my God!" Park gasped and instinctively jumped back. She couldn't help but take in the bizarre sight: a fat woman dressed in a maid's uniform, her blond wig hanging off her head to reveal a polished bald scalp. Only when Park looked more closely at the body did she realize that the blue-tinged face was familiar—and it wasn't a woman at all. An image of last night's crazed photographer flashed in her mind. He was lying on his back, his eyes open, a stream of blood trickling from his mouth. A bright pink scarf was wound tightly around his thick neck.

"Jesus H. Christ!" Steven Hillby bellowed. "What the hell is that?"

Her breath coming harshly, Park slowly raised her eyes and stared at Jeremy.

"I—I went to the closet to get my coat from off the hanger," he stammered nervously. "And . . . when I opened the door she—he—she . . . *it* fell out!"

"I'm calling the cops," Steven said. "Nobody move!"

Park had backed herself into the wall. She couldn't believe her eyes. She couldn't believe it was happening all over again. "Jeremy," she whispered faintly. "You've got blood on your hands."

15

A Body, a Suspect . . . and
a Little Bit of Polyester

It took the cops a little more than an hour to positively identify the body of thirty-six-year-old Diego Marsala—aka Chicky. The black handbag he'd been sporting contained a driver's license and several other aliases, along with a bogus press badge, a tube of lipstick, and a package of extra-large fishnet stockings.

It was this last detail that made Lex shudder. A French maid's uniform with fishnets? One didn't have to be tacky to be kinky.

She and Madison had rushed down to the lobby upon hearing the ominous cry of sirens. By the time they jumped out of the elevator, the front entrance of the building was sealed off and the street was ablaze with lights. Park had been huddled in one corner of the room, Jeremy in the other. Madison had taken one look at the body and screamed. Lex, her stomach getting stronger with each new murder, had merely stared in shock.

Now she was standing just outside the antechamber, watching the uniformed men tiptoe around the corpse. It was an uglier sight than Zahara Bell on the coatroom floor. Chicky Marsala, the psycho photographer, had not made an attractive plus-sized woman. Lex moved her eyes over the curve of his big belly as it strained against the black dress. She studied the misshapen forms of his stuffed-bra boobs. The whole getup was wrong. Why, she wondered, hadn't he worn a belt? It would have hugged his waist and added some contour to his otherwise square figure. If not for the Triple Threat scarf wrapped around his neck, Chicky Marsala would have gone to fashion hell.

She looked up at the closet across the room. It was fairly large and held several uniforms worn by the doormen and maintenance workers. According to what Jeremy told the cops, the body had fallen out when he'd closed his hand over the knob to retrieve his jacket. He'd pushed it away, screaming, and gotten some blood on his hands.

"*Excuse* me, Miss Hamilton," a voice boomed sharply in her ears.

Lex turned around and saw Detective Charlie Mullen standing over her. He was dressed in the same ugly blue pants and black loafers as the night before, and he looked as though he hadn't slept in years. "Oh, hi," she said offhandedly. "I'm glad you're here. There's something I want to show you."

His face flushed. He raised his arm and pointed to where Madison and Park were standing, a clear ten feet from Jeremy. "Please go and wait with the rest of your little crew. I have official business to take care of here."

"I know, Detective, but so do I." She stepped into the antechamber and walked toward the body. Standing directly over it, she studied the front of Chicky Marsala's French maid's uniform. There was a small rip in the black fabric just above the navel. "You see that?" she said to Mullen, pointing down at the jagged tear. "That's evidence of a struggle. This uniform is three parts rayon, one part Lycra. A very tough fabric combination. It doesn't rip easily."

"And how do you know what fabric the dress is, Miss Hamilton?" Detective Mullen asked her doubtfully.

"Just by looking at it. If you glance at the label, I'll bet you anything it was also manufactured in Asia."

He sighed. "And why should I care?"

"Because it proves that Mr. Marsala struggled with whoever attacked him, silly," Lex said with certainty. "I know you think my sisters and I are guilty of something, but if *we* were responsible for this, don't you think we'd have injuries? Mr. Marsala, as you can see, was a large man. We couldn't have strangled him."

Mullen crossed his arms over his chest. "According to Park, Mr. Bleu was in this room alone for several minutes before the body appeared. Since you're playing at cop so well, why don't you tell me why *he* isn't guilty?"

"Simple," Lex replied. "Park was out of this room, but she was still well within earshot. If Jeremy Bleu killed Mr. Marsala, Park would have heard the struggle and come back before Jeremy started screaming. So it's obvious that Mr. Marsala gained entrance to the building through the side service doors, was killed, and then was moved here, into the closet. How else would Marsala have gotten in? The doorman would've spotted him walking in through the front doors, don't you think? It was Jeremy's hard luck that he happened to be the one to open the closet door."

"And so the mysterious killer vanishes again," Mullen said with a chuckle. "But not before tying a pretty little scarf that belongs to *you* around the victim's neck. You're gonna have a hard time explaining yourself to a jury."

Lex rolled her eyes. The initial shock and horror of seeing a Triple Threat scarf wrapped around Chicky Marsala's neck had subsided. Those first few seconds, she and Madison had been horrified, then angered. Lex couldn't believe how terrible the scarf looked on a person wearing so much polyester-based black. She said to Mullen, "The fact that another article of clothing from my closet is tied to another crime scene only proves that the killer stole more than one thing from my closet."

"You have all the answers, don't you, Miss Hamilton?" Mullen reached into his blazer pocket and pulled out his notepad. "Now, we've already spoken with the doorman. Who else would have access to this building—other than you and your sisters?"

Lex thought about it. "Our housekeeper, Lupe Ramirez, and our chauffeur, Clarence Becker. But they have nothing to do with this."

"Why not?"

"I spoke to Clarence early this morning," Park said, stepping forward. "When I called him and asked him to go and pick up Jeremy and bring him here, Clarence was at home, in his apartment in Queens. He went there last night."

"And Lupe was with us all night," Madison said,

also coming forward. "But I guess every tenant of this building has access to it, right? I mean, if that was your question . . ."

Before Mullen could reply, one of the crime scene technicians stepped between them and held up a small plastic bag; inside were several dark strands—not hair, but something thicker. The tech explained that the strands had been extracted from beneath Chicky Marsala's fingernails.

Lex reached out and plucked the plastic bag from the technician's hand before Mullen could take it. She held it up to the light. "Polyester," she said. "A very poor fabric. But why would it have been . . ." An instant later, the information spinning through her mind clicked. "Oh! I've got it! This was under Mr. Marsala's fingernails because he fought his attacker. The killer was wearing something made of rayon. I was right—sign of a struggle. So now—"

Detective Mullen snatched the plastic bag from Lex's hand. "That's enough!" he bellowed. "I'm tired of your interference. Wipe that smile off your face, because you haven't proven anything! I'm here on official police business and there's not enough room for the *both* of us in the investigation!"

Lex flashed him an irritated look. "Well, maybe if you lost a couple of pounds, there *would* be."

Mullen's eyes nearly popped from their sockets. "What did you say?"

Park cleared her throat. "At your age, Detective, you should be getting colonics regularly. I'm sure that's what my sister meant. I could recommend an excellent spa."

He stared from Madison to Park to Jeremy. Finally, he expelled a breath and shook his head. Then he locked his eyes stiffly on Lex. "Have you even taken stock of your mammoth closet yet, Miss Hamilton?" he asked her. "How many other items are missing? First your dress, and now this scarf. What else?"

"I don't know," Lex murmured. "I haven't examined my closet. I haven't actually taken a full inventory yet."

"Why the hell not? Aren't you the least bit curious to see what else is missing?" Mullen pressed.

"Well, of course I am!" Lex crossed her arms over her chest. She knew disappointment and worry finally showed on her face. "But a full inventory of my closet and everything in it—day wear, evening wear, designer couture, ready-to-wear, my own label, plus accessories and shoes—would take *days*. I haven't had the courage to start yet, okay? I'm scared."

"Well, I suggest you do it *soon*." Glancing over at the body, Mullen scrawled something in his pad. "Now, why do you think Mr. Marsala came here? Why do you—"

"He came here to kill us!" Madison shouted.

"Your other police people told us that Marsala had a gun in that ugly purse of his."

"I'm aware of that," Mullen said through gritted teeth. "I mean, what reason could he have had to want to kill you? Why would he go through all this trouble? Maybe he thought you girls saw something at the gala that could get him into trouble? Or incriminate him?"

Lex glanced quickly at Madison and Park. *The camera,* she thought suddenly. *He came to get that damn camera back. But we can't turn it in. Not yet.* "I have no idea why Mr. Marsala wanted us dead," she blurted out. "Maybe *he's* the one who killed Zahara Bell and tried to frame us by using my dress. Did you ever think of that?"

"Yes, but that still leaves *his* murder unsolved," Mullen replied quickly. "Could Mr. Marsala have had access to your penthouse at some point in the past?"

Lex shook her head. "Totally not. But since we're talking about murder and danger and all, there's something I think I should show you." She reached into the pocket of her jeans and pulled out her cell phone, showing Mullen the frightening text message.

His eyes widened. "You were the only one to get this?"

"No." Park spoke up quietly. "We all got it."

"I'll need your cell phones," he told them. "That has to be entered in as evidence."

Lex and Madison erupted with shocked sounds—cries that might have followed a gunshot or an explosion, cries that signaled complete and utter fear. "Don't *even* think about taking our cell phones!" Lex gasped. "What would you expect us to do without them?"

"Insane," Park whispered.

Mullen drew a hand across his face in a gesture of frustration. Then he turned, and his eyes lit on Jeremy. "Mr. Bleu," he said with mock cheer. "You're certainly very quiet here. You were present last night at the gala. You were there when Zahara Bell's body was found. *And* you were right here in the same room today. Is there anything you'd like to say?"

Lex gulped as she watched the color drain from Jeremy's face. He had moved closer to Park, and right now, Lex couldn't help but see him for what he was: a good-looking guy with a lot of bad luck. Suddenly, inexplicably, her suspicions about Jeremy Bleu dissipated, and she couldn't figure out why. Could he really have pulled off all this?

"I didn't do anything wrong," he said. "I'm just as innocent as them."

"I never said they were innocent." Mullen's voice was firm.

"Oh! The *nerve* of him!" Madison snapped, glancing at Park and Lex as she pointed at Detective Mullen. "And to think *our* tax dollars pay *his* salary . . ."

Jeremy cleared his throat nervously, shifting his weight from one foot to the other.

"What made you come here this morning?" Mullen asked.

For the first time, Lex found herself posing the same question. In the ensuing panic and mayhem of finding Chicky Marsala's body, she and Madison hadn't thought to question Park about Jeremy. Why *was* he here? She glanced at Madison, whose eyes also registered quiet confusion.

Jeremy licked his lips. He cleared his throat again. He tightened his grip on Park's shoulder and responded quietly, "Park called me and asked me to come over."

Mullen shifted his gaze. "Park? Why did you ask Jeremy to come over?"

"Because I wanted to talk about what happened last night," she said evenly. "And because I . . . I missed him."

Bullshit, Lex thought. *I can see right through you.* She and Madison and Park were excellent liars, but not when it came to lying to each other. They had shared the same limelight for too long.

Mullen didn't seem to be buying it either. His eyes narrowed, and his silence was nothing short of scary. "When was the last time you were in the Hamilton penthouse, Mr. Bleu?"

Jeremy shook his head. "Never. I've never been in the Hamilton penthouse."

Mullen laughed. "This isn't the time to try to keep your girlfriend outta trouble, Mr. Bleu. Even

if she isn't supposed to be bringing boys home after school."

"He's telling the truth," Park said stiffly. "And just
for the record, I've never brought a boy home *after
school*. I'm usually very busy after school."

"Uh-huh." Scratching his chin, Mullen turned
around and pushed past the three crime scene technicians who were still collecting evidence. He studied the body of Chicky Marsala closely. Then he
walked back to Jeremy's side. "Give me your jacket,
Mr. Bleu."

"Excuse me?" Jeremy's voice broke.

"Your jacket," Mullen said forcefully. "Give it
to me."

Stepping away from Park, Jeremy hesitantly handed
over his leather Chip & Pepper jacket.

Mullen grabbed it by the collar, holding it out as
though preparing to examine it under the light. He
looked at Lex. "Miss Hamilton, would you care to do
the honors?"

Lex leaned toward the jacket and gave it a quick
once-over. "It's genuine leather," she said. "And the
lining is one hundred percent nylon."

Mullen, holding the jacket open in front of him,
stared down at the black lining. It was worn. And
there, on the bottom right corner, was a diagonal rip.
"Miss Hamilton, I'll need your expertise again—"

"I can explain that very easily," Jeremy cut in

quickly. "That got torn last week in L.A., and my publicist saw it happen."

Mullen ignored Jeremy's explanation and motioned Lex forward.

Frowning, Lex ran her finger over the tear, then bit down on her lip.

"Well?" Mullen asked.

"The filler of this jacket is polyester," she said. "Black polyester."

"That's crazy!" Jeremy blurted out. Eyes wide, he looked desperately at Park. "I paid eight hundred dollars for that jacket—there's no way the lining is man-made. I didn't do it. Please believe me. This guy"—he pointed at Mullen—"is just trying to set me up."

Lex remained silent. Madison and Park followed suit.

"There's no reason to get so worked up, Mr. Bleu," Mullen told him. "I'm just trying to figure things out." With a smirk, he bunched the jacket in his big hands and slung it over his arm. As he did so, something tumbled from one of the pockets and hit the floor with a *ping*.

It landed directly between Park's slippered feet.

Lex watched as Park bent down and picked up what had fallen. Then she watched as Park's eyes widened and lips parted.

"What?" Madison said. "What is it?"

Park raised her hand; pinched between her thumb and forefinger was something thick and silvery. "This is a key to our penthouse," she whispered. Her wounded gaze found Jeremy. "And it was in your jacket."

"I didn't do it!" Jeremy cried. "And that's not mine. I swear—it wasn't me!"

Detective Mullen reached for the handcuffs on his belt.

16

Run, West, Run!

Sporting his usual baseball cap and Prada sunglasses, Theo stood just inside Central Park, a few feet from the Seventy-second Street entrance. He had a clear view of Fifth Avenue. More specifically, he had a clear view of the building where Madison, Park, and Lex lived. And as his eyes took in the unfolding scene, he kept repeating the mantra that comprised his whole freakin' life.

Stay cool. Don't call attention to yourself.

The front of the apartment building was flashing

with lights—police cars parked one after another, two ambulances, a fire truck, three unmarked vehicles sporting sirens in their windshields. The corners that encompassed the building were sealed off. Traffic had ground to a halt, and now the crowd of curious onlookers was thickening.

Theo couldn't quite believe his eyes. He knew he should have felt fear in his blood, but he was actually experiencing a strange sort of calm, something akin to peace. It felt a lot like the euphoria that accompanied an Ecstasy high. He was floating, and yet his heart was beating quickly. He was seeing the chaos erupt just across the street, and yet the reality of it wasn't registering. If there had been strobe lights above him and a dance floor beneath his feet, everything would have made perfect sense. But that wasn't the case. Nothing about the moment was enjoyable.

He slipped his hands into the pockets of his Zegna coat and unfolded the newspaper tucked beneath his arm. He had read the main stories. He had expected the front-page headlines and the first whisperings of a major scandal. But in truth, he was surprised the scandal hadn't broken *completely.* That was what he had prepared himself for. All night long he had lain awake in bed, imagining his own face plastered across the pages beside Madison's. And yet, here he was, as inconspicuous as any dog-walking passerby.

Could it be that no one had discovered the truth yet?

The park was growing more crowded by the minute. It was a bright sunny morning, the air fragrant with spring, and the Manhattan fitness buffs were on the streets for their customary three-mile jogs. The second they hit Fifth Avenue, however, they all stopped to stare at the crazy scene unfolding in front of the building. It resembled something straight out of a movie.

Theo kept casting sidelong glances to make sure no one was staring at him. The last thing he wanted was to be noticed. And eventually, someone *would* notice him. The shameless curiosity of the general public never ceased to amaze him. No matter where he was or what he was doing, people asked him bluntly about his family's corporate empire and which new business deals were on the horizon. They asked him about the publishing division West International owned, about the two buildings his father, Richard, had recently purchased on the Hudson River, and whether the Wests would be erecting those long-awaited high-rise luxury condos. And sometimes they even asked him personal questions—such as how it felt being in the same school with the Hamilton sisters and knowing that the Hamilton empire was always threatening to bust up West International in a hostile takeover. To that, Theo rarely replied politely.

Right now, though, he was calm. The baseball cap and sunglasses disguise had worked well for him in the past, and he felt confident that no one had seen him making his way across town in the chill blue of dawn. He had walked the long distance from his family's town house on West End Avenue. All the while, he'd reviewed the details of his plan, going over every last word, every last action. It was necessary. The truth would have to come out. Last night, at the gala, he thought he'd done the right thing with regard to Zahara Bell. Now he knew it had been a stupid move. As always, his rage had gotten the best of him and his big mouth had taken over. And although he had snuck beneath the radar unseen, he was certain the truth would be revealed soon.

He thought back to the night before, to the fight that had erupted between him and Annabelle. Defending Madison—even talking about her—had been wrong and stupid, but his emotions had won out. Feelings of a romantic nature, coupled with a big mouth, didn't mix well. Seeing Madison in such a delicate state had grated against his heart. Standing so close to her in that buzzing and crowded corridor, surrounded by cops and a brewing scandal, he had yearned to throw his arms around her, to whisper sweet words in her ear. She'd wanted that too. He had seen the fire in her eyes. But he'd been smart and kept his emotions in check. It was the hardest thing he'd ever done, especially with his nerves wound so tight.

Where were you, Theo? What did you do?

Annabelle's voice echoed in his head. He forced it away. He didn't want to think about those awful ten minutes in question, when his heart had raced and his blood had run cold. That wasn't any of Annabelle's business. And besides, she wouldn't understand. Only Madison would understand.

Why can't you tell me where you were, Theo? What are you hiding?

The answer to that question actually made him chuckle. *A lot,* he thought. *A whole lot.*

He wondered if the heat was showing in his cheeks right now. The plan he had pieced together only a few hours ago wasn't going to work. He realized that now. Coming over here had been a mistake, a notion motivated by fantasy. But how else was he supposed to get to Madison? How else was he supposed to explain this whole terrible mess?

Suddenly, a chubby woman in shorts and a sweat-stained T-shirt came jogging through the crowd. She stopped when she saw the police cars and the sirens, the lights illuminating Fifth Avenue like a stage. "It's all over the news," she remarked to the other onlookers. "There's been a murder in that building, and the Hamilton triplets are supposedly tied to this one too!"

Whispers fluttered on the air.

The calm feeling left Theo's body. He turned around and pushed his way through the crowd, heading back across Central Park to the West Side. When he rounded the first bend of shadowy trees, he broke into a run.

17

A Clue in the Closet?

Through the long hours of the afternoon, reporters gathered on the sidewalk in front of 974 Fifth Avenue. The news of Chicky Marsala's murder had swept across the airwaves like wildfire, compounding an already sensational scandal. The day only got worse when it was released to the public that Jeremy Bleu had been taken into police custody for questioning.

Lex couldn't remember a single instance in her life when so many media people were gathered in one spot. Even from way up in the penthouse, she could see the stretch of Fifth Avenue ablaze with lights. The building's security staff had been beefed up, and any residents who wanted to leave had to do so with an escort. One murder in the lobby was enough, thank you very much. After coming back upstairs with Madison and Park, Lex had finally found the time to peruse all of the day's newspapers. The headlines weren't as lurid as any of them had expected. It was clear from the tone of the articles that no one *really* thought they were guilty of committing any crimes, but ultimately, that didn't matter. The Hamilton name—and the billions of dollars attached to it—was being dragged through a big pile of horseshit.

Lex felt particularly odd when she saw the countless mentions of her Triple Threat line. It was gratifying. It was exhilarating. But it was also horrifying. She didn't want her designs revealed to the world this way. She had worked hard, and now the global fashion enterprise she had envisioned was synonymous with dead people. Where was the glamour in that? Where was the bright side in any of it? She couldn't help but wonder if she and Madison and Park would ever recover from this mess. It wasn't merely a scandal of the fleeting kind. It was a damn saga designed to sabotage them.

Now Lex was standing at her bedroom window, hundreds of thoughts churning in her brain. She stared out at the purple sky. Night was falling slowly over the city, but the colors of twilight were lost in the glare rising up from the street. She knew the reporters and photographers and news crews wouldn't be leaving any time soon. Several hours ago, Madison had disconnected the phones in the living and dining rooms because of the sheer volume of calls flooding the apartment. No, she and her sisters didn't know why Zahara Bell had been murdered. No, they didn't have any connection to the dead photographer named Chicky Marsala. On and on it went, without a moment of quiet. Lex felt like climbing the walls. Her restlessness was too strong to contain. She wanted to go and comfort Park, but both she and Madison knew that Park dealt with difficulty on her own. Park didn't want a shoulder to cry on.

Adding insult to injury was the strange story that was also being covered on the evening news. In the last twenty-four hours, retailers all over Fifth Avenue had reported shockingly low sales and almost no customers. It was a mystery, a dark phenomenon. Nobody understood what was happening—except Park. She knew the legend of the Avenue diamond was taking hold. Park took the whole thing very seriously; it depressed her more than anything else, even more than what had happened this morning. And despite the blood on Jeremy's hands and the key in his pocket, Park had yet to say that she thought him guilty of two murders.

For the record, Lex wasn't sure she believed Jeremy Bleu was guilty either. Even in the midst of the chaos earlier today, she'd caught the glimpses Jeremy had thrown at Park, and they were nothing short of steamy. He was hot for her. So if he hadn't killed Zahara Bell or Chicky Marsala, he had been framed. Lex believed that Jeremy's scarf could have fallen off his shoulders at some point during the gala. But it clearly didn't matter what she thought. Park hadn't had much choice but to reveal that bit of information to Detective Mullen, and now it would be used against Jeremy with crushing weight.

But if Jeremy hadn't murdered Zahara Bell, who had? Lex reviewed the facts in her head, listing them one by one. The killer was *definitely* a man. The killer was someone who had been at the gala last night. The killer had broken into this penthouse and raided her closet at some point in the recent past. And the killer had struck again this morning, because the crimes were obviously connected.

So what does that explain?

Well, nothing. No one would understand a single thing until they all knew *why* Zahara Bell had been killed. Robbery? That didn't make sense. Why go to the trouble of using the Triple Threat cocktail dress just to steal the diamond?

Sighing, Lex turned around and brightened the track lights in the bedroom. She pulled the blinds closed, protecting herself from helicopters with telephoto-lens cameras. The last thing she wanted was her private sanctuary revealed to the world. The bedroom was, of course, her favorite part of the penthouse. She had designed it herself, the light pink walls accentuating the sky blue color of the ceiling. Her canopy bed was fluffed with snow white pillows. The marble bureau held several of her favorite photographs: Lex with John Galliano, Lex with Betsey Johnson, Lex with Alexander McQueen, Lex with Sarah Jessica, Lex with Angelina, Lex with Princes William and Harry. She would have a lot of explaining to do next month at the various fall fashion shows. She couldn't imagine what people would be saying. One of her best pieces and it had to go and end up on a dead woman. Thinking back on it now, Lex was comforted slightly by the fact that Zahara Bell's thin body had, in fact, looked good on the floor of the coatroom. The cocktail dress should have been hiked up a little higher for cleavage purposes, but Zahara's poor boobs would never bounce again.

Lex walked into the very center of the room and faced her closet doors. They were closed. She *always* left them closed. She hadn't wanted to face them last night or this morning. But now it was absolutely necessary. For the first time, she regretted not getting a lock and key for them as Park had suggested several months ago. Maybe that would have stopped whoever had broken in from actually stealing the dress. She tried to imagine just how it had happened. In her mind's eye she pictured a masked figure slipping in through the front while they were all out, tiptoeing into her room, and quietly opening the closet doors. She saw gloved hands reaching past the hangers that held her everyday designer clothes. She saw long fingers curling around the black garment bag emblazoned with the Triple Threat emblem. And then the getaway: the swift padding of feet across the carpeted floor as the thief rushed out. At the very least, she hoped the bastard hadn't come in here wearing poorly fitting leather gloves, an acrylic ski mask, and sneakers.

Eww.

She gritted her teeth, utterly perturbed. She glanced at the small circular desk at the far end of the room, where her personal datebook sat open on its spine. She didn't have to flip through it to know that the past few weeks had been inordinately busy. In addition to classes and the usual social engagements, she had visited the Badescu salon several times for facials and body wraps. She'd flown to Milan last month to select fabrics for several evening gowns she had designed. And then there'd been the impromptu trip to Los Angeles when Hamilton Holdings completed its hostile takeover of that silly global real estate company. The penthouse had been practically empty for weeks. And with Lupe coming and going whenever she pleased, the thief could've even uncorked a bottle of champagne and taken a dunk in her very own Jacuzzi, for God's sake!

She tried to remember the last time she'd actually seen that particular cocktail dress, but her memories were fuzzy. On her daily trips to and from her closet, she didn't stop and count the articles of clothing hanging everywhere. *That* would take at least three hours—*with* a personal assistant.

She mustered all her strength and marched toward the closet. She threw open the double doors. The light, a sensor, flicked on automatically. It was like illuminating an opulently furnished warehouse: the walls were floor-to-ceiling cedar shelving filled top to bottom with shoes and accessories; the floor was carpeted, and tall full-length mirrors with built-in track bulbs comprised all four corners. In the center of the closet was a three-level brass mechanism that came alive at the push of a button. Lex called it the clothing carousel. It held hundreds of occupied hangers and was organized to accommodate the demands of a busy social life. The bottom level was for daily, funky wardrobe, especially designer jeans: True Religion, 7 for all mankind, Sergio Valente, Habitual, Citizens of Humanity, Chloe, Blue Cult. There were rows of shirts as well, from Morphine Generation and C&C, Heatherette and Itsus. The second level comprised designer pieces suitable for business meetings, power brunches, or evening galas; there were sleek and sophisticated suits by Giorgio Armani, Donatella Versace, agnès b., Roberto Cavalli, Marc Jacobs, Stella McCartney; absolutely gorgeous—and brilliantly outrageous—gowns by John Galliano and Jean Paul Gaultier; Vera Wang evening wear; blazers and coats by Vivienne Westwood; her favorite Issey Miyake Pleats Please skirts.

The third level was reserved for her own designs. To date, the Triple Threat label included gowns, cocktail dresses, assorted minis, blazers and coats, and various accessories. Her designs had been created using only the finest fabrics. The silks: chiffon and china, crepe de chine, charmeuse, jacquard, noil, douppioni, tussah, fuji, georgette. The wools: superfine merino, medium merino, Border Leicester, Corriedale, cashmere. The leathers: vegetable tanned, chrome tanned, buckskin, suede. Her choice of exquisite fabrics was matched only by the versatility of her designs. There were bright flashy gowns with leopard-print trains and strategically placed hand-embroidering; elegant but provocative suits with plunging necklines; blazers that revealed just a glimpse of skin beneath the navel; waist-hugging purple and black jeans that flared dramatically at the ankles; several pieces of lingerie that accentuated a young woman's sweet parts; thick leather belts studded with wisps of pink down, and various other accessories. Daring. Unique. Seductive. It was not fashion for the faint of heart.

She tapped the little beige button on the wall to her right, and the intricate system of spiral-shaped poles came to life. Hundreds of hangers shook in their places. A beep sounded. Then the dozens and dozens of clothes moved down the track and back around, much like a carousel. She only had to press the button to stop the spinning, which brought a selected item right to her fingertips. But she didn't stop it. She stood rooted to the spot, eyeing her collection of clothes, paying special attention to the uppermost level.

And then she saw it—a space right in the middle of the perfectly organized rows; it wasn't more than six inches wide, but it revealed a big part of the mystery swirling in her head. That was the spot where the Triple Threat cocktail dress had hung. Someone had taken it right off the damn track.

But who?

Images flashed in her mind. She had countless friends, both at St. Cecilia's Prep and outside of the school. Girls, guys, slightly older college boys. They had all hung out right here in this very room over the past few months, sporadic little get-togethers that usually ended with drinks and cognac-dipped cigars. Had one of them planned this? Had one of them—or two of them?—stolen the dress when she was in the bathroom, or the kitchen, or rummaging through the forbidden bar in the library? It seemed preposterous. But then again, everything that had happened in the last several hours seemed impossible to believe, and yet the ugly events had unfolded before her very eyes.

She turned and stared at the wide expanse of her bedroom. She hadn't noticed anything out of place recently. Nothing else was missing. She faced the closet again and walked to the opposite side of the moving rack. To her left were the cedar shelves that held her shoes. To the right of those were the shelves that held her accessories. The shelf piled high with scarves was messier than the rest, as if it had been rifled through. And it *had*, Lex realized, remembering the pink scarf tied around Chicky Marsala's neck.

Damn you, mystery man. When the hell did you do this?

Exasperated, she dropped to her knees and began crawling around, scraping her hands gently over the carpet in search of clues. She had seen the detectives on the cop shows go about crime-solving this way. According to prime-time TV, criminals always left traces of themselves when doing their business. She didn't have a magnifying glass or one of those feathery fingerprint-finding tools, but there was no time to worry about that now. She wanted answers. She wanted a swift resolution to this messy murder problem.

She moved her fingers back and forth over the carpet, pinching at the fibers. The immediate area was clean. Refusing to give up, she knotted her hair in a bun, crouched down, and then got onto her stomach. She squirmed into the small space under the clothing carousel, holding her breath as she did so. It was like slithering beneath a very pretty rock. Shadowy and dense, the space smelled of perfume and moisturizer. She navigated it inch by inch, stretching her arms out against the carpet and then moving them up and down. Before she knew it, her thin frame had disappeared completely beneath the carousel. She squirmed some more. She exhaled and drew in another breath. She was about to curse and give up when the fingers of her right hand coursed over something small and hard and very cold.

A button? A coin? Lex grabbed the thing and then quickly jiggled her way out from under the carousel. Resting on her knees, she stared into the palm of her open hand. The thing was oval-shaped and gold, but otherwise empty. Suddenly she realized that she was looking at the flat backside of a charm; detached from its chain, it had obviously hung from someone's neck. And that *someone* hadn't realized that it had fallen or been dropped onto the floor of her closet.

She didn't recognize the charm. It wasn't hers, nor did it belong to Madison or Park. Whose was it? She turned it over in her palm and saw the three letters etched deeply into the face of the gold.

T.A.W.

It took a moment for the letters to compute. But when they did, Lex gasped and angrily closed her fingers over the charm. *Holy shit,* she thought. *This explains everything.*

T.A.W.

They were initials, and they stood for *Theodore Aaron West*.

18

The D-as-in-Dead List

Julia Colbert Gantz exited the cab in front of 4 Times Square and thanked the driver with a discernible tremor in her voice. It was past midnight. The wide stretch of Broadway was packed with traffic and tourists, but the customary chaos actually quelled her nerves. There was safety in numbers.

She wondered if the fear was evident in her eyes or in the quick steps she took toward the building's entrance. It was certainly alive in her blood, churning like waves in a storm. She had never in her life been this scared. Throwing a glance over her shoulder, she pushed through the revolving doors and averted her gaze from the two uniformed men sitting behind the large front desk. At this hour of night, the security guards were usually pretending to be on the job, glancing up from their magazines or books without really *looking* at who passed them by. Julia hoped that would be the case now. She didn't want to make small talk, but men generally felt the need to speak to her, no matter the time of day or hour of night.

Tall, toned, and beautiful, Julia's twenty-eight-year-old body still looked seventeen, and she had retained the distinctive sashay of her supermodel days. Strawberry blond hair tumbled past her shoulders in thick tendrils. Her milky complexion was accentuated by the heart-shaped pout of her lips. At *Catwalk* magazine, she was often referred to as the only fashion expert with *real* experience in the business. Julia herself knew it was true, but she had never been one for taking sides or making enemies. She was pleased with her job as the executive assistant to the editor in chief. She and the infamous Zahara Bell shared an amicable working relationship, which was a mystery that defied solving.

Now, of course, there was a much bigger mystery to solve.

As Julia walked past the desk, she heard one of the guards clear his throat.

"Ms. Gantz," he said, a little too loudly.

Julia paused and turned to face him. "Hello, Ralph. Busy tonight?"

"I can't believe what happened to Ms. Bell!" he said breathlessly. "It was like a circus here yesterday and today. So many people. So many cops. It just calmed down a few hours ago."

"Yes, I know. I'm still in shock. I just can't believe it." She pulled a crumpled tissue from the pocket of her Miu Miu trench coat and dabbed at her nose.

"And then today—that guy killed in the Hamiltons' building. Man!"

Julia's breath caught in her throat. She didn't want to hear about it because, God knew, she had spent the last twenty-eight hours agonizing about it. *Are you going to do something and solve this mess?* the little voice in her head kept asking in an outraged tone. *You can't hide forever. You can't let the fear get you.* Now she squared her shoulders and gave Ralph a terse nod. "I have things to do upstairs. If you'll excuse me . . ."

"You need any help? Can I carry anything for you?" He stood up.

"No, not at all. But thank you." Julia turned and headed for the elevator bank. The building housed several corporate offices that operated around the clock, so it wasn't too deserted. She stepped into the first empty elevator and rode it to the seventh floor. The executive offices of *Catwalk* magazine were decorated in hues of white and red, with splashes of earth tones on the reception area carpet and large mahogany frames that held covers of the magazine's previous editions. Now the entire suite was dark and empty. Julia listened to the hum of computers left idle on desks, a clock ticking in the nearby conference room. Swallowing her fear, she walked across the floor and hung a right down the first corridor. She passed her own small cubicle and headed for the office at the very end—the one she had never before entered without permission. She paused when she reached it, breathing heavily.

Stop being so stupid. There's nothing to be afraid of.

The voice resounded in her head, but she didn't quite believe it.

Julia wasn't afraid of her dead boss. She was afraid of the person who had killed her.

The person who had found out Zahara Bell's secret plan to scandalize and ruin lives.

The person who was still out there, waiting to make another vicious move.

A chill snaked up her spine. She knew what she had to do, and she had to do it quickly.

She turned the knob and threw open the door. She flicked on the light and took in the spacious corner office with its piles of paper and magazines, overflowing out-baskets, and swatches of colorful fabric. There were files on the floor, pens and paper clips scattered across the desktop, drawers left open. The cops had scoured the office thoroughly, looking for clues. In truth, the mess was reminiscent of Zahara Bell, who had not been a slave to organization. She had left those mundane tasks to Julia, along with fetching coffee and managing an active social calendar. But in the past few months, Zahara had let Julia in on a number of highly classified projects aimed at taking *Catwalk* magazine to a whole new level of distribution. Magazine publishing was a competitive market, and readers wanted more than just articles about clothes, hair, and makeup. They wanted gossip. Hell, they wanted *dirt*.

Julia remembered clearly the day she had stumbled across Zahara's notes; the pages comprised several paragraphs of shocking claims and allegations about celebrities and CEOs, actors and rock stars, socialites and celebutantes. In certain places, Zahara had scrawled cryptic messages and codes illegible to the untrained eye. Julia had panicked and opened her mouth.

Are you crazy, Zahara? This is dangerous stuff. You can't publish this.

Of course I can. I worked damn hard to dig up that junk.

So then . . . it's all true?

Of course it's true! Airtight sources. It's exactly what the magazine needs—a nice helping of salacious truths.

I'm trusting you to keep quiet about this, Julia. Play your cards right and you could be promoted to executive editor within the year.

And so Julia became Zahara's unwilling—but nonetheless curious—confidante. Julia had watched Zahara take the hush-hush phone calls, watched her scribble more dirt onto those crinkled sheets of paper. On and on it went. The list of famous names kept growing. The scandalous secrets got downright filthy. There were times when Julia had literally feared the publication of that first column, imagining a day filled with gun-wielding celebrities eager to open fire right here in the office.

Now she shuddered. The fact of Zahara's murder hadn't hit her yet. She kept thinking it was a mistake, or a joke, or some idiot's way of trying to create media waves. But the news teams hadn't been wrong. Julia had watched the story unfold from her own television, and she'd known instantly why Zahara had fallen prey to a killer.

The list. The column. Too many dangerous secrets revealed.

She walked over to the desk and kneeled down behind it. Carefully, quietly, she opened the thin uppermost drawer that held pens, Post-its, paper clips, and rubber bands. She slid it out as far as possible. When it caught and froze, she wrapped her fingers around the edges and gave it a hard tug. It popped out, nearly emptying itself over Julia's chest. At the very back of the drawer was a small manila envelope that almost blended into the brownish color of the wood. Julia snatched it off and held it. Then she cautiously maneuvered the drawer back into place.

Rising to her feet, she opened the envelope and pulled out the folded sheets of paper. She flipped the edges up, instantly recognizing the scrawl, the odd little symbols, the unmistakable codes beside the names of celebrities and their soon-to-be-printed secrets. The pages were carbon copies. Julia didn't know where the originals were. She had gone looking for them last night, neatly ransacking Zahara's town house. She'd managed to find a few of the proofs, but nothing substantial. She had spent almost an hour going through the big spacious rooms. Leaving the town house with an armful of papers and photocopies had been a risk. Thankfully, she hadn't been caught.

Now she glanced down at the pages in her hands. She skimmed the first few paragraphs, fully aware that they contained the contents of the inaugural gossip column, which would have been published in next month's issue of *Catwalk*. The targeted names made her stomach shake.

Madison, Park, and Lexington Hamilton.

Actors Jeremy Bleu, Rebecca Lintz, and Sharon Donavitch.

Theo West and the West family.

Dangerous dirt.

Julia extricated the first page from the others and held it in her hand. Then she returned the other pages to the envelope and slipped it into the pocket of her blazer. She wondered who among those names had found out about Zahara's plans to run the column. It was hard to imagine any of them resorting to murder, but that was what had happened. Julia knew it. There was simply no other motive.

She took a deep breath. Her job—for now, at least—was done. She had succeeded in getting Zahara's information before the police, and she was sure the police would show up here and ransack the office again tomorrow. Julia couldn't let them have the list. Not yet. It was the equivalent of several million dollars, and it belonged to *Catwalk* magazine. One day soon, when she was promoted to editor, Julia would carry out the column on her own. And, just like Zahara Bell, she would know power and fame.

She flicked the light off and made her way quietly down the corridor. As she rounded the corner, she heard the *ding* of the elevator and froze. The doors opened, and several men exited. One was tall and older, the other three were in uniform. Cops.

Shit, Julia thought. *Am I busted? What should I tell them?*

The older man smirked and took two steps toward her. "Ms. Gantz, I presume? The security guards at the front desk said I might find you here." He opened his wallet and flashed his shield. "Detective Charlie Mullen, NYPD."

Julia nodded. Her heart was pounding. "Yes. Hello. I came back to the office because I forgot some work here. I usually never work on Saturday nights," she said, hoping her reply sounded authentic.

"Technically, it's Sunday morning," Mullen told her. "Almost one a. m. We left you two messages—one late Friday night and one this morning. We even came looking for you at your apartment."

"Yes, I apologize." Julia fought to keep her tone steady. "I was running around a lot today."

Detective Mullen smirked at her again. "Uh-huh. What have you got there in your hand?"

"Nothing," Julia replied, but her voice sounded strained. *Don't give in. Don't drop the bomb. There's too much info you can still use.*

Detective Mullen nodded perceptively. "Come with me, Ms. Gantz. Let's have us a little chat."

19

Motive for Movie Star?

"Jeremy!"

In the wee hours of the morning, he was released from police custody. It felt like an eternity since he'd inhaled fresh air, since he'd felt the spring breeze on his face. He could barely keep his focus steady. As the door to the precinct opened and he stepped outside, cameras flashed wildly.

"Mr. Bleu! Did you kill Zahara Bell?"

"Did you kill Chicky Marsala?"

"Jeremy!"

He didn't know what to say or how to react. Exhaustion seeped into his blood like anesthesia. If it hadn't been for the woman beside him, her arms linked firmly inside his, he would have likely passed out right here on the pavement.

"Are you and Park Hamilton a couple? Why were you at the Hamilton building?"

"Jeremy!"

"Jeremy!"

He blinked as the white light from six different cameras assaulted him. The reporters were an aggressive little bunch, crowding the sidewalk like rabid fans. He saw everything in quick spurts: microphones shaking, hands reaching out to him, lips moving as they formed new questions. It took loads of willpower not to lash out and slug every last person there. But that, of course, was what they wanted, and Jeremy wasn't about to create more negative publicity for himself. He had enough sense to at least keep his cool.

Now he leaned into the woman whose strong hands were holding him up. As usual, she was navigating the crowd with expert ease.

Felicia Rafferty was slim and elegant, her face pulled tighter than a trampoline. She had been Jeremy's publicist for two years, although his name was only one of a dozen on her client list of Hollywood superstars. Felicia liked to call herself a "mistress of media mayhem." All the important high-powered people knew her. More significant, however, was the fact that she knew a whole lot about those high-powered people's messy private lives, which worked beautifully when a little professional blackmail was needed. She had one of those scalpel-happy West Coast faces that looked forty and sixty in the same glance.

"*Out* of the way, please!" she shouted. As they neared the waiting limousine, her right hand flew up and landed directly on a paparazzo's wide-angle lens.

Jeremy kept his expression stony as Felicia popped the back door of the limo and ushered him inside. As his butt hit plush leather, the noise finally dissipated. For the first time in several hours, he let his whole body go loose. A strangled sigh escaped him. *Please,* he prayed, *let this nightmare be over.*

Felicia jumped inside and slammed the door closed. She was dressed in a tight black suit that showed none of the wear and tear of a red-eye flight. She had flown in from L.A. upon learning of Jeremy's alleged involvement in the murders of Zahara Bell and Chicky Marsala.

The limo sped away from the precinct. Jeremy uncapped the bottle of water sitting in the bar before him. He drank in long gulps, letting the drops spill out of the corners of his mouth and dribble along the sides of his neck. At long last, his nerves were beginning to stabilize. Just sitting close to Felicia made him feel calmer. He was her youngest client and sometimes felt downright unworthy of all the time and effort she invested in his career. His was certainly a household name, but Felicia also dealt with several legendary luminaries: Robert, Al, Tom, Brad, both Jennifers, Halle, and Ms. O. Jeremy knew that without her he'd end up buying a house on Shit-faced Lane.

Now he leaned deeper into the seat and sighed. "Be honest," he said quietly. "Tell me how bad it is. Am I over? Am I finished?"

"Of course not," she snapped. She flipped open her cell phone and tapped off a text message to someone. "The good news is that official murder charges weren't filed against you, and that's because the evidence the cops have is all circumstantial."

It was. Throughout the long hours, Detective Mullen and several other ill-dressed men had pressed Jeremy as he'd sat in that stinky interrogation room, circling him like fat wolves narrowing in for the kill. *Did you pay someone off to get that key to the Hamilton penthouse? Did you break and enter the last time you were in New York?* Jeremy had remained steadfast in his denial. He had answered their questions, but he hadn't volunteered any information. Smart celebrities never did.

"Anyway, that's not our biggest worry right now," Felicia said. She stared at him intently as the limo hit a pothole and hung a left down Fifth Avenue. She reached into her large white leather bag, retrieving from it three folded newspapers. She chucked them onto Jeremy's lap. "Copies of today's papers," she told him. "But they haven't hit the newsstands yet. The *real* scandal is about to bust open."

Jeremy picked up the *New York Post*. His eyes widening, he glanced at the *Daily News* and the *Times* as well. The front-page headlines were all variants of the first: ZAHARA'S BOMBSHELL; SLAIN EDITOR'S NOTES REVEAL MORE THAN JUST MOTIVE. There were grainy snapshots of Madison, Park, and Lex leaving the Met Friday night, and one small picture of him on the bottom right corner of the *Post*; the shot was an old one, but he looked good in it.

"The police tore up Zahara Bell's apartment on West Fifty-sixth, and the town house in the West Village, and then they ransacked her offices at *Catwalk* magazine looking for information that might shed light on why she was murdered," Felicia explained. "A few hours ago, they shook down her assistant, Julia Colbert Gantz, and Julia cracked under the pressure and spilled some interesting beans." Felicia reached into the pocket of her blazer and pulled from it a crinkled sheet of paper. She unfolded it and held it out. "Apparently, Zahara Bell was planning on publishing a new gossip column in her magazine beginning next month. According to what Julia told the cops, it's supposed to be one of those major scandal-breaker columns about socialites and celebrities that upset a lot of people but also sell a lot of magazines."

Jeremy held his breath. He knew what was coming.

"In addition to a lot of dirt on the Hamilton triplets and several other celebrities, Zahara Bell came up with some dirt on you, Jeremy. The dirt you and I both wanted to forget." She shook the sheet of paper at him.

Jeremy felt his stomach flip into his throat. No. Not that. It couldn't be what he was thinking. They had been so *careful* about keeping it concealed.

"Zahara Bell found out about your prior arrest," Felicia said quietly. "And she figured out that it was the reason you were dropped for the Locasio print campaign."

Closing his eyes, Jeremy grunted. The very mention of those words—*the Locasio print campaign*—made him physically ill. The Alfredo Locasio menswear line was the hottest thing on the international fashion scene; Locasio, a young designer from Naples, Italy, had already drawn comparisons to Giorgio Armani and the late, great Gianni Versace. At this year's Academy Awards, Brad Pitt, Johnny Depp, and Usher had all worn Locasio. The line of suits and accessories was classic and cool, and last December, the eccentric Alfredo Locasio had handpicked Jeremy to be the line's international poster boy. A three-year, five-million-dollar contract for standing around in awesome clothes and smiling for the camera. It had been big news.

Jeremy, thrilled and honored, had even flown to Milan for an impromptu dinner with Alfredo Locasio. But two days later, while vacationing on Lake Como, Jeremy made the mistake of getting behind the wheel of a red Ferrari after too many shots of grappa. He'd been partying recklessly, hastily, *and* illegally. Speeding along one of the dark twisting roads, drunk as a senior on graduation night, he skidded off the pavement and flipped the Ferrari. By way of sheer miracle, he emerged from the wreck unscathed. In the pocket of his jeans, police found two ounces of marijuana and several tabs of Ecstasy. Within an hour he'd been arrested, processed, and booked. Felicia, who knew a high-ranking judge in the nearby city of Turin, had managed to douse the scandal before it made international headlines. She'd cut one of her secretive under-the-table deals, but Alfredo Locasio caught wind of the news and, fearing negative publicity, dropped Jeremy from the ad campaign.

Statements had never been made in the press. Jeremy refused to answer questions about why the mammoth contract had been pulled out from under him. It was one of those lukewarm Hollywood mysteries that raised only a few eyebrows, but both he and Felicia knew that if the story ever broke, it would tarnish his rising star. He would never have gotten the lead role in his upcoming movie, *Knight*. His millions of young fans would have begun seeing him as a careless teenage druggie and not a promising young actor with an Oscar-filled future.

And now the past was coming back to bite him savagely in the ass.

It made perfect sense. Of course. He could still hear the cops' guttural shouts echoing in his brain: *When did you figure out what Ms. Bell was up to? When was the last time you spoke to her? Tell us what you know, Jeremy.* Thankfully, he hadn't responded.

Now he took the piece of paper from Felicia's hand. It was a grainy carbon copy that looked as though it had been faxed hastily. Jeremy read through the notes that were half typed and half written in what he assumed was Zahara Bell's hand. She had gotten every last detail correct; the bitch had pegged him as a druggie with a gorgeous face and abs of steel. It wasn't good. He looked at Felicia. "How did you get your hands on this? These are copies of Zahara Bell's actual notes!"

Felicia smirked. "They were leaked to me by one of my police sources," she replied simply.

"So, how did Zahara find out about the Locasio campaign?"

"Probably through one of Locasio's people," Felicia said. "But it doesn't really matter now. The word's out. The same excerpt that was leaked to me was leaked to a few reporters. There's mention of it in the *Post,* along with everything else."

Jeremy stifled a heave of tears. One stupid mistake and he'd be paying for it with the remainder of his career. *Good-bye to the chance of working with you, Mr. Scorsese. Farewell, Mr. Spielberg.* "Did that Bell bitch think she'd get away with this?" he said, suddenly angry. He held the sheet of paper up. "There's major damage here. This stuff could cost people millions of dollars. It could even cost them their lives!"

"It cost Zahara Bell her life, and it'll certainly cost the Hamiltons a lot."

Skimming through the notes again, Jeremy found exactly what Felicia was referring to. He read over the details Zahara Bell had jotted in her messy scrawl about Madison Hamilton and Theo West, and the forbidden affair they'd had. "Oh, my God," he whispered. "That can't be true. Everybody knows the Wests and the Hamiltons are enemies. Talk about the shit hitting the fan!"

"Yes," Felicia said. "And it isn't even the affair itself that creates the problem. It's the fear that in the midst of their little tryst, Madison and Theo may have revealed corporate secrets to each other. It'll create quite the shake-up."

"Can't they just deny it?"

Felicia frowned. "They can, but people like Zahara Bell don't publish this kind of gossip without airtight sources. The affair between Madison and Theo is very likely true, just like the story about you is true. It wouldn't make any sense for you to deny it, because somewhere back in Italy, there's at least one piece of paper on file that proves you were technically arrested. But right now, believe it or not, this little bombshell is gonna help you."

"Why?"

"Because it proves that several people had reason to want Zahara Bell dead, including the Hamilton triplets and Theo West."

"And what about that guy—the paparazzo, Chicky Marsala? The police think I killed him too."

Felicia shook her head. "He went to the Hamilton residence looking for *them*, not *you*. That says a lot right there. Maybe those girls aren't as innocent as they seem."

An image of Park filled the empty space before him. Even now, exhausted and at the bottom of the barrel, he totally wanted to be alone with her. He felt Felicia's hand on his, and he turned his head to look at her.

"You can be honest with me," she said gently. "Did you have anything to do with these crimes? Are you hiding any other secrets? Now's the time to talk, Jeremy. You can't afford any more surprises."

He stared out into the waking dawn. He didn't answer.

20

A Confession . . .
and a New Company!

Madison screamed. For the third time in less than ten minutes, she let out a high-pitched wail that practically rattled the windows and shook every chandelier in the penthouse. She was sitting on her bed surrounded by five open newspapers. The headlines were making her sicker than spoiled caviar and cheap champagne.

According to the *Post*, Zahara Bell's inaugural gossip column, slated to run in next month's issue of *Catwalk* magazine, was going to explode upon the

New York and Hollywood social scenes with the force of an atom bomb. Zahara's assistant had confessed all she knew to the police late last night and forked over what she had of Zahara's notes. And in those notes was the scathing truth about the relationship Madison and Theo had tried to keep hidden from the rest of the world, along with damaging comments about Jeremy Bleu and several other well-known actors, musicians, and models. The notes also included a few references to St. Cecilia's Prep, and how the school's "diploma-buying" policy spoiled its celebutante students.

There were four pages dedicated to the story. Madison stared down at the pictures of herself, Park, and Lex and felt her anxiety level soaring. Damn reporters hadn't really bothered with the fact that two major crimes had been committed; instead, they had exaggerated the whole chain of events, casting suspicion on the people Zahara had been planning to trash in her column.

And we're three of them.

Madison shut her eyes, holding back tears. It was okay to scream in frustration, but a spell of crying would do no good. Besides, she had already showered and applied her makeup. She had worked several extra minutes to conceal the dark circles under her eyes—the direct result of a sleepless night—and pulled her hair into a ponytail. She was wearing her favorite pair of Habitual jeans with her favorite cashmere TSE tank top. She should have felt marginally comfortable. But as she hurled all the newspapers onto the floor, she felt only fury and fear.

It wasn't that the whole world now knew she and Theo had slept together. It wasn't even that Hamilton Holdings would suffer from all the negative publicity as a direct result of her carelessness. It was the simple fact that she had allowed her emotions to shadow her intellect, and that just wasn't her style. She'd known from the start—from the very moment their eyes locked and lit—that whatever passion she and Theo West shared would have harmful repercussions. But the threat of exposure had been no match for the fire in her heart. The danger of a personal meltdown hadn't eclipsed the attraction between them. Under the spell of his kiss, she had felt transformed, uplifted, nearly complete. She'd lost her ability to reason analytically.

And even now, with the whole mess splashed across the papers and everyone revving up to talk, Madison still couldn't deny her true feelings. She loved Theo West. She yearned for his attention, his affection, his touch. But it had nothing to do with sex. She was beyond the physical components of desire. He was the only guy who would ever understand her odd little insecurities, her fears and hopes and goals. He was the only guy who knew that she sometimes dreamed about what life would be like without the cameras and the media coverage and the pressure to constantly be the best. One failure and the whole damn country heard about it. One simple mistake and it ended up on Page Six of the *Post*. Yes, she had been born into a world of unimaginable beauty and privilege, but fame had its price. Wealth had its price too. Most people would never understand the reasoning behind the occasional disenchantment, yet Theo did. And those were the moments Madison couldn't relinquish—the ones of true intimacy, when they'd spoken honestly and openly, exposing their innermost feelings to each other. She was certain she would never find that level of comfort with a guy again.

Sitting on the edge of her bed, she wondered what he was thinking right now. Was he freaking out? Was he petrified of how his parents were going to react? Yes, of course. And what about Annabelle? She'd very likely freak when she heard the news.

And what about me? she thought nervously. *What's Dad going to say? How can I explain this?*

It was a mess. A total mess. Madison imagined the disappointment that would darken Trevor Hamilton's face when she admitted to him that the story in the papers was true. *Madi, how could you? I thought you had more sense that that. I thought I raised you to put duty before all else.* Just thinking about it broke her heart.

Gauging the depths of the whole scandal, however, twisted her brain.

The proverbial tangled web, she thought. When you play, you pay. And Zahara Bell had played a little too hard this time around. According to the newspaper reports, the intent of that first gossip column had been to ruin lives, companies, entire industries. The affair between Madison and Theo, Jeremy Bleu's arrest, actor Sharon Donavitch's illicit affair with a pre-operative transsexual mechanic—they were just the tip of the iceberg. It was no wonder Zahara Bell had been silenced.

A knock sounded on her bedroom door. Without waiting for a reply, Park and Lex walked in. From the looks on their faces, Madison knew they had already scoured the newspapers.

"Honey, I'm sorry," Park said, coming around the bed and throwing her arms out.

"Thanks," Madison replied. She welcomed the embrace. She held on to it longer than usual, then felt Lex's hands on her shoulders. The support lifted Madison's spirits instantly.

"Well," Park said quietly, "I guess now we know why Julia Colbert Gantz was in Zahara Bell's town house at the same time we were."

"She was looking for this stupid column!" Madison sniffed. "Maybe we should've wrestled her to the ground and gotten ahold of all her notes."

They sat in a semicircle on the massive king-sized bed as the usual cacophony of Manhattan traffic drifted into the silence. Madison glanced at her sisters, recognizing the hard, fixed expressions on their faces. She was wearing the same one. It was the look of strategy, of tactical plotting. In just a few hours, there would be statements to make, interviews to grant, press releases to approve. There was a whole scandal they had to turn around and use to their collective benefit. Madison usually initiated duties like these. She knew Park and Lex were waiting for her to speak.

But before Madison could open her mouth, Lex stepped off the bed, crossed her arms over her chest, and sighed loudly.

"What is it?" Madison said. "What's wrong?"

Lex looked first at Park, then forced her gaze to Madison. "I stayed up all night trying to convince myself that what I found wasn't true, but it's important, Madison, and it'll eventually all come out into the open anyway."

"What are you talking about?" Madison asked. She watched as Lex reached into the pocket of her pink silk robe, retrieved something from it, and then held her hand out. Madison felt her heart skip a beat. The small gold charm was all too familiar. She listened as Lex explained where it had been found, all the while feeling sicker and sicker.

"I don't know exactly what it means," Lex said gently, "but it does place Theo West in my closet, and that's where the dress was stolen from."

"My God," Park whispered with a shake of her head. "So that *really* explains it. How the dress was stolen, why Zahara was killed. Theo was scared the column would be published and that everyone would know about the relationship, but instead of just killing Zahara, he plotted the crime so that it would be pinned on *us.*"

"The lengths people will go to when they're desperate," Lex said quietly.

Madison got off the bed and slowly paced the room. She had never thought it would come to this. Why had she been so *stupid*?

"Unbelievable," Park whispered. "And to think that Jeremy was taken into police custody. That *he's* the main suspect. I'll bet Theo planted that key on Jeremy Friday night at the gala."

Just listening to her sisters was making Madison dizzy. They were building an erroneous composite of a crime. She knew that firsthand—and without a doubt. But admitting it would throw another dash of fuel onto the fire. Finally, she faced Lex and Park, squared her shoulders, and said, "Theo didn't kill Zahara Bell. There's a perfectly good explanation for why that charm with his initials on it was in your closet."

"There is?" Park asked quickly.

"Yes. And it's totally embarrassing." And then Madison told them. She told them about the unexpected rendezvous she and Theo had shared three weeks ago. How they'd spoken about things at school, and how she'd invited him back to the penthouse—an *absolutely, positively* forbidden move. There'd been no one home. Madison's bedroom, in the final stages of a renovation, was a mess, so she and Theo snuck into Lex's bedroom. It was supposed to be a chat, a gentle heart-to-heart. But Theo hadn't been able to contain himself and Madison had gotten those butterflies in her chest and before they knew it . . .

Tears smarting her eyes, Madison stopped explaining. She felt too ashamed to continue. She wished the ground would just open up and swallow her whole.

"Wait a minute," Lex said, holding up a hand. "Are you trying to tell me that you and Theo got busy in my *closet*?"

"Not your closet, your room. My room was too messy," Madison blurted out. "The walls were covered in plastic and plaster. There was paint everywhere. I never meant for it to happen and I—I . . . I'm sorry. To both of you. To Daddy. To the company. I'm sorry. I've ruined everything with this stupid nonrelationship."

Lex, her cheeks flushing with rage, looked as though she were about to explode. She huffed. She puffed. She clenched her fists together. And then she said exactly what was on her mind: "*Eeewwwww!* That's *rank*. How could you do a thing like that?"

"I don't know. Passion, I guess." Madison wiped a tear from both of her eyes. "But that's why Theo's charm was in your room. Afterward, as he was getting dressed, he mentioned to me that it wasn't around his neck, that he'd lost it. I guess it fell off while we were . . . you know . . . and maybe when I walked out of your bedroom I kicked it into the closet without even realizing it. But he's not a murderer. He didn't have anything to do with this."

"Actually, I think he did."

Madison and Lex whirled around.

It was Park who had spoken those five powerful words, Park who was sitting cross-legged on the bed with Madison's purse spilled out before her and the forgotten digital camera in her hands. Now she lifted the camera like a prize. "Did you happen to see the rest of the pictures in here?" she asked, posing the question at Madison. "That chicken man certainly knew what he was doing, and it explains why he came here looking for us. It explains *everything.*"

Madison grabbed Lex's hand, and together they went around to the opposite side of the bed. "I haven't seen anything in that camera," Madison said.

"I don't want to think about it! I would've thrown it away if you hadn't found it."

"Then brace yourself." Park held the camera out so that its screen could be viewed more clearly. She clicked the Forward arrow, and the first picture came up. It was of the museum's Grand Ballroom, all glittery and crowded in the initial stages of the gala. Several more followed—of various socialites standing together, of Madison at the podium giving her opening remarks, of the stunning floral centerpieces that had adorned the tables. But it was the fifth picture that Park froze and zoomed in on.

It showed Theo West standing next to a very live Zahara Bell, in what looked like the corridor where the coatroom was located. They weren't smiling. In fact, the next picture—taken only seconds after the previous one—was of Theo's red and seemingly enraged face; his lips were pulled back from his teeth, and he was clearly in the process of berating Zahara Bell. The pictures followed in chronological order, five in all of Theo West, Zahara Bell, and their tense standoff. In the final picture, Theo's right hand was closed around Zahara Bell's wrist; she was turned to one side, as if trying to break away. The photographer had obviously captured them in moments of struggle and outright discord. It was plainly evident from the clarity of the pictures that Theo and Zahara had been fighting about something.

Madison stared down at the little screen, unable to believe her eyes.

"And there's the outfit Zahara Bell had been wearing when she first arrived at the Met," Park said. "Not exactly a Lex Hamilton original."

"It's actually Dior," Lex said, leaning over to get a better look at the gorgeous dress in the picture.

"Maybe Theo had the Triple Threat cocktail dress hidden in the coatroom," Park offered calmly. "He forced her in, strangled her, and then dressed her. And all so that he could draw us into this and try to ruin us. But why would he steal the Avenue diamond? He doesn't need the money."

"Isn't it obvious?" Lex snapped. "To throw off the police. To confuse everybody. He probably never imagined that Zahara's assistant was going to spill the beans about the gossip column, or that she even knew about it. Taking the diamond makes it look like a total robbery."

Madison shook her head. "This doesn't prove anything," she stated firmly. "The pictures, the charm—it's all circumstantial evidence. Theo's not a killer. I know he didn't want our relationship being broadcast, but he would not have killed for it."

"But he *did* kill for it!" Lex shouted. "We've solved the damn crime!"

"Stop it!" Madison yelled back. "That's not true. We didn't solve anything."

"Let me ask you something," Park said, turning to

face Madison. "Think back on your little rendezvous with Theo in Lex's bedroom. At any time, did you leave Theo alone?"

Madison opened her mouth to speak, intending to blurt out an instant and forceful *no*. But as the question seeped into her brain, she froze. Her breath caught in her throat. She stared guiltily at Lex.

"Well?" Park prodded. "What's the answer?"

"Yes." Madison closed her eyes. "Afterward, I went into the kitchen to get us both something to drink. It didn't even take me three minutes."

"Twenty seconds is all you need to grab the dress off the carousel and stuff it in your backpack," Lex told her. "Did he have his backpack with him?"

"Yes."

"And did it look bunchy and full?"

"I don't know." Madison sat down again on the edge of the bed. "I didn't actually see Theo leave. I was standing in the kitchen when he called out to me from the foyer. He said he had to get going. By the time I got there, he was on the other side of the door, and I only saw him from the neck up."

"Ha!" Lex snapped. *"Hellloo?* I spy a killer. Somebody get me an electric chair."

Madison dropped her head into her hands.

"I think we should all get dressed and go to the police station," Park said evenly. "We have to turn this evidence in to Detective Mullen."

"Wait!" Madison cried suddenly. She reached out

and gripped Park's arm. "I know Theo didn't do this. I know it's all just a misunderstanding. What about the other people Zahara Bell was planning to trash in that column? You can't just forget that Jeremy was at the gala too. That his scarf was around Zahara's neck. That he was in the antechamber when Chicky Marsala was killed. He's just as allegedly guilty as Theo."

"On the face of it, he is," Park said gently, slowly. "Everybody is, including us. But when did Jeremy ever get into Lex's room? When would he have had the chance to steal the dress from her closet?"

"He had a key, he could've come in here anytime!" Madison shot back.

With a sigh, Park looked down at the camera in her hands. She pressed the little button, and another picture flashed into clear focus. It was of Jeremy Bleu, his black scarf—the first murder weapon—hanging loosely around his neck. Park clicked again. The next pic popped up. Behind her, Lex gasped in horror. It was a clear shot of Zahara Bell in death, lying on the coatroom floor, the black scarf wound around her neck. Next shot: a close-up of the scarf and the blue-tinged pallor of Zahara Bell's skin.

"Oh, my God," Lex whispered. "*This* is why the paparazzo went crazy when we got hold of the camera. He walked into that coatroom and took these disgusting pictures of Zahara Bell. He knew she was dead long before he snapped the pic of you and Jeremy."

Park nodded. "Chicky Marsala saw something. He saw *someone.* But he decided to take these pics so he could sell them for a lot of money instead of opening his mouth and saying something. What does he gain from reporting what he saw to the cops? Nothing. No money." She held the camera up, staring intently at Madison. "It's obvious what these pics are."

"A chronology of the murder," Madison stated flatly, her tone grim. "And so you think it all points a finger at Theo. That's what you're saying." She gulped over the lump in her throat. "You're saying I'm in love with a killer, right? Well—I won't believe that!"

Park stood up. "Look, Madison, facts are facts, and right now the facts paint a very suspicious picture of Theo—and Jeremy. Maybe one of them did snap. Maybe one of them knew Zahara was planning to publish that column and thought killing her was the best way to stop it from being published. I don't know the answer. But I *do* know that *we're* going to suffer from this, and so is the company. Whoever killed Zahara Bell wants to take us down with him, and it's poor Lex who's gonna get the brunt of it."

The anger left Lex's face. A moment later it was replaced with genuine hurt. "I worked *so* hard to design those clothes," she said. "And now it's going to be the laughingstock of the whole industry. Of all the dresses in the world, why did Theo—or the killer—have to pick one of *mine*?"

"It was a smart plan," Park admitted quietly. "We are, after all, archenemies of the West family. What better way to ruin us than to tie us to two murders? Theo totally knew what he was doing."

Madison listened. She knew what Park had just implied—that the rendezvous she and Theo had shared three weeks ago had been nothing more than a calculated piece of his plot. By gaining access to her heart, he had inevitably gained entrance to the penthouse. Thinking about it in those terms was painful. Considering it as the truth made her want to crawl under the bed and die. But what if it was true? Maybe she didn't know Theo totally and completely.

Suddenly, the silence was shattered by the ringing of cell phones—all three of their cell phones, in unison, announcing the simultaneous arrival of text messages. They stared at each other. They reached for their phones. The message typed out on all three screens couldn't have been more direct:

GO TO THE POLICE AND YOU DIE IN FLEECE

"Fleece!" Lex shrieked, slamming the phone closed. "This killer is a sick puppy! Who dresses in fleece, for God's sake? *Fleece?* Ugh."

"Relax," Park said. "None of us is going to die in fleece. I think the killer is just trying to be catchy or something."

Madison locked eyes with Park. She waved her cell phone in the air, indicating the text message. "Jeremy or Theo? One of them is playing games."

Park nodded. "I don't know. But we have to find out."

Madison stood up. She went over to the window and drew back the drapes. She stared down at the empty stretch of Fifth Avenue, at the mob of reporters clogging the front of the building. Her family's name. Her father's respect. Both would crash and burn if she didn't take hold of the reins and tackle the situation. There was too much at stake. There was too much to fear. She couldn't let emotion guide her.

You know what you have to do. You were raised to handle scandals like this. When the publicity is bad, turn it around and use it to your advantage.

Inwardly, Madison nodded. Yes, she knew what she had to do. What they *all* had to do. It was basic math, a simple equation in the complicated scheme of their lives. She turned around and stared at her sisters. "You're right—we have to move on this. We'll make a statement to the media declaring our innocence." Her eyes suddenly hardened into a no-nonsense gleam. "But let's do it in style. Lex, go to your closet and select Triple Threat outfits for me and Park to wear. And put one on yourself. We're going to hit the Avenue and show the world that we aren't guilty of anything—and that we have nothing to be ashamed about."

Park folded her arms across her chest. "So we're not going to bring the camera to the cops?"

"Not yet," Madison answered. "Don't you see? This has turned into a game. Our little killer is desperate. He doesn't know what to do next. He got rid of Zahara Bell, and that didn't work. He got rid of Chicky Marsala, but *we* have what Chicky wanted. If we turn the camera in, we can't shake him down—and I *want* to shake him down. But I still think there's something else— something we have or know that the killer wants."

"Like what? He's bound to make another big mistake soon," Park said. "The killer has the Avenue diamond, and the diamond's curse is starting to take hold. We *have* to get that diamond back."

"Yes, we do." Madison bit down on her lip. "That would brighten our reputations again. That would put us back on the right track. We need to control the publicity now so that it'll work in our favor. And if we turn that camera in to the cops, it'll look worse for us."

Park was half smiling, half shrugging. "So you want to hit the Avenue in Triple Threat clothing. The same clothing that Zahara Bell was found dead in. The same clothing that's being splashed all over the newspapers. Are you thinking what I *think* you're thinking?"

Madison nodded firmly. "Yes. We're going to announce the start of a new company today, a new division of Hamilton Holdings, Inc. We're going to launch the Lex Hamilton/Triple Threat fashion line for the world to see. And we're going to do it *now*—while we can take advantage of the publicity. Someone's trying to bring us down, and this is the best way to make sure we stay on top."

"My own label!" Lex shouted, smiling from ear to ear. "You've finally come to your senses!"

"I guess I have," Madison whispered. She turned and stared out the window again. A huge plan was unfolding in her head. She saw a well-lit runway, beautiful clothes, hundreds of glowing headlines eclipsing the negative ones of today. *Triple Threat Fashion—A Global Enterprise.* What better way to turn bad press into profit? Trevor Hamilton had taught them well; he wouldn't expect anything less than a smart, bold plan right now—a plan that would ultimately bear his very name.

Madison felt a sudden surge of energy shoot through her blood. If she, Park, and Lex played the game correctly—if they navigated the media storm exactly as they had been raised to—the Hamilton name would be more powerful than ever in just a few days.

Together, they were a force not even a killer could stop.

21

On the Avenue

The media frenzy erupted the moment Madison, Park, and Lex stepped out of the lobby and onto Fifth Avenue. Scores of reporters began shouting their names. Photographers zoomed in from behind blue police barricades. Across the way, television cameras started rolling as newspeople dropped their coffee cups and grabbed their microphones.

"Madison!"

"Park!"

"Lexington!"

They stood a few feet from the building's main entrance, calmly soaking up every last ounce of the chaos. A full minute passed. The shouts got louder. It was all part of the plan, and Madison, at the head of the line, cocked her head slightly to one side and winked at the closest photographer. She wasn't surprised when the flashes moved downward, enveloping their Triple Threat outfits. Neither was Park. And Lex, of course, hadn't expected anything less than the whirlwind of adoration. That was the main point, and it was working beautifully.

Madison, glamorous and sleek in Triple Threat, wore an off-the-shoulder chocolate suede dress that hugged her waist and accentuated her cleavage. Stunning Manolo Blahniks and a matching Jimmy Choo hobo completed the look. The dress fell to her ankles in a straight line. Anything but plain, it was an eye-grabber that drew prolonged stares and several direct camera kisses. She had chosen the dress herself, seduced by its lustrous form and subtle sexiness.

Park inched forward slowly. Hands on her hips, eyes hidden behind Chanel sunglasses, she was the epitome of cool. She was wearing a Triple Threat pantsuit that hugged her body like a glove. Black silk, the blazer had only one large button, and it had been cut to accommodate peeks of flesh: the front lower half rose up to form a sharp triangle that exposed her navel. A top hat gave the outfit an androgynous edge.

Lex had decided on one of her flashier designs. She was wearing a white satin dress with lace trim that stopped well above her knees; thin straps tapered to a plunging neckline. A white mink scarf wrapped her neck several times and trailed down her middle. White boots—leather, of course—rose up past her knees. She called it her "last-day virgin" look. She had blown her hair out, and now it fell over her shoulders in bright blond masses. The constant flashes made her blink repeatedly. Nestled in the crook of her left arm was Champagne; a smooth white doggie-coat sheathed his furry little body, and he yipped as the commotion intensified.

As if on cue, one voice suddenly rose above the rest; it was that of a female reporter, and she posed her question without a hint of irony: "Who are you wearing, Madison?"

As microphones crowded around her, Madison smiled. "We're all wearing Triple Threat originals," she said brightly. "My sister, Lexington, happens to be an accomplished designer—as you can all see."

"Are you planning on launching this new label?" a second reporter shouted. "And if so, is there any specific reason you're launching it at *this* particular time?"

"The line will be unveiled in a private fashion

show later this week," Park replied coolly. "It has long been our intention to launch the Triple Threat brand, and our decision to do so at this time—instead of at Fashion Week—is not motivated by anything other than excitement, and a belief that our product will be universally loved."

"Lex, how did you come up with the label's . . . *interesting* name?" yet another reporter called out.

Lex took the question for all it was worth. Madison's publicity mantra—*the less affected by the scandal we appear, the more power we commandeer*—resounded in her head. She didn't flinch as a dozen microphones flew in her direction. "The Triple Threat label is designed with young women in mind, and so all of my clothes naturally evoke sexiness and freedom. My clothes are about the body, its beauty and its primal demands. I was inspired by my sisters and our three very different identities. Sophistication. Sexiness. Intelligence. When you wear a Triple Threat design, you feel empowered and ready to take on whatever the world throws at you."

The cameras exploded in a stream of flashes.

"Madison, how do you respond to allegations that you and your sisters played a role in two murders?"

Lex gave a start as Champagne suddenly lurched forward in her arms with a ferocious snarl. He clamped his little jaws down on a bobbing microphone and gave it a hearty yank.

There was a startled "Oh!" of protest from the middle-aged man holding the microphone. He jerked his head back quickly, causing his sandy-colored toupee to shift and slip down the left side of his face. A bright red bald spot came into view.

Lex bit down on her tongue to stifle her laughter. She wanted to tell the man that he *desperately* needed a few ounces of Badescu buttermilk moisturizer, but instead of opening her mouth, she pulled Champagne into a tighter hold and cleared her throat.

Madison picked up the cue. "My sisters and I are not in any way connected to the murders of Zahara Bell and Diego Marsala," she stated firmly. "In fact, our own investigation is ongoing, and we believe that a heartless killer is using our name and our public to mask his own dark motives."

"Madison, is it true that you and Theo West—heir to the West family empire—were involved in an ongoing romantic relationship?"

She didn't hesitate before replying. "At this time, for matters that relate directly to my personal safety, I will say only that Theo West and I have known each other our entire lives, and that I am always wishing him well."

The crooked-toupee reporter stepped forward again and thrust his microphone into Madison's face. "Wouldn't an affair between the two of you compromise

Hamilton Holdings' corporate assets?" he asked, a bit too aggressively.

Champagne went on the attack again, jutting out from Lex's arms and unleashing a flurry of barks that sent several reporters stepping back.

Madison gritted her teeth in annoyance. Being upstaged by a dog was totally embarrassing and completely unacceptable. What was this—a canine press conference? She turned her head toward Champagne, cut him her coldest stare, and emitted a low growl from the very back of her throat. It sounded guttural and raw, like a wolf's predatory warning.

Quivering, Champagne sank into the crook of Lex's arms.

The momentary silence was tense, but Madison quickly gained control of it. She squared her shoulders and swept her eyes over the cameras. "*None* of our corporate assets has been compromised," she said firmly. "Proof of Hamilton Holdings' corporate strength is evidenced by the imminent launch of the Triple Threat label, which will likely become a global brand. Hamilton Holdings, Incorporated, is—and will remain—the most powerful media empire in the world."

"According to what Zahara Bell was going to publish in her gossip column, Hamilton Holdings is planning a hostile takeover of West International. Is that true?"

Madison felt her lips go dry. *Of course it's true,* she thought. *But no one's supposed to know about it.* She threw her head back and said, "Zahara Bell's informants had their facts jumbled. You can't believe everything you read in gossip columns."

"What has your own investigation into the murders revealed?" a reporter screamed from the back of the thickening crowd.

Park had expected the question from the moment she'd stepped outside. She'd even welcomed it. This was their chance to lure the mysterious killer in, once and for all. Choosing her words carefully, she said, "We have come across—and are in possession of—valuable evidence that we believe will ultimately reveal the identity of the murderer."

A flurry of whispers hit the air.

"Do you think the Avenue diamond will be recovered?" someone shouted.

Park nodded. "Absolutely. As you all know, the Avenue diamond is inextricably bound to the Hamilton family—especially to our mother, Venturina Baci. I believe the diamond's power will triumph, and that it'll find its way home very soon."

"Park, what's the nature of your relationship with actor Jeremy Bleu? He's been questioned by police about the murders. Do you know why?"

"I consider Jeremy a friend," Park replied. "I do not know why he has been questioned by police, or whether he has any connection to the crimes."

Lex stepped forward. She surveyed the crowd, noting that it had spilled into the street. Through the mass of bodies surrounding her, she caught a glimpse of the traffic; it was backed up for several blocks. She turned her attention back to the cameras and said, "At this time, we ask your cooperation in respecting our privacy and our safety. My sisters and I will be available to answer your questions as this terrible scandal comes to a close—and we haven't any doubts that it will end soon. We look forward to working with all of you as we launch the Triple Threat label."

It was Madison who threw a glance over her shoulder and back into the lobby of the building. She was relieved when Clarence stepped through the doors and gave her a nod. He came up behind her, his arms hovering over Park and Lex as well, and together they navigated their way past the reporters and cameras.

"Stay close," Park said to Clarence as the flashes went off again.

He nodded. "I'm right here. I've got ya covered. I'm following your every step."

Madison, Park, and Lex cleared the crowd and began walking down Fifth Avenue side by side. They were aware of the several reporters still trailing them, aware that dozens of cars had stopped, passengers staring through windows to get a glimpse of the fashionable spectacle. They were aware of the news chopper that suddenly appeared in the sky, its blades beating the air. They tried not to make eye contact with the pedestrians who lined either side of the street—and by the hundreds, it seemed—because the whole point of this very public appearance was to *attract* attention, not *give* attention.

"It's definitely working," Park murmured, standing, as usual, in between her sisters.

"It totally is," Lex agreed. "But I *hate* helicopters."

Madison nudged Park as they walked. "Both of you, hush," she said quietly. "If we're asked any more questions about the scandal, just reply by talking about the fashion line. Remember: we have to turn all this front-page news into profit."

The trail of publicity followed them as they continued down the avenue. They walked for nearly thirty minutes, purposely prolonging it, striding past Tiffany and Bergdorf's, Bendel's, and Prada. At Rockefeller Center, directly across the street from Saks, they paused amid a second flurry of activity, then waited for Clarence to join them.

"I'm here," he said, his hands on Madison's shoulders. "You girls gotta move fast. The press is closing in again."

He led them into the building's main lobby and to the elevators.

Once indoors, Madison, Park, and Lex were finally able to breathe deeply and regroup. The building's security desk had been alerted to their arrival, and the press were being barred from entering. In the elevators, they stood close to each other, Madison breathing a sigh of relief as Clarence's shadow loomed over them. They rode up to the tenth floor, then emerged into the executive offices of Hamilton Holdings, Inc.

Decorated in muted tones and dark wood, the offices were mercifully empty on this Sunday afternoon. Clarence stepped out first, doing a quick sweep of the reception area, poking his head under the front desk and down the back corridor that led to the employee kitchen. "Coast is clear," he assured them.

Madison led the way to Trevor Hamilton's huge corner office, using her key to unlock the door. Large windows soaked up the afternoon sun, but the bright light did little to mitigate the tension in the air.

"I'm scared," Lex said suddenly. She was standing beside one of the couches to the right side of the large, L-shaped desk.

"I am too," Park replied. "But we're safe here. We're together. And Clarence is standing by the elevators, guarding us."

"And there happens to be a lot of work to do," Madison added, leaning across the desk and booting up the computer. She threw a quick glance over her shoulder. "Have either of you checked our messages? I know Coco's been trying to call. And by now, Mom's probably called too."

"It wouldn't surprise me if Mom called Coco to try to get ahold of us," Park said. "They're both prone to anxiety."

"It doesn't matter." Madison shook her head. "We have to stay focused on what we're doing. We can't talk to anyone but each other just yet."

"It's almost like we invited the killer here," Lex continued, ignoring them both. She cuddled Champagne tightly against her chest, as if seeking warmth from a chill only she could feel. "By making those statements to the press—I mean, what if he's watching? What if he's coming here right now?"

"That's exactly what we want him to do." Madison plopped into the big leather chair, inhaling a lingering trace of her father's cologne. "It's either Jeremy or Theo, and the three of us can totally take either one of them down." She turned her attention to the flashing screen. Recalling the lessons her father had taught her, she used a series of encrypted passwords to gain entrance to one of their joint personal bank accounts. In a few swift clicks, she allocated $25 million to a temporary business account and earmarked it with the words *Triple Threat National Start-up Fees*. She knew it would take at least that much money to launch the fashion line quickly and successfully.

Of course, none of those bucks would actually transfer until Trevor Hamilton approved the move, but Madison was certain he would agree with them once he got home. If luck was on their side, they would generate enough hype from the scandal to gain a hefty return on their investment.

But it was a tricky move.

Using short-term notoriety to attract long-term publicity had its dangers. Trevor Hamilton would have called it a "calculated risk." It was like the school slut turning around and deciding to run for student council president *after* everyone knew she'd screwed half the guys on the football team. It was like the class snitch vying for a place with the in-crowd *after* he'd ratted out the coed pot party in the girls' bathroom. *Oh, now I'm supposed to like you?* Sometimes it worked and people followed the media wave. But there were other instances when the smoking gun backfired, and those bullets *totally* hurt.

What Madison feared most was that the public at large would react negatively to their announcement of the Triple Threat label while two murder investigations were still ongoing. She knew it was a tasteless move, but there was no other way to shift the spotlight. Besides, it had been done a million times before. Half the world's celebrities had benefited from turning their own dirt into diamonds.

"I'm not going to break my nails fighting a killer,"

Park said. "You can take him down yourself." She went into the outer office and revved up another computer. She logged on to the Internet and hit Yahoo!. The appearance and statements she, Madison, and Lex had made little more than a half hour ago were in the top five bulleted headlines. HAMILTON TRIPLETS SPEAK OUT, CLAIM TO HAVE EVIDENCE. On another site: HAMILTON TRIPLETS LAUNCH FASHION LINE IN THE MIDST OF GROWING SCANDAL. And yet another: HAMILTON TRIPLETS LOOKING DROP-DEAD GORGEOUS. She knew from past experience that the headlines would go on for at least twenty-four hours.

She reached for her purse, unzipped it, and pulled out the digital camera. She hooked it up to the computer. It took all of three minutes to transfer the JPEG files onto the screen in front of her. Staring at the little thumbnail images, she clicked on the two that showcased the dead Zahara Bell. The first was a complete body shot. Park maximized it several times, looking for anything strange or out of the ordinary. Nothing jumped out at her. On the second shot, however—the close-up of Zahara Bell's neck and the scarf that strangled it—Park noticed something odd. Again, she maximized the image to its highest possible degree and saw what hadn't been visible on the camera's small screen.

There, running along the side of Zahara Bell's white face, was a smattering of small black spots—

not pimples or blemishes, but obviously some sort of residue. Park remembered clearly the very moment she had set eyes on the body in the coatroom Friday night. The residue had not been on Zahara's skin; her face had been smooth and blue-tinged, and its pallor would have revealed any such residue immediately.

She flipped on the printer beside the desk and printed out the image. Then she got up and went back into the office, carrying the picture in her hand.

Madison was busy clacking away at the keyboard.

"Here," Park said, tossing the picture onto the desk. "Tell me what you think."

As Madison snatched up the pic, Lex came around and studied it as well.

"I don't know what that is on Zahara Bell's face," Park told them. "But it wasn't there when *we* first saw her lying on that floor."

"No, it wasn't," Madison agreed. "It looks like . . . dirt."

"Dirt?" Park wrinkled her nose. "So someone cleaned off her face before we found her, but not before Chicky Marsala took the photo?"

Lex grabbed the pic and held it close to her face. She turned, examining it in the weak light pouring in through the windows. "This isn't dirt," she said with certainty. "These little things on Zahara's face . . . when you look closely, you can see that they're solid, that they're kind of like . . . long and all different shapes. And they're kind of thick too. This isn't dirt."

"Then what is it?" Madison pressed.

Lex brought the pic as close to her eyes as possible. "It looks like ashes."

"Like from a cigarette?" Park asked.

Lex nodded. She chucked the picture back onto the desk.

"It does look like ashes," Madison agreed. "But how come this wasn't on Zahara's face when we found her?"

"Maybe the little bits of it flew off her face when you threw open the coatroom door," Lex suggested. "Like maybe the draft cleaned off her face. Or—wait—don't you remember? When you turned on the light in the coatroom, you also turned on the overhead air-conditioning vents. I totally felt it. And if that's what happened"—she smiled—"the police wouldn't know about it, because *they* saw what *we* saw, and *not* what Chicky Marsala photographed."

Park circled the desk, both hands on her hips. "So the killer is on his knees, leaning over Zahara Bell, choking her, and—what? Maybe there was a pack of cigarettes in his pocket, and little flecks of tobacco leaves fell out of his pocket and landed on her face? It's possible. I mean, think about it. Zahara Bell must've been struggling against him, maybe there was sweat on her face, her skin was damp. The ashes—or whatever—would stick."

"And you don't think the killer looked down and saw the residue and tried to wipe it all off?" Madison asked.

"He was working quickly, and he knew he had to hurry up and get the hell out of that coatroom," Park answered. "He also turned off the light when he left the room, which turned off the air vents."

A silence fell. Through it, Madison whispered, "Theo smokes."

"So does Jeremy." Park nodded. She ran both hands through her hair. "This is all starting to make sense to me, especially when you consider the time. It's almost exactly forty-eight hours since Zahara Bell was murdered and the Avenue diamond was stolen. And according to the legend, the diamond will be found forty-eight hours after it's stolen. One of them has that diamond, but he doesn't know that it's flushing him out."

"*So* not true," Lex said. "*We're* the ones who're flushing him out. *We're* the crazy ones who're waiting here for something to happen. I just hope"—her voice dropped to a whisper—"I just hope no one else ends up dead."

Madison stood up. She buried her face in her hands, then turned to stare out the window at the city below. It was nearly dusk. Again. She felt as though they were all living in a vacuum, completely disconnected from the world. She had lost her sense of time and distance. She had lost her sense of security. The frustration grated on her nerves and tears welled up in her eyes. She turned around to face Park and Lex. "I just can't bring myself to believe it," she said. "How could Theo—or even Jeremy Bleu—be capable of this? How could either one of them resort to murder? And how could either one of them actually threaten us with fleece for a damn camera? The truth will get out eventually."

"How?" Lex said. "It won't get out unless we turn this camera in to the cops."

Park went over to the desk and logged on to the Internet again.

Madison wiped the tears from her eyes. "It still doesn't make sense. It's all too crazy to believe."

"Crazy or not, we have to consider other alternatives here," Park said firmly. "There've got to be two hundred headlines online saying that we know who the killer is, that we have evidence, that we're in the middle of our own investigation. It won't be long before Detective Mullen comes looking for us."

"I won't turn that camera in!" Madison shouted, angry. "Not until I speak to Theo, face to face. Not until I ask him why he did this, and why he turned on us—on *me*—so viciously. I want to hear it from his own lips."

"What if it's Jeremy we're waiting to hear from?" Lex asked quietly.

Suddenly, Park gasped. She double-clicked. She

pointed to the flashing computer screen. "Latest headline," she said. "Breaking news."

Madison and Lex stared, unable to believe their eyes.

Celebutante Theo West, wanted by police for questioning in the murders of Zahara Bell and Diego "Chicky" Marsala, was missing.

22

Knight in Armor

Jeremy closed the bedroom door of his penthouse hotel suite, blocking out the noise that had been buzzing around him for hours. In the living room area, his publicist, Felicia Rafferty, was arguing with some hotshot Hollywood attorney named Gavin Kaminsky. They were going on about what to do, talking as if Jeremy were a freaking serial killer haunting the streets with a butcher knife. He couldn't stand listening to them anymore. What he hated most was the fact that they were discussing the whole scandal as if he were truly guilty.

Assholes, Jeremy thought. *Both of you.*

Following the ordeal of the last twenty-four hours, he had come back to the hotel and crashed on the couch. Sleep had not touched him. He had lain awake, trying to piece together what he could about yesterday morning. That was what concerned him most. How had the damn key gotten into his pocket? He wasn't about to go on trial and lose his life for some bullshit psycho who'd framed him.

First the scarf, then the key. Could it get any worse?

He *had* lost the scarf Friday night at the gala. Of that he was certain. But when? And where? More importantly, who had picked it up and used it to kill Zahara Bell?

He lit a cigarette. He started pacing. He was on the edge of insanity, being locked up in this hotel suite while two people hammered out the plan he would have to follow for the next several weeks. They hadn't even bothered to listen to him earlier today. What *he* wanted suddenly didn't matter, because if charges were filed against him, lots of people would lose money. That was what this whole damn scandal was about: cash, fame, other people's lives. Felicia had spent the morning on the phone with the producers of his upcoming movie, *Knight,* assuring them that no matter what, Jeremy would make his scheduled appearances on *The Tonight Show, Oprah,* and *Access Hollywood.* Had any of them even asked if he was feeling well? If maybe he wanted to sit down and talk about what this was doing to his mind? Hell no. It was just the same load of bullshit, over and over again. What he had to say. How he had to look. Whose ass he had to kiss next.

Well, fuck it.

He was pissed. He was tired too—tired of everything and everybody. Was this how trained circus monkeys felt? Always having to wait and see if their next step was okay? The realization hit him as he puffed hard on the cigarette and stared around the cold room: he wanted out.

Not just out of this hotel, but out of the whole world that had swelled up around him.

So much fame. So much money. So much power.

And yet so little freedom.

He felt like a caged animal. Was this what he had spent his whole life dreaming about—being controlled by publicists and lawyers and agents who would forget him the moment he stopped being hot? He thought of his old friends back in Iowa. They were probably partying right now, kicking back beers with their girlfriends, not worried about a damn thing. Maybe that was where he wanted to be—with people who cared. With a girl who'd put her arms around him and make all the uncertainty and angst go away. He knew exactly who that girl was, but he couldn't go near her. He couldn't even pick up his phone and call her because *that* was forbidden. *A bad publicity move,*

Felicia would say. *A potentially incriminating act,* Gavin would tell him. It was paramount that Jeremy think about his career, his fans, his ever-increasing pay scale.

Up until a few hours ago, that *was* what he cared about, but the loneliness and chaos of this whole experience had totally zapped his brain. Now all he felt was empty. He felt disconnected from everything.

And he wasn't going to stand for it.

Suddenly, the bedroom door burst open and Felicia appeared on the threshold. "Splendid news!" she shouted. "Theo West has run away—disappeared. He's trying to avoid the police because they want to question him about the murders."

Jeremy folded his arms over his chest. "And why the hell is that good news?" he snapped.

"Well, darling . . . it's basically an admission of guilt." She smiled. "It's all over the news. Theo West killed Zahara Bell because he thought it would silence her from publishing that story about him and Madison Hamilton. And before long, the police will tie him to yesterday's murder too."

"What about Park?" he asked her quickly.

Felicia's face registered confusion. "What about her?"

"If Theo West is a killer, and he's crazed and running on empty, how do you know he isn't on his way to hurt the Hamilton triplets right now?"

"I don't know. But I'm sure those girls have good security around them. Now, Jeremy, we need to discuss your next statement, and what you're going to say about this whole ordeal on *Late Night*. I think—"

"I *don't* wanna talk about it." Turning around, Jeremy grabbed his coat from where it hung off one side of the bed. He shoved into it, his heart beating fast. What if his hunch was right? What if Park really *was* in danger? He couldn't think about it without feeling sick.

As he stormed past Felicia, Gavin Kaminsky appeared on the threshold. He wasn't a big man, but he had strength. He shoved Jeremy back into the bedroom. "Easy does it, kiddo. Easy does it."

"Let me go!" Jeremy shouted. "What the hell are you doing?"

"Jeremy!" Felicia said. "You can't go outside!"

"I can do whatever I want!" he bellowed back. But Gavin had shoved him onto the bed, and now he and Felcia were darting for the door. They ran out, closing it behind them. Jeremy heard a *click* and knew that he was locked in.

Breathing heavily, he stood up and looked frantically around the bedroom.

"It's for your own good," Felicia said from the living room. "You can't be seen in public yet!"

Dropping his head into his hands, Jeremy heaved a sigh. He felt like crying. He felt as if the world were about to end. How was he going to get out of here? He had to get to Park. He had to tell her that he needed her, that he had never meant for any of this to happen, that he thought he was already in love with her. . . .

23

Message from . . . ?

By nightfall, the media crowds had thinned considerably, but the news was all about Theo West and his apparent flight from the police. The television broadcasts were airing small biographical pieces about him, as if his life were already over. Where had he fled? What was he hiding? Why hadn't the West family made a statement yet? The manhunt was officially under way.

Madison, Park, and Lex sat in the spacious entertainment room of the penthouse, watching the story unfold. At Park's insistence, they had closed up the executive offices and come home. There was no point in staying, she'd said, and the familiar confines of the apartment building would provide them with more safety. Now the television flashed from channel to channel, spewing out the same headlines.

Park took it all in with her usual blend of composure and reserve. More than anything, she wished she could give some of her innate calmness to Madison, who was huddled on one corner of the couch, crying quietly. Park went to her and gently placed a hand on her shoulder. She couldn't imagine how awful Madison felt. Despite the eternal feud between the Wests and the Hamiltons, Madison had truly fallen in love with Theo, and her pain at losing him—at having been betrayed by him—was heartbreaking to watch. Sitting there, Park felt a stab of guilt in the pit of her stomach. Should she and Lex have been more supportive of the relationship from the beginning? Maybe if they'd told Madison to follow her heart instead of her duties, none of this would be happening now.

"Hey," Park said. "You can't go on crying forever. This will all be over soon."

Madison sniffled. "I know you don't believe me, but everything that's going on, the way it's unfolding— it's so totally not Theo. I know him, and I just don't believe he lied to me and used me and then killed two people."

Park didn't answer. There was nothing she could

say that Madison didn't already know. She watched as Madison got up and walked over to one of the large windows that overlooked Central Park, her footsteps heavy, her mannerisms sluggish.

"Even when we were together three weeks ago, Theo seemed so . . . genuine," Madison went on. "We talked about a lot of things. We talked about college and how we both want to go to Princeton. He seemed fine." She crossed her arms over her chest. "How could I have not noticed him stealing the dress from Lex's closet that day? *How?*"

"You were just caught up in the moment," Park offered. "It's understandable."

"What if Theo isn't missing?" Madison asked. "What if he's out there somewhere, falling apart, even thinking about hurting himself because he knows he can't get away from this mess?"

Park didn't answer.

"And you know what else I don't understand?" Madison turned to face her. "If Theo also killed Chicky Marsala, it means he came here yesterday, that he was downstairs at some point. Did he come here wanting to talk to me?"

Lex, sitting in a chair across the room, was still examining the photographs from Chicky Marsala's digital camera. Rapt in thought, she paid no mind to the television flashing a few feet away from her. Without looking up she said, "Do the math, will you? Theo figured out that we had the camera. Chicky Marsala came here to get the camera back, and Theo came here making sure the camera wouldn't get into the wrong hands. They crossed paths, they had a confrontation, and Theo fried him—using a scarf he also stole from *my* closet that day he was here." She sighed. "Stranger things have happened, and when people get desperate, they'll do just about anything."

"That's *exactly* the response I expected from you, Lex," Madison snapped. "You're always ready to point out Theo's bad points just because he's a West."

"I'm sorry," Lex mumbled, rolling her eyes. "I tend to point out a person's bad points when he's tied to two murders."

"*Allegedly* tied to two murders!" Madison ranted, her eyes welling up again.

"You *have* to calm down," Park told her gently. "Your makeup is a mess, and all that running mascara is totally going to make you break out."

Madison bit down on her lip. "I don't even care what I look like anymore. I'm too upset to care. The *last* thing on my mind is my complexion."

Lex gasped in shock. But, just as quickly, her shock turned to anger. "Don't you *ever* say something that horrible in my presence! Take a good look at the world out there, Madison. Without good complexions, we're nothing."

Madison's shoulders slumped in a gesture of defeat. "Sorry," she mumbled. She quickly ran her fingers across her cheeks, wiping away the residue of watery makeup.

"You're doing that all wrong." Park got up, grabbed a tissue box from the coffee table, and walked across the room to where Madison was standing. She whisked several tissues into her hand, then began dabbing them gently along Madison's cheeks. "Quick, easy pats," Park said. "Otherwise, all that gook will clog your pores. Your next facial would take, like, three hours."

Madison nodded, trying to hold back her tears.

Lex got up as well. Hands on her hips, she circled her sisters like a stylist in the critical ten seconds that preceded a photo shoot. Then she stepped behind Madison and began working her fingers through Madison's hair. "A nice French twist will cheer you up," she said. "Park, go into my bedroom and get my styling tools."

"No," Madison replied quietly. "Really, I don't think now is the—"

"Why not a chignon?" Park asked. She grabbed a new wad of tissues and, with the tip of her forefinger, began working it around the edge of Madison's lower lip. "Let's do something more dramatic. Like a chignon."

"*Ugh.*" Lex made a sour face. "That's *so* New

Jersey prom night. Maybe we should do some red highlights—"

Suddenly, Madison's cell phone rang loudly, shattering their banter like a gunshot. They all jumped at the sound.

"Dammit," Lex mumbled, letting go of Madison's long locks.

Whirling around, Madison ran to the coffee table and picked up her phone. It had only rung twice, announcing the arrival of a text message.

Park stood up and hovered over Madison. Lex followed.

"It's from a restricted number," Madison said. "It's got to be the same person who sent us the previous two messages."

"But this time, the person only sent it to you," Lex pointed out.

Madison flipped open the phone and the message came into view.

IT'S THEO. MEET ME AT THE CORNER OF 110TH STREET AND 1ST AVE IN HALF AN HOUR. PLEASE? I'M SORRY. . . .

Madison gasped. "Oh, Theo," she whispered.

"Forget it!" Lex shouted instantly. "There's nothing he can say to you on a street corner that he can't say in a police station."

"Of course there is!" Madison shot back, closing the phone and pushing it into the pocket of her jeans. "Don't you see? He wants to explain everything to me. He doesn't want it to end this way."

"Madison!" Lex's voice went rigid. "Wake up and come out of your love trance! He's trying to lure you somewhere so he can get what he wants and finish this whole mess."

"That's not true! I know it's not true!" Madison covered her face with her hands.

"You're not actually thinking of meeting him, are you?" Park asked. She shook her head. "That would be crazy. And for the last time: *please* keep your hands *away* from your face!"

"I *am* meeting him," Madison replied firmly. "He just wants to talk. He wants to tell me something. He wants to explain. No one's going to hurt me."

Suddenly, Park heard a knock on the front door. She listened as Lupe answered it and ushered someone inside. A moment later, Clarence came into the living room.

"I just sent the last of the reporters away," he said sullenly. "I told them you girls wouldn't be making any other statements. Believe it or not, the front of the building is pretty clear. Is . . ." He eyed the strain on their faces. "Is everything okay?"

"Oh, everything's just dandy," Lex quipped. "Madison here wants to go and meet a killer in the dark."

"What?"

Park explained the text message to Clarence.

Instantly, his eyes widened in shock. "Absolutely not!" he screamed. "At least not without me!"

"And me!" Lex echoed.

"And me too," Park said quietly. "It's either we all go, or none of us goes. You can call the police and tell them everything, Madison, but you can't put your life in danger."

Drying her eyes, Madison walked to the center of the living room and squared her shoulders. Looking at each of them, she said, "I am going to meet Theo in half an hour. Clarence, you can drive and accompany me—but that's it. I won't make a circus out of this. Whether or not you all want to hear it, Theo means a lot to me, and I know in my heart that there's a reasonable explanation for all that's happened. I'll talk to him, and then I promise I'll take everything to the police." She paused, letting her words sink in. "Now that's my final word, and I won't discuss it anymore."

Park sighed. She knew arguing would be useless. She shot a glance at Lex, whose eyes also registered defeat.

Five minutes later, they were all gathered in the elevator. They rode down to the lobby in silence. Madison had grabbed her purse and coat, and Park and Lex had done the same, despite the fact that they weren't leaving the building any time soon.

"I just want to go on record as saying that I'm *completely* against this," Lex announced as they stepped into the lobby.

Madison turned to face them.

Park caught the longing in her eyes, the look that was equal parts desperation, fear, and hope.

"I have to do this," Madison said quietly. "Not only for all of us, but for myself. Once I hear what I need to hear, I'll be able to put everything behind me. And I'll get the diamond back for us—for everyone." She clutched her purse tightly. "I'll call you soon. We'll all go the police station together."

Park nodded. She looked at Clarence, who was waiting by the front desk, the limo keys in his hand. "Watch her," she said, an edge of warning in her voice.

Clarence nodded and gave her one of his you-think-I'll-hesitate-to-kick-someone's-ass-tonight? looks.

Holding her breath, Park watched as Madison exited the building, ran toward the limo, and disappeared into the night.

A tense silence fell; it seemed to fill the entire lobby, choking the air like smoke.

Park and Madison paced the reception area, unable to draw themselves away from the wide front double doors. At this point, Park didn't care if a stray reporter snapped a picture of her. She didn't care if someone walked by and caught sight of her with her face pressed to the glass like a gawking child. She felt the hard thumping in her chest and kept telling herself that it would be okay, that Madison had done the right thing, that Theo wouldn't hurt her with Clarence there.

Outside, the night was clear and dark. Traffic wasn't crazy. She calculated that it would take Clarence about ten minutes to make it to the odd location Theo had asked Madison to meet him at. Why 110th Street and First Avenue? It was a pretty seedy area. Was that where Theo had run to, where he'd been hiding all this time in order to avoid speaking to the police? And what, she wondered, did he hope to gain from Madison?

"I can't stand this," Lex said as she pressed herself up against the front desk, where the doorman, Steven Hillby, was glaring at her quietly. "I've never been so nervous."

"Me either," Park admitted.

Five minutes ticked by.

Ten.

Fifteen.

Twenty.

And then Park looked outside again and let out a frightened gasp.

A heavily clothed figure stood on the sidewalk just beyond the closed front doors. He was tall and lanky, and only his eyes were visible beneath the wool cap that covered his head and the thick scarf wound over his mouth and nose.

Park froze. She felt Lex's hand close on her arm.

Who the hell is that?

The figure unwound the scarf and yanked the cap off his head as he took two steps toward them.

It was Theo.

24

The Third Victim

Madison stared out the open window of the limo and watched First Avenue drift by. The wind felt good on her face, and as it whipped through her hair and down into her shirt, she realized that she was sweating. In fact, she was shaking. Her right leg was bobbing up and down nervously. Her fingers wouldn't keep still. She felt as if she were headed into uncharted territory, into the scary unknown—as if she were en route to Macy's or Kmart for the first time.

She turned and fixed her eyes on Clarence. He

was driving tensely, both hands locked on the steering wheel. He didn't shift his gaze to look at her in the rearview mirror. Madison was glad for the silence. She didn't know what to say or even what to think. Despite Clarence's presence, she was afraid of what might happen next. Not for a moment did she believe Theo would try to hurt her, but in his obviously desperate state, would he break down and beg her to help him? There was nothing she could do at this point except talk to him. All the money in the world couldn't erase what he'd done, and trying to understand his motives would only lead to more heartache.

She wouldn't let that happen.

She wasn't doing this to reestablish what was left of their impossible romance. She was doing this for herself, for her own peace of mind, and maybe even to look Theo in the eye and tell him how fucked up he was to have put her and Park and Lex through this.

"We're almost there."

Clarence's voice broke her reverie. Nodding silently, Madison clutched her purse to her chest and took a deep breath. She glanced out the window, noticing how the landscape had changed in so short a span of blocks. The tall doorman buildings of the Upper East Side had given way to the shabby structures of a neighborhood that had witnessed too much crime and not enough caring. The streets were dark. Why on earth had Theo chosen this area? Did the

Wests own real estate here? Was he hiding out in one of these shadowy apartment buildings?

The limo came to a crawl as they approached 110th Street. Clarence hung a right and pulled up to the curb. "This must be it," he said grimly.

Madison stared outside. She was looking at an abandoned warehouse that rose up at least three stories and stretched all the way to the next corner. Up along the top floor, several windows were either cracked or completely blown out. She saw no sign of lights or people anywhere.

She popped open the door and climbed out. Clarence emerged from the driver's side and immediately went to open her door. She stared at him. "Why don't you wait for me here?" she said. "If Theo sees that I've come with someone, he might not want to talk. Or he might even run away without doing anything."

Clarence shook his head. "I'll walk you in, and if I think it's okay, I'll wait just outside the door. But you can't go in there alone."

Throwing a glance over her shoulder, Madison walked up to the abandoned warehouse. She followed the scarred walls down to what had obviously once been an entrance. Two huge doors, barely on their hinges, creaked as a gust of wind blew through the streets. She pulled open the first one. A musty odor assailed her senses. It was pitch-black inside.

As she took slow steps forward, she reached for Clarence and breathed a sigh of relief when his hand closed over hers. She kept going, trying to etch out of the shadows something that would tell her she wasn't in an underground cave. The wind howled outside. The rafters high above shook with a clatter. She let out a little yelp when she heard the front doors slamming shut.

Now she was sure they were standing somewhere in the middle of the wide, uneven floor.

She cleared her throat nervously. It was time to declare herself. "Theo?" she called out. Her voice spiraled through the darkness. Then she heard a loud *pop* that made her heart jump into her throat.

Above her, a series of lights clicked on. They ran along the ceiling, illuminating the broken windows, the rutted ground, and a tall scaffolding that wound all the way up to the third story.

"Theo?" Madison shouted again. "Theo? Can you hear me?" When the silence enveloped her, she turned around and saw Clarence standing a few feet away, beside an open fuse box. She hadn't even felt him leave her side.

He was staring back at her. The gleam in his eyes was cold. He reached into his lapel pocket and pulled out a half-smoked cigar and a book of matches. "Theo isn't here," he said, the matchbook slipping from his shaky fingers.

"What?" Madison's voice was a whisper.

"Theo isn't here," he repeated quietly. "And he isn't coming."

She watched as Clarence bent down to retrieve the matchbook. As he did so, a sprinkling of loose to-bacco poured from his lapel pocket and into the air; the little black remnants swirled and spun, hitting the floor soundlessly. And in that terrifying moment, Madison understood everything. She knew exactly why she had been brought here—and for what grim purpose.

25

Let's Head West

"Just *listen* to me!" Theo shouted.

He was standing inside the lobby, pressed up against the wall. Park and Lex had each grabbed pillows from the couch in the reception area, and now they were holding them out like weapons. Steven Hillby stood just to Theo's right, a threatening look in his eyes.

"What the *hell* are you doing here?" Lex screamed back. "Don't try to kill us, because we're armed."

"That's . . . that's right!" Park said. She touched a

hand to the pocket of her jeans and held it there, as if reaching for a gun.

Theo let out a long sigh. "Search me if you want to! I'm not here to hurt you—I'm not a killer."

"Two murders don't make you a killer?" Lex snapped. She swung the pillow and slammed him broadside in the head.

Theo let out a grunt as the impact shook his jaw. "Don't you understand? I came here to explain everything to Madison," he said breathlessly. "Where is she?"

"You should know, moron!" Lex answered. "You're the one who directed her to 110th Street!"

"What are you talking about? I haven't even spoken to her!" Theo's tone was tense but firm, the look in his eyes was serious.

"Fine! *Texted* her!" Lex shrieked. "If you don't come clean, I swear to God, Theo, your balls will be hanging on our Christmas tree this year!"

"Wait a minute!" Park's voice rose high into the air. Slowly, cautiously, she lowered the pillow she'd been holding and took a step back. She grabbed Lex's arm, instructing her to do the same. Then she stared at Theo and said calmly, "What's going on? You have exactly thirty seconds to tell us. The truth, by the way."

The doorman grabbed Theo's shoulder as if to rough him up.

With a wave of her hand, Park ordered him to stop. He did.

Theo stepped away from the wall, wiped the sweat from his brow, and took a deep breath. "For the last sixteen hours, I've been hiding out with my parents at my uncle's condo on Sutton Place," he began. "*I* wanted to talk to the cops and explain myself, but my parents wouldn't let me—not without their star lawyer, and he's flying back from Sydney right now because of this mess. I—"

"You're babbling," Park told him coolly. "Get on with it. Why the hell did Annabelle turn you in? Why does everyone think you're guilty—including us?"

"Annabelle did it to get back at me," he replied quickly. "She and I had a fight Friday night. We broke up. She knows that I"—he gulped—"she knows that I love Madison."

Staring at him, Park flashed back to the pictures Chicky Marsala had snapped of Theo and Zahara Bell—and their very obvious confrontation. "We know you saw Zahara Bell Friday night just before she was killed," she told him. "We have proof of that."

"You're right, I did see her," he admitted flatly. "But I didn't kill her. And I didn't know about the gossip column she was planning to publish."

"But you argued with her," Lex said. "You were angry with her. Why?"

Theo cleared his throat and looked down at the

floor. His shoulders sagged, as if too much weight were upon them. "West International—the whole company—is going through some serious financial trouble right now. My parents are freaking out. Investors all over the world are freaking out. It's not something the general public knows yet, but Zahara knew. And I knew that she knew. She's always hated my father—hated all my family."

He paused and took another deep breath. "Anyway, on Friday night, I *did* leave the ballroom for the ten minutes Annabelle's blabbing about. I needed a break. I was upset seeing Madison there. I got totally emotional and I felt really fucked up. I thought maybe I'd go outside and smoke a joint. But on my way out, I saw Zahara coming in. She was on her way to the bathroom. Our eyes met. I guess I must've given her a dirty look, and that's when she sniffed and raised her nose in the air and . . . and insulted me."

Park, listening attentively, dropped the pillow onto the floor. "What'd she say?"

"She had a little smirk on her face," Theo explained. "And she looked at me and said, 'I'm glad you can still afford Armani.' Then she chuckled. And *that's* when I totally fucking lost it."

"You grabbed her arm," Lex muttered. "It was a pretty physical confrontation."

Theo's eyes widened slightly, as if in shock. "Yeah, I did. How'd you know? You saw it?"

Lex shook her head. "*I* didn't see it. Neither did Park or Madison. But someone did."

"And then what happened?" Park pressed, her eyes locked on Theo's face. "That couldn't have taken you ten whole minutes."

"It didn't," he said. "The whole argument lasted maybe twenty seconds. I was all worked up. I went out through the sculpture garden and had a smoke. I guess I stood there in the quiet for a few minutes. Then I went back to the ballroom. That's what really happened, and Annabelle's trying to pass it off as something suspicious just to get back at me." He raked a hand through his hair, visibly on edge. "I *swear* I'm telling you the truth. You think I snuck out of my uncle's place in disguise and made my way over here to play more games? When twenty thousand reporters are waiting to snap my pic? When the cops are waiting to arrest me?"

"Why didn't you just explain that to Annabelle Friday night?" Park asked him. "Wouldn't that have saved you a lot of trouble? I mean . . . *duh.*"

"I didn't wanna tell her that I'd gotten into an argument with Zahara Bell just before Zahara was killed," Theo replied. "I didn't want to tell anyone. But Annabelle went and opened her big mouth anyway, and that's why I'm wanted for questioning. Now, can you please tell me where Madison is? I came here to explain everything to her."

"She's gone." Park told him about the two threatening text messages they had all received, and about the one just under an hour ago that had sent Madison on her way.

"What?" Theo shouted. He grabbed his own cell phone from the pocket of his jeans and held it out. "Here. Go through everything if you don't believe me. I had *nothing* to do with any text messages."

"But then . . ." Park threw a confused glance at Lex and began pacing the floor again. She reviewed the facts in her mind—Theo's initialed charm in Lex's closet, those missing ten minutes, his refusal to speak to the police, even the ashes in the picture of Zahara Bell's face. Hello? It all spelled guilt. But then why the hell was her gut telling her to believe what Theo was saying? When she looked up from the floor, she saw her own uncertainty reflected in Lex's eyes.

Who the hell is doing this to us?

"Then it can only be one other person," Lex whispered.

Park knew she had insinuated Jeremy. The very thought of it infuriated her, but the anger quickly died away and was replaced by frustration. She lowered herself into a chair. Tears welled up in her eyes and spilled over her cheeks, causing her mascara to run. "Lex," she said weakly, "please give me my purse."

Lex did her sister's bidding, going over to retrieve

the purse sitting on the coffee table in the main reception area.

Park took it and quickly unzipped it. Then she sat up straight in the chair and sighed. "This isn't my purse. This is Madison's purse." She inspected the brown leather hobo handbag. "Shit. She took my purse by mistake. They look so similar. I guess . . . I guess she got confused."

"Just use her mascara," Lex said.

Park began rifling through the handbag. She saw the digital camera, Madison's sunglasses and favorite pair of cashmere gloves, several pens and ballpoint markers, scraps of paper emblazoned with the St. Cecilia's logo. Even now, in the midst of all this confusion, it amazed her that Madison was so damn *messy;* she appeared neat and organized, but the proof was in this handbag. Park gave it a good shake and reached inside. Her fingers closed over something hard and smooth. She pulled it out. It was a black Chanel compact case, the edges scarred and nicked. She held it up. "This isn't Madison's," she said.

"No, it isn't." Theo stepped forward. "She doesn't use Chanel. She uses Clarins. We both use Clar—" He stopped short of admitting what no guy with great skin wanted to admit.

"Whose is it?" Lex asked.

Park opened the compact and knew immediately that it wasn't actual makeup. Not exactly. The mirror was dirty, and the round spongy applicator looked old and crusty. The floor of the compact was loose, a hairline crack running along one side of it. A tiny piece of paper stuck out from beneath. Park flipped the compact over; both the mirror and the applicator fell into her hand, and the small rectangular floor swung out as well.

There, pressed into the very bottom of the dismantled compact, was a folded sheet of white paper. Park carefully tugged at one edge. It slid into her fingers. She unfolded it slowly, careful not to tear it. Her eyes began skimming the neat print, the little nuggets of gossip grouped in descending order beside names and dates. And as her breath caught in her throat, Park knew she was staring at the final piece of the puzzle—Zahara Bell's list of informants, the very sources who had enabled her gossip column. The people who had spilled their intimate knowledge and fueled a campaign of ruin.

"Oh, my God."

Lex and Theo, both leaning over Park's shoulder, gasped.

The piece of paper shook in Park's fingers as she found the entry bearing Madison's name and, just beside it, Theo's name. Beneath the names Zahara Bell had written two damning sentences: *Forbidden love spells corporate chaos. Thanx, Chauffeur Clarence.* The Hamilton entry continued, listing several facts about Hamilton Holdings, Inc., that were not public knowledge—including the intended date of the long-awaited hostile takeover of West International that Trevor Hamilton and his executive board had been planning for years.

No. It can't be.

Park shot to her feet. She couldn't believe her eyes. It was impossible. A lie. Another piece of Zahara Bell's vicious propaganda. But even as the shock soared through her brain, Park knew the sheet of paper was the single most irrefutable piece of evidence they had.

It's Clarence. He was Zahara Bell's informant. He killed her.

"I can't believe it!" Lex shouted. "How could we not have seen it?"

Park looked down at the handbag. "How—how did this end up in Madison's purse? This is Zahara Bell's compact—Zahara's handwriting. How the hell . . . ?" She stared at Lex, desperately seeking an answer.

"Never mind that!" Lex shrieked. "It's Clarence! And Madison is with him *right now*!"

"Where?" Theo's voice rose anxiously. His hand snapped around Lex's wrist.

Park quickly folded the sheet of paper up, stuffed it back into the compact, and dumped it into the handbag. "110th and First Avenue," she said. "Come on! We have to get there now!"

They burst out of the front doors, leaving Steven Hillby gaping behind them. Fifth Avenue was mercifully quiet. Park stopped at the curb, suddenly remembering that without their limo, they had no ride.

"Let's just hail a freaking cab!" Theo said.

"There's no time!" Park shouted back.

"Look!" Lex pointed to the cab parked across the street. The driver had gotten out, and he was disposing of a McDonald's meal in an overflowing trash can. The driver's-side door was ajar, the engine still running.

Without a word, they ran across the street.

"Sorry kids, I'm off duty," the driver called out as they approached.

Lex grabbed the handle of the driver's-side door and hopped in behind the wheel. Park and Theo dove into the backseat.

"Hey!" the driver screamed, running toward the car. "What do you think you're doing? Stop! Stop!"

"Sorry, sir!" Lex yelled. "We'll be back as soon as possible."

"*Hurry!*" Teeth gritted, Park kicked the back of the driver's seat.

Lex jumped. And then she threw the cab into gear and slammed her foot down on the accelerator.

26

A Smokin' Bad Time

Her lips dry, Madison stared at Clarence as he puffed on the cigar and then exhaled a thin stream of smoke. Every muscle in her body had gone tense. She felt rooted to the spot, even as the voices in her head screamed for her to run, to get out, to try to escape before it was too late. As fear rose in her throat, she said, "Tell me why, Clarence. Why did you do this?"

He looked at her, then looked down. "I didn't want to do it," he replied. "Please believe me when I tell you I didn't want to do it. I never meant to hurt you and Park and Lex. But Zahara Bell left me no choice. I had to kill her."

"Why?"

"Because I was her informant," he stated flatly. "I was the one who told her about you and Theo, and about a lot of other things I overheard your father talking about. Stuff about the company, about business deals, about money. All the dirt that was gonna make it into her column."

"When did you even meet her?" Madison asked. "How did you even get involved?"

Clarence rolled the smoldering cigar in his fingers. "Two months ago, I drove Lex to a fashion show at the Armory and waited outside for it to be over. Zahara Bell arrived late, and I was standing there when she got out of her own limo. She was rushing to get inside, but she tripped and almost killed herself right there on the sidewalk. I caught her. Saved her. She was grateful and acted all sweet. Then she asked me who I was, who I drove for. When I told her I worked for you gals, she perked up right away. She gave me her business card and told me that if I wanted to make some extra cash, I should call her. Two days later, I did."

Madison felt the knot in her stomach tightening. "And she agreed to pay you for any dirt you could dig up on us, right?"

"Yeah. She was just starting to put together some

gossip column for her magazine. I never meant to get so deeply involved in it, ya know? But I was making money, and I just couldn't help myself. The arrangement worked out nicely for a while, but then she did the wrong thing."

"And what was that?"

He pursed his lips together and shook his head. "She stopped needing me. She said I'd given her everything she needed. And when I got pissed off, she warned me that if I didn't back off, she was gonna publish my name along with everyone else's in that gossip column. That was her plan, anyway. She was gonna use her informants and then rat us out in the next issue. Ruin our lives. I'm not the only one. She had lots of other informants in her little datebook. But I wasn't about to be exposed and fired and maybe even put in jail. And that's exactly what your father would've done—slapped me with a lawsuit."

He sighed. He shook his head. The look on his face was one of disappointment and regret. "I really never meant for it to happen this way, Madison. But what other choice did I have?"

"So in order to stop Zahara from ratting you out, you killed her," Madison said slowly. "But how? When did you steal the dress from Lex's closet? How did you manage to keep people from seeing you?"

"I stole one of Lupe's spare keys," he answered. "I knew Friday night would be my last chance, so last week, when your father left for his business trip and you girls were at school and Lupe was out, I went into the penthouse and took the clothes from Lex's closet. No one saw me. I exited through the side of the building, brought the stuff back to my apartment."

"The key," Madison said. "That's the one you planted in Jeremy's jacket. And you killed Chicky Marsala too, then stuffed his body in the closet."

"Now *that* was a total stroke of luck." Clarence chuckled. "That fat pig was hiding out next to the lobby yesterday morning. I had just gotten to the building. I knew Park had figured out about Jeremy's scarf, and I was worried. I happened to go into the antechamber, all the way through to the service entrance, and I saw Chicky hiding out there, dressed like a maid. We started arguing. I figured out who he was. Then he told me that he thought he recognized me. He was right. He'd seen me leaving the coatroom right after I killed Zahara. I thought about that, and about the pics in his camera. I got scared, so I killed him too."

Madison swallowed over the lump in her throat. "And you tied Lex's scarf around *his* neck," she said.

"Yeah. I had to. I was originally gonna use that on Zahara, but when I found Jeremy Bleu's scarf on the floor just beside the men's room, it was just too perfect. A great idea. Threw the suspicion on him for a while, until Theo West made himself the prime suspect." He brought the cigar to his lips again.

"So the fabric found under Chicky Marsala's nails, the polyester—it was from your blazer," Madison figured. "There was a struggle, and he almost got you."

"Almost," Clarence agreed. "But that blazer is in the trash now. And Jeremy Bleu probably won't ever remember that I'm the one who took his jacket from him and hung it up in the closet. He didn't even see me do it. He was too spaced out to notice." He flicked ashes onto the floor. "Believe me, Madison—I never meant for it to happen this way. But you and your sisters—you started prancing around like little detectives. I never expected that."

Keep him talking, Madison thought. *You have to keep him talking.* "The Avenue diamond," she blurted out. "Why'd you steal it? Where is it?"

Another smile spread across his face. He reached into the inside pocket of his blazer and pulled from it a black silk handkerchief. He unfolded it. He linked his fingers inside the chain and lifted the diamond up.

Madison couldn't help but gasp at the bright shimmer of light it cast. It nearly transfixed her.

"I never planned on this little baby," Clarence said. "But after I finished with Zahara, I realized that after I disappeared, I'd need some money. You know how much I can get for this rock on the black market? A few million at least." He folded the handkerchief over the diamond again and dropped it back into his pocket. "After I finish up my job here, I'm headin' for the airport. I'll be doin' the cha-cha in Argentina by the time they arrest Theo West for—"

"For what?" Madison asked in an injured tone. She already knew the answer.

Clarence sighed loudly again. He didn't meet her eyes. "For killing you," he whispered.

Madison's blood ran cold. She blinked back tears, determined not to cry. "How did you send those encrypted text messages?" she asked. "We all know your cell number. Did you buy yourself an extra phone just to send those cute little notes to us?"

He nodded.

Madison heaved a sigh. Her heart was beating painfully in her chest. Attempting to sound calm, she said, "I still don't get how you pulled it off. How did you kill Zahara without anyone seeing you?"

"Oh, people saw me," he said. "But they just haven't made the connection yet. Who the hell am I? A lowly little chauffeur among rich famous people who only have eyes for other rich famous people. It was easy, Madison. Easier than I expected. I swear, killing with a crowd nearby is the best way to do it."

She tightened her fingers around her purse, unable to think of anything else to say. She looked up, to her left and right. There was no way to escape.

"Now come on," Clarence said, his voice weary but firm. "Give me the purse and let's get moving."

"Here." She flung the purse at him. "The camera's in there. Take what you want and just let me go."

"It's too late, Madison. I'm sorry. Really, I am." He slipped the purse under his arm and, with his free hand, reached into his blazer pocket. He pulled out a small handgun. He held it out and leveled it.

"No!" Madison cried, throwing her hands up in reflex. "Don't shoot!"

"I won't. Not yet." He motioned toward the scaffolding. "Get moving. Come on. Time is short."

As Madison turned around and neared it, she saw the steel staircase leading up to the top of the scaffolding. It creaked beneath her as she started up the first flight. She felt Clarence behind her, felt the muzzle of the gun digging into her back. Her entire body trembled as they cleared the first landing. She made the mistake of looking down and nearly lost her footing. They were high off the ground.

What's he going to do to me? she thought. *Is he going to kill me and leave my body here? People will find the text message and blame Theo. And what about Park and Lex? Will they get blamed for everything too? Will people take pictures of me when I'm dead—with my hair such a mess?*

The first tear streaked her face just as the doors two stories below burst open. The sound boomed through the entire warehouse.

"Madison! Where are you?"

It was Park's voice.

Madison gasped, relief flooding her. Pressing her feet into the unsteady floor of the scaffolding, she froze even as the gun jabbed into her back. "I'm up here!" she screamed.

"Shut up!" Clarence barked.

A moment later, Madison dared herself to look down again. When she did, she saw Park, Lex, and Theo dashing across the wide ground floor of the warehouse.

"Clarence! Stop!" Lex shrieked.

The entire scaffolding creaked the moment Theo jumped onto the staircase.

Madison screamed as Clarence's hand went around her neck. She felt herself being spun around, pulled toward him. She closed her eyes as the gun dug into her side.

"Okay!" Theo shouted, throwing up his hands. "I'll stop. Just . . . just don't hurt her!"

"Stay back, all of you!" Clarence's voice was desperate.

"We know everything," Park said, coming up behind Theo on the staircase. She reached into the purse, pulled out the compact, and held it up. "This is what you really want, Clarence. You took it when you killed Zahara Bell, and then you dropped it when you climbed back into the limo Friday night. You restocked the bar like you always do and it must've fallen right out of your pocket when you were leaning over. Madison picked it up off the floor of the limo by mistake when she spilled her own purse."

His eyes widening, Clarence took the purse Madison had given him and, realizing that it served no purpose, hurled it over the side of the scaffolding. "Give me that," he ordered, staring at Park. "Give it to me or . . . or I'll kill her!"

Madison let out a yelp as his arm tightened around her neck.

Park reached past Theo and chucked the compact onto one of the stairs.

"Let her go, Clarence," Lex called out. "It's too late. You can't get away with this!"

"Take the damn compact," Theo told him, trying to sound calm. "But let go of her."

Madison held her breath. She felt Clarence's arm loosen slightly from around her neck as he leaned forward and grasped for the compact. She couldn't see him, but she knew he was straining to maintain his grip on both her and himself. The gun left her side for an instant. *Now,* she thought, *do it.* In a split-second move, she bit down on Clarence's hand and broke from his hold.

He cried out. He stumbled back as his fingers grazed the compact. But his hand caught Madison's sleeve and shoved her forward.

She slammed into the railing. The force knocked the breath from her lungs, and the dizziness that followed made her stumble and pitch forward as the scaffolding shook violently.

Lex shrieked again.

Park struggled to maintain her balance.

And Theo dove toward Clarence.

Their bodies slammed together like enraged bulls, crashing to the floor with a thud. They struggled. They wrestled. Theo jabbed Clarence with an uppercut to the jaw.

Madison watched the fight as she regained her balance. With nowhere to go but up, she raced across the next landing and headed for the second staircase. But she was too frightened to climb it. She whirled around and saw Lex pushing past Park and powering toward the fight.

With a roar, Clarence thrust Theo to one side and rose to his feet. Gasping for breath, blood trailing from his nose, he raised the gun and pointed it at Lex.

She froze.

Theo hoisted himself up and swept his arms across the bottom of Clarence's legs.

"Watch it!" Park screamed.

As Clarence stumbled, the gun in his hand went straight up and discharged.

The boom of the shot thundered through the warehouse, sending a flock of pigeons scurrying across the ceiling.

"Get down!" Madison cried.

It was the moment Lex needed. She grabbed the magic purse from around her shoulder, raised it high, and swung it in typical propeller fashion. The full force of the blow caught Clarence squarely in the face.

His head snapped back. His eyes rolled. He looked as though he were seeing stars and fireworks as he dropped the gun and pitched forward onto the railing. His body lurched precariously, and the black handkerchief fell out of the pocket of his blazer and into the air.

"Park!" Madison wailed. "The diamond!"

Her eyes blazing, Park flew down the stairs and across the ground floor. She looked up just as the black material unfurled. The Avenue diamond spun through the shadows, emitting rays of brilliant light and color. And Park literally took to the air. As if in slow motion, she dove forward, arms outstretched, hair fanning out behind her. She slammed to the ground an instant before the diamond grazed her palm. She closed her fingers over it. "Oh," she muttered. "That totally hurt."

"Mads!" Theo ran across the landing. Despite the scaffolding's tremors, he reached out and pulled her to him, enveloping her in a tight embrace.

Madison drank in the scent of him. She buried her head in his shirt and, for the first time in a long time, felt her body melt.

"That'll teach you!" Lex's voice resounded through the warehouse. She was squatting down just behind Clarence's off-balance body. She kicked the gun away, grabbed his belt, and pulled him back with all her might.

He slid off the railing like a bag of sand. He landed flat on his ass, then let out a bloodcurling scream as one of his diamond-shaped hemorrhoids burst.

27

Triple Threat

For the second time in exactly one week, the Great Hall of the Metropolitan Museum of Art was glittering. A fashion show not waiting for Fashion Week was unorthodox, and so the unveiling of the first Triple Threat collection had attracted massive amounts of press from around the globe. No expense had been spared in creating a truly elitist ambiance. Huge Andy Warhol–esque posters of Madison, Park, and Lex covered an entire wall. The Hamilton Holdings, Inc., insignia—three skyscrapers shadowed by the letters *MPL*—hung from the arched entryway. A long catwalk stretched down the center of the floor, rose petals scattered along its edges.

In the last few minutes before showtime, Lex stood backstage, cuddling Champagne, watching as the customary chaos that comprised all fashion shows took hold: girls running half-clothed to their designated dressing stations, makeup artists frantically doing their final primps, stylists checking and rechecking wardrobe. As chief designer of the line, Lex wouldn't be modeling any of the clothes. She had, however, instructed Coco McKaid to round up nearly thirty of their closest friends from St. Cecilia's Prep to get the job done. The gene pool at St. Cecilia's ensured a better selection than any modeling agency in the city. And here they all were—freshmen, sophomores, juniors, seniors—eager to commandeer the catwalk in Triple Threat.

Cuddling Champagne against her chest, Lex watched as Coco darted into the center of the crazed room and clapped her hands loudly.

"Listen up, girls!" she shouted. "Five minutes till showtime. All of you take your damn places!"

Lex stifled a laugh when Coco shook her head and wiped the sweat from her brow. "Hey, you're doing a great job. The girls look sensational."

Coco smiled. "I know. I'm so glad it all came together. And by the way, I'm so totally never serving as

Madison's special assistant again. Next fashion show, I'm only modeling. I can't take all the stress!"

"Deal." Lex touched her shoulder, then scanned the room. No sign of Madison or Park. They were likely still getting touched up. She turned and walked out to the very edge of the threshold. Craning her head sideways, she was able to see the ballroom in its entirety. It was packed. The din of voices drifted on the air as people rushed to take their designated seats. High-profile fashion editors and celebrities occupied the first two rows on both sides of the catwalk, followed by assorted socialites and a handful of other celebutantes. Every major news organization was represented.

And there, cordoned off to one side, was the Italian Fashion Power Club: Donatella, Miuccia, Giorgio, Domenico, and Stefano; seated smack in the middle of the stellar group was Venturina Baci. Venturina was wearing the only Triple Threat piece that wouldn't be modeled on the catwalk—an elegant figure-hugging black gown trimmed in lace. She clutched a framed picture of Madison, Park, and Lex in her lap.

Smiling broadly, Lex cut her eyes to the opposite side of the room, where Trevor Hamilton sat waiting patiently for the show to begin. He was surrounded by his executive team: three personal assistants, two attorneys, his publicist, and several members of

Hamilton Holdings' board of trustees. Yesterday, upon his return to New York, he had officially given the Triple Threat label his blessing.

Excitement surged through Lex's body, but it was quickly eclipsed by feelings of gratitude and peace. After the ordeal of the past week, she was eternally grateful that Madison hadn't been hurt, that Theo and Jeremy had been vindicated, and that Clarence Becker had been hauled off to jail following extensive rectal surgery. There was still a lot that had to be figured out and dealt with, but she was determined to adopt Park's example of composure and utter coolness.

The lights above her flashed. Showtime. Lex dashed through the backstage area and took an adjacent staircase down to the main floor. Quietly, she opened the door that brought her to the very back of the ballroom. Well out of sight, she stood pressed up against the wall, eager to see her dreams unveiled.

The lights dimmed. A series of strobes blasted the catwalk. Then music cut up the air: trance and techno set to a backbeat.

Coco opened the show. Dressed in a stunning lily-white party gown with matching lace gloves and a corseted middle, she powered down the catwalk with her arms flung out and her head bobbing to the beat. A cheer instantly went up in the crowd. Cameras flashed like wildfire. Two, three, four, five: it was model after model, exquisite piece after exquisite piece. Lex kept her eyes on the fashion editors, pleased when they nodded and quickly inked their notepads.

Then it was Park's turn on the catwalk. She was clothed in Triple Threat day wear; her low-cut leopard-print jeans tapered down evenly to black stilettos, and a black tank top wrapped her upper body. She held a richly textured quilted bag with a gold chain strap. And there, sparkling at her neck, was the Avenue diamond. In gratitude for having recovered the rock, Tiffany had insisted that Park wear it. She was practically swooning as she stood there, enveloped by its magical light.

Suddenly, a male figure came striding down the catwalk. It was Jeremy Bleu, in his first official public appearance since the scandal. He was dressed in the only Triple Threat menswear piece Lex had ever designed—a black double-breasted suit complemented by a sky blue shirt, silver cuff links, and a gold silk tie. A long black scarf hung loosely from his shoulders. He came to a stop directly behind Park, basking in the overflow of flashes. Then, in a purely sensational gesture, he yanked the scarf from his shoulders and slowly wrapped it around Park's neck. He planted a kiss on her bare shoulder as whispers fluttered through the crowd.

It was Madison who closed the show. She drew

the greatest round of applause, coming down the catwalk in a tan floor-sweeping gown that was both ethereal and bold; intricately detailed, it was a backless beauty that rose up and around her neck in a delicate swirl. The gown's frayed hem dragged over matching stilettos.

Lex nodded proudly, then found herself scanning the crowd until she found Theo West. He was sitting in one of the back rows. He looked good but inconspicuous, and a bright smile played across his lips as he stared up at Madison. Lex felt a stab in her stomach. What would become of them? she wondered. How would their complicated romance play out? Would it survive the inevitable swells and dips—especially now, with Hamilton Holdings secretly and strategically plotting to take over the entire West empire? She decided that it didn't matter right now. In this moment, both Madison and Theo were as happy as they could possibly be.

As the show drew to a close, a spotlight cut across the front row and illuminated the one chair that had purposely been kept empty. On it was a glossy issue of *Catwalk* magazine. The crowd rose to its feet in honor of Zahara Bell, who would surely have been present today.

Lex ran back up the staircase and through the backstage area. It was time to take her bow. She stepped onto the catwalk as the spotlight brightened amid waves of applause. Madison and Park were waiting way down at the end. Lex walked to them, smiling and waving to both sides of the room. They linked hands and posed for the cameras.

When the music died down, a reporter in the front row called out, "So what's next for the Hamilton triplets?"

Lex lowered her gaze and shot him a mysterious wink. "Don't you worry," she said. "We'll be back *very* soon."

ACKNOWLEDGMENTS

Talk about a cool job: I get to spend my days writing about fashion, diamonds, murder, and Manhattan. It's all good stuff, and none of it would be possible without some very awesome people.

Michael Bourret, for his professionalism, encouragement, and steadfast support.

Krista Marino, who edits with intelligence, enthusiasm, and style to spare. Thank you for shaping this manuscript into a book.

Beverly Horowitz and the excellent team at Delacorte Press, for being the best.

A special shout-out to Angela Carlino, for her seamless creative vision.

And, of course, endless gratitude to my family: I am blessed to have you.

Antonio Pagliarulo was born and raised in New York City and still calls the Big Apple home. He attended Fiorello H. LaGuardia High School of Music & Art and the Performing Arts and SUNY Purchase College, where he earned a BA in sociology. Though he has never lived in a penthouse, owned a Chihuahua, or flown his private jet to Borneo, he *does* enjoy window shopping on Fifth Avenue and hopes to one day own a Dolce & Gabbana suit. *The Celebutantes: On the Avenue* is his second book for young readers.

Madison, Park, and Lexington Hamilton
are back, and this time they're . . .

IN THE CLUB
The Celebutantes

coming in spring 2008